Asset Management

Annette Mori

Asset Management

Annette Mori

Affinity
eBook Press
NZ
2015

Asset Management

© by Annette Mori 2015

Affinity E-Book Press NZ LTD
Canterbury, New Zealand

1st Edition

ISBN: 978-0-908351-08-4

Editor: Nat Burns
Proof Editor: Alexis Smith
Cover Design: Irish Dragon Designs

Acknowledgments

Probably the most important person to acknowledge, besides my wife, is Erin O'Reilly, because she continues to provide gentle and kind guidance. Erin spent numerous hours teaching me, encouraging me, and helping to polish this story. When I got stuck, she brainstormed with me a way to get unstuck with the plotline. She helped me plug my holes and address problematic timeline issues. I continued to pester her nearly every night and without fail, she would review and promptly respond to my attempts to correct the issues identified. I am honored to call her a friend and she continues to mentor and guide me. I would also like to express my gratitude to

Affinity Press and the wonderful trio (JM Dragon, Erin O'Reilly and Nancy Kaufman) who continue to support this new and somewhat unconventional writer. I am eternally grateful for the opportunities they give me to let my stories see the light of day.

On my journey, I elicited feedback from my older sister, Val, who gave me valuable feedback that helped shape the final version of the story. She continues to be an incredible encouragement to me. My other family members who were also very supportive, include my nephew, Aaron and his wife, Chelsea, my wife's nephew, Chad, and my little sister, Kim. On more than one occasion, I heard my mother's voice in my ear.

Books always need editing and my mom gave me a good baseline education for which I am eternally grateful. Although my mom is no longer with us, I am sure she would have loved this book. It is exactly the kind of book she tended to gravitate to.

Kay Carney was a delight to work with again as my beta editor, and Nat Burns did her magic again as the final editor. Inevitably there are those pesky final errors that slip through and I am thankful that the final proof editor, caught those before the book went to print. Nancy Kaufman is a rock star with her covers and this one is definitely hot.

Finally, my wife, Jody, continues her support even when it interferes with our weekend time.

Dedication

To my mother who if there is a heaven is surely spreading her joy and compassion. I miss her every day. This is the type of action packed book she would have loved to read. To my wife who I love dearly for her patience when I get in a groove and ignore her during "our" weekend time.

Table of Contents

Also by Annette Mori

The Incredibly True Adventure of Two Elves in Love

(Affinity 2014 Christmas Collection)

The True Story of Valentine's Day

Love Forever, Live Forever

Chapter One

Washington, DC was the beating heart of the political machine and a favorite location for networking and high-dollar fundraisers. The Republican Party always took advantage of this particular venue because there were so many rich, conservative donors who lived nearby. Most of the supporters of the fundraiser considered the décor of the enormous ballroom elegant with its imported marble floors and handcrafted crystal chandeliers. Toni, however, was oblivious to her surroundings.

"At least I get to play bartender for part of the evening. Look at all these fat cats stuffed into their too tight tuxedos," she grumbled into her wireless communication device. "God, how do their wives crawl in bed with them every night? Don't their big old potbellies get in the way? Kim, make sure to steer Byron to my bar as soon as they get here. I'd rather not cut this too close."

Toni carefully scratched under one side of her ash blond wig. It and hazel contacts created the illusion of a typical college student picking up extra cash by working the special event.

She sighed, unable to shake the feeling that something terrible would happen tonight. Ha, feeling. Toni chuckled aloud. At least that was one thing she and Sophie had in common. She knew Sophie didn't put any weight on all that mumbo jumbo crap that Kim was always talking about. Toni and Sophie dealt in facts and things you could actually see and hear.

Toni shifted uneasily behind the bar as she thought of the fateful night when a similar suspicion had burrowed into her unconscious brain. As it turned out, that feeling of doom proved spot-on.

Can't think about that now.

The only good outcome from that night was Sophie's resignation from the FBI and the subsequent partnership and joining of forces with her two best friends. The price paid was brutal to everyone. Sophie lost her partner, Nat, and Toni felt the loss of a good friend. In addition, Nat's death left Sophie bitter and suspicious of almost everyone.

Sophie entered the ballroom, offering her escort for the evening a quick smile as she excused herself.

Toni whispered into the comm link. "I don't see Kim. Where is she? That bastard better show."

"Calm down, Toni. I just saw Kim and Byron out front. They should be here in five. I'll direct her to you as we planned," Sophie replied, when she was well away from prying ears.

Sophie's transformation, in her salmon-colored evening gown that hugged her curves in all the right places, amazed Toni. She also noted the admiring glance that Kim quickly masked as she resumed her character for the evening.

Kim's ability to adopt any persona they needed constantly shocked Toni. As a former theatre graduate from Stanford, Kim was, by far, their most talented undercover player.

"I've got a bad feeling about tonight. Did you place our contingency disguises where the cameras can't track the change?" Sophie asked.

"Of course. The paranoia of these bank execs sometimes works to our advantage. The hotel always has to have a few very private locations for their guests. I've found every one of them and used the schematics for the building to ensure safe hiding places. I see Kim coming in now so you'd better hurry back to your date. Kim picked out a nice dress for you, by the way, so I can't wait to see what she picked out for me. She certainly has a flare for selecting just the right outfit. Whoa…"

"What? Something wrong? Is Kim okay?" Sophie asked.

"Yeah, yeah. Check out the redhead coming in behind Kim and Byron. Wow. I definitely need to meet her."

"No. No way, Toni, you do not have time tonight. Didn't I just say I have a bad feeling?"

"Shh, date alert at two o'clock, intercept in less than three." Toni distracted Sophie, narrowing her focus in the direction where the two couples were connecting.

Sophie turned and accepted a glass of wine from her escort.

Byron and Kim approached Sophie and her date.

Byron glanced at Sophie and his eyes traveled up and down her body, spending an extra couple of seconds seemingly admiring her cleavage.

Toni listened intently to the conversation of the two couples as she continued to serve drinks.

"Hello, Ted. I hear the divorce is now final. I see you haven't wasted any time. Who is your lovely companion?"

"Byron. I'm glad you could make it. This is Amanda. Amanda, this is Byron and…?"

"Oh, how rude of me, this is Wendy," Ted added.

The two couples shook hands.

"I see you already have drinks. I hope the bars are stocked with the good stuff and not some inexpensive off brand," Byron remarked.

"I overheard someone saying that only some of the bars are carrying the more expensive liquor. I believe that bar there is one of them." Sophie pointed to where Toni was serving.

"I'll come with you. I'd like to ask about their wine options." Kim took Byron's arm.

Toni's eyes were surreptitiously on Kim and Byron as they walked to the bar where she was serving. "Good evening, sir, what can I get you to drink?"

"I'll have a scotch, neat. If you don't have anything better than Glenlivet eighteen, I suppose that will suffice, but do not give me any Johnny Walker Red or other similar brand." Byron turned to Kim. "Wendy, what would you like, dear?"

"Can you tell me what options you have for white wine?"

"We have either a chardonnay or a Riesling," Toni replied.

Kim frowned, then expertly turned Byron's attention to her while Toni poured an inexpensive Johnny Walker Red. "Perhaps you can indulge me later in your room if they don't serve a pinot tonight with dinner."

"Here you go, sir."

Byron took a small sip of his scotch and immediately scowled at Toni. Setting the glass on the counter and pushing it toward her, he growled in irritation, "I specifically requested not to have an inexpensive scotch. Will you please check to see what other options you have?"

"Oh, I am terribly sorry, sir, let me check." Toni used her most apologetic tone.

4

She casually retrieved the glass, carefully avoiding the sides and turned around while she used the special latex to capture his prints for fingerprint recognition. She pulled a bottle of Glenlivet from the hidden shelf, along with a bottle of pinot. Carefully placing the latex inside a napkin, she turned around and smiled at Byron and Kim. Pouring from the Glenlivet bottle, she handed the new drink to Byron.

"I found a pinot. Would you like a glass, miss?" Toni asked.

Kim smiled at Toni. "Yes, that would be lovely, thank you."

Toni handed her the glass of wine, fumbling it and spilling it on Kim's hand and the edge of her sleeve. "Oh, my God, I am so sorry. Let me get you some napkins."

Toni began wiping Kim's hand and sleeve and then handed her the napkin with the latex print.

Kim discreetly placed that napkin in her purse and used another to wipe at her sleeve.

Toni watched closely and registered Byron's irritation at her clumsiness, but fortunately, he didn't appear to take notice of the exchange between them. They had choreographed their subterfuge well.

The commotion drew Sophie and Ted to the bar.

Ted smirked at Byron. "It seems your requirement for a particular brand of scotch is more trouble than it's worth. We should just skip the before dinner drinks and instead, enjoy an after dinner cocktail in our rooms. Separate rooms—I wouldn't want to crash your party, Byron."

Byron's irritation seemed to dissipate. Although they'd planned for this, Toni was uncomfortable with the knowledge that he probably recognized this as the perfect opportunity to get Kim to his suite. She suspected Sophie was having a full-fledged shit fit right now about his apparent eagerness to get Kim alone.

5

"Quite right, Ted." Byron turned to Kim with a broad smile. "I do hope you will join me in my room later. I'm sure I can arrange to have a bottle of pinot brought to the room."

"I'd like that, Byron. Thank you for the offer and for inviting me tonight."

"I assure you, the pleasure is all mine."

Toni glanced over, saw the look of loathing in Sophie's eyes, and glared at her. Blowing their cover with a display of obvious emotion wasn't an option. Sophie needed to remember that Kim was a pro and had the situation under control.

Toni had no concern about Kim's ability to get close enough to capture a high-quality picture of Byron's retina, using her specially designed camera embedded in Kim's colored contacts. Byron was not a tall man, so she knew that Kim's three-inch heels would provide the perfect angle to capture a high-quality shot of his iris. And Toni knew it would require a closer, more intimate atmosphere for her to get the job done.

"I better head to the ladies' room and see if I can try to salvage this dress," Kim announced.

"I'll come with you. I might even have something to help remove any possible stain," Sophie offered.

"We'll meet you at the table by the podium after we've had a chance to network a little bit," Byron said.

Sophie and Kim strolled to the bathroom while Ted and Byron mingled with those around them.

As soon as they were well away from their dates, Kim whispered into her comm link. "Time to start phase two, Toni. Your style change is in the west wing hospitality bathroom. I hid it in the ceiling tile above the first stall. Cameras are deactivated." Kim chuckled.

"I know that laugh. What the hell kind of outfit did you pick for me? I better look hot. I need to connect with that stunning redhead," Toni whispered into her comm link.

"Oh, you'll look hot all right, but the amount of cleavage might be a bit risqué, even for you, Toni. It will definitely be a completely opposite look compared to your normal combat boots, leather jacket, and ripped jeans."

"Perfect. Thanks, Kim."

"Don't get sidetracked by that redhead. I may need your help later with the transfer of images. The lens is your prototype and I'm anxious to see the results," Sophie added.

As soon as Kim, Sophie, and their dates left the bar area, Toni slipped the pill that would simulate the symptoms of food poisoning into her mouth. It wouldn't take long before she developed a sudden need to visit the bathroom and had the excuse she needed to leave her bartending station.

†

Sophie entered the bathroom and made a quick sweep of the stalls to ensure they were alone. Kim carefully extracted the latex hidden in the napkin and handed it to Sophie who delicately placed it in a plastic zipper bag. Sophie gently pushed back an errant lock from Kim's expensive wig. She placed her hands on Kim's arms and absently stroked down Kim's well-defined triceps.

Kim smiled.

"Listen, I want you to be extra vigilant with Byron. I've heard some things about him that I don't like. Even if we have to abort the mission tonight, don't hesitate to call for reinforcements. Don't take any chances and don't let that slime bag take things too far just to get a good picture. Toni

7

and I will be listening in, so all you have to do is say the magic word and we'll be there in a jiffy."

"Don't worry about me. I've done this a thousand times. I'm an expert at wiggling out of an unwanted embrace. He's a banker, for God's sake. I think I can handle him."

"Your welfare is more important to me than completing this mission. I, um…"

Kim took one of Sophie's hands and interlaced her fingers. "I know, Sophie."

†

Toni burst into the bathroom, rushed to the toilet, and vomited.

"Damn, I thought it would only look like I was getting sick. I didn't actually think I would be puking up my burrito. I'll never eat Mexican food again." Toni yanked a generous supply of toilet paper off the roll and wiped her mouth. "Hey, do either one of you have a mint or something?"

Kim pulled a stick of spearmint gum and a roll of mints from her purse. "Here. You still look a little peaked, but it should wear off quickly, especially after the big purge. Sorry. I guess the side effects are different for different people."

"You're looking kinda cozy there, did I interrupt something?" Toni grinned.

Sophie frowned. "We better get back and Toni, you need to get dressed."

"Relax. I'm on it. I'll hang out here for another minute or so. I don't want them connecting us, even while I look like Cathy College. I still don't like that you two are in such close proximity to one another tonight. Don't forget to avoid the cameras. Sorry, Kim, but we'd better not recycle any of these disguises—both of you really stick out. I know we're supposed to capitalize on your looks to get close to Byron, but nondescript disguises put us less at risk."

"Good point. I personally would rather we use a different tactic in the future than put Kim in danger of being mauled by some disgusting middle aged bank exec," Sophie added.

"See you later tonight. Break a leg, Kim. All we need is that picture, then Sophie and I can work our magic."

Kim and Sophie exited the bathroom just as Toni's stomach acted up again.

"Shit, I am never volunteering to do this again," Toni grumbled.

Toni leaned over the sink and tossed cold water on her face. A warm hand touched her back. She looked into the mirror and was surprised to see the stunning redhead.

"Are you okay? Can I get you anything?" a husky alto voice inquired.

"Thanks. I'll be fine, just a touch of food poisoning, I think. I'm heading home right now."

"Would you like me to call you a cab?" The woman was looking closely at Toni. She appeared to show genuine concern, but alarm bells were going off in Toni's head.

"No, but thank you. I'm good now."

Toni rushed out of the bathroom in search of her next disguise, hoping Kim left a toothbrush and toothpaste for her.

†

Toni glided into the ballroom and watched as several heads turned in her direction. She was scanning the room hoping to set her sights on the redhead.

Almost as if she felt her scrutiny, Toni turned her head right and locked eyes with her object of desire for the evening. A practiced glance at the table revealed an open space. The dinner portion of the evening was almost ready to start and she wanted to make sure she was sitting at the same table. Toni made a beeline for the table before her golden opportunity passed her by.

"Is this seat taken?"

"It is now. We were wondering who would be brave enough to join our boring little group."

Toni noticed the woman openly appraising her dress. Gaydar intact. *Yep, she definitely plays for our team.* Toni quickly glanced at the other table guests who were all distracted with their own conversations. Several others in the group pinged her gaydar.

Toni raised one eyebrow. "Boring, huh. Well in that case, I ought to seek out another table. I was hoping this was the one to start the table dancing."

"Attorneys never table dance. We buy the table dancers. How much?"

"How much what?"

"How much will it take for me to get you to table dance?"

"A kiss and you have to join me."

The woman chuckled and her husky laugh sent shivers down Toni's spine.

Damn this woman is sexy, even her laugh causes me to tingle.

"Touché. You are certainly going to liven up my evening," the attractive redhead remarked.

"Camille." Toni offered her hand. "At your service."

The woman extended her hand. "Heather. I'm glad you decided to join us. Can I ask an entirely rude and inappropriate question?"

"Such a sweet talker. How can I resist such a request?"

"Why are you here by yourself?"

"Oh, that's easy. My date had a sudden onset of food poisoning and she insisted I go."

"Hmm, it must be going around, I just met a woman in the bathroom who also mentioned having food poisoning. I hope it didn't originate in this hotel."

"No, definitely not. Probably just a coincidence." Toni paused. "How come you aren't here with a date?"

"I'm married to my work, so I have very little, if any time for a social life. When I'm lucky, like tonight, I snare unsuspecting women into my web."

"Promises, promises."

"Would you like a glass of wine? White? Red? Take your pick." Heather pointed to the two bottles of wine on the table.

"White, please."

"At the expense of sounding cliché, what do you do when you're not attending boring fund-raisers and livening them up with table dances?"

"Oh, a little of this and a little of that—mostly related to technology." Toni learned a long time ago that the best cover stories usually have an element of truth to them, so she offered up this partial truth. This woman seemed like a person who could detect a bullshit cover easily.

After graduating from Stanford with a degree in computer science, Toni had expanded her knowledge base by entering into the fascinating world of biometric security. Learning how to break nearly fail-safe security systems led to her prototype development of a high-resolution camera that would capture near perfect retinal displays—good enough to break any biometric security installed. Her crowning achievement was placing the camera into a paper-thin contact lens.

"Technology, huh? Sounds riveting."

"Are you making fun of me?" Toni asked, smiling flirtatiously.

"No, never. I am a bit of a geek myself in my limited spare time."

Waiters began delivering salads to each table and the women's conversation subsided momentarily. Toni was well aware of her prior commitment to complete the mission and assist Sophie with the security breach and asset movement, but she couldn't help inquiring about this beautiful woman's plans.

"So, do you have any specific plans for the evening, after this little shindig ends?"

"I thought maybe I would hit a strip club or two, get a lap dance, and gamble away my entire inheritance. You?"

Toni burst out laughing. "Oh, I plan to accompany you to those strips clubs, give you that lap dance, and steal several of your thousand-dollar chips while you are distracted and getting drunk on cheap liquor."

"Perfect, shall we begin our festivities at ten p.m. on the dot?"

"I think it might take us a bit longer to get to Vegas, unless we take your private jet. You do have a private jet, don't you?"

"Of course, but we'll have to find a different mode of transportation to get us back to DC, because I plan on putting up my jet as collateral and I am sure to lose that at the roulette tables."

"Fine, I'll call my buddies to spring us from jail and provide first-class transportation back to the land of politics."

"Wait, why will we be in jail?"

"Oh, I plan on counting cards and then telling them that you put me up to it. Then you'll vigorously deny the accusation. I'll take that as my sign to throw a punch at the smelly security guard you're in a nose-to-nose argument with, but the police have already been called and gun beats fists any day of the week," Toni joked.

"Will you finally make a pass at me in our cozy jail cell?"

"I've been making passes at you since I sat down at your table," Toni quipped.

"You do realize that before the night is through you and I will be in a passionate lip lock."

"I'm definitely not opposed to a quick bathroom break."

"I thought you would never ask." Heather smiled.

"I might as well find out whether you are a good kisser, before we start our wave of crime."

"I don't think you will be disappointed."

"No, I don't expect I will." Toni stood up and offered her hand to the redhead. "Shall we?"

Toni glanced at her watch to make sure she had enough time to enjoy her rendezvous in the bathroom. She knew that Kim hadn't had time to get a picture yet and suspected she would have to join Byron in his hotel suite.

†

In an effort to maintain a certain sense of decorum, Toni resisted the urge to race to the bathroom, despite her craving for the beautiful redhead. A quick glance around the restroom confirmed that they were alone. Toni luckily remembered to turn off her comm link—a few minutes of silence wouldn't be the end of the world.

Toni tugged the redhead into the handicapped stall and locked the door. "More room," she offered.

"I see you've done this before."

Toni's eyebrow lifted in mock surprise. "You haven't."

"I didn't say that. Just making an observation," Heather responded.

"While I've thoroughly enjoyed all the witty banter—a total aphrodisiac—no offense, but stop talking."

Toni pushed the redhead against the bathroom door and crushed her mouth, finally satisfying her need to capture those luscious lips.

Heather closed her eyes and Toni thought she saw her surrender to the kiss in a way that was more emotional than physical.

Toni ran her hands up and down the outside of her dress and almost lifted up the dress to access her panties, but for reasons unknown to her she stopped.

Too bad I had to meet this intriguing woman while on a mission and in disguise.

Toni couldn't believe she was about to stop herself from fucking the redhead in the bathroom stall—but something seemed totally wrong about the situation. Heather was way too classy for a cheap one-night stand.

Toni broke from the kiss, panting, and looked directly into the woman's eyes. She thought she saw arousal and maybe something else, before the woman pulled back. She recognized the mask of controlled interest. It was a role she played often.

A look of inquiry replaced the mask. "Why did you pull away? It was just starting to get interesting," Heather asked.

Toni offered an uneasy cough. "Um, I wouldn't want your tablemates to start spreading rumors. We ought to get back to the table and force ourselves to suffer through the remainder of the speeches. I was dying to feel your soft lips and that's enough for now."

"To be continued, then…"

"Absolutely." Damn, if only it were that simple. All the subterfuge was killing her chances to develop any kind of real relationship. Toni knew that eventually Kim and Sophie would acknowledge their feelings for one another leaving her the only one to continue to flit from woman to woman.

I wonder how I might run into her as Toni.

For some reason she wanted to get to know this woman and playing one of her twenty other aliases was damned inconvenient.

✝

Toni and Heather sauntered back to their table and received knowing smiles and nods from their tablemates.

Toni looked at the other tables and noticed that Byron and Kim were no longer at their table. *Good, it won't be much longer now.*

She knew that Byron probably convinced Kim to have a drink in his room, which is exactly what they needed. Toni smiled to herself as she noticed Ted sitting by himself. *Nice work, Sophie.* It amazed her how Sophie always managed to wriggle free from dull politicians and businessmen.

Toni turned her head noticing Heather's sudden intense scrutiny.

"Have I smudged my lipstick?"

Heather shook her head. "No. I was just thinking about going to Vegas with you."

Toni raised an eyebrow. Something told her that was only a ploy. "I believe you said we'd be meeting for that later tonight at ten."

Heather smiled. "That I did," she said, before picking up her fork and taking a bite of her salad.

✝

Kim flashed Byron her most charming smile as she entered his suite. "Thank you for inviting me tonight, Byron. I've had a lovely evening. If you don't mind, I really only have enough energy for a quick after dinner drink. It's been a long, hectic day so I think I'd better retire to my own suite after that."

"Of course, my dear. Let me just open up this bottle of pinot that I asked them to send up and we can relax for a few moments."

Byron crossed to the bar and opened the wine. Kim had a flash of discomfort when she wasn't able to see exactly what Byron was doing as his back was turned toward her. The comment Sophie made earlier about hearing things about Byron resonated before she tossed it aside and focused on her mission.

Byron smiled at Kim as he handed her the wine.

Kim, sitting on the loveseat, shifted to make room for Byron to sit close to her. *Perfect.* She turned to face Byron, looked directly into his eyes before touching the button concealed as a sequin on her dress. Pressing it three times, she sighed in relief. Three shots should do it. Now to get out of there.

Their glasses touched in a toast.

Byron, with a lust-filled expression, looked directly into her eyes. "To our next Republican President."

Kim took a small sip. "It's a done deal," she said. She was ready to make her excuse to leave.

Byron frowned. "Is the wine not to your liking? I can have them send up a different bottle."

Kim, not wanting to make her exit too obvious, decided to finish the glass before making a graceful exit. "Oh no, the wine is lovely, but I do really need to leave after I finish this drink." Kim took a larger sip from the wineglass.

Byron smiled.

The faster she finished, the quicker she could join Toni and Sophie. Just as she took another big sip, Sophie's words came rushing back to her. She began feeling dizzy and noticing Byron's satisfied smirk, she knew he had spiked her drink. The previous warning settled too late into her consciousness, yet she still had enough wherewithal to let Sophie know the score.

She touched another button—I'm in trouble—while attempting to clear her head. "I don't know what is wrong with me," she slurred. "I suddenly feel dizzy and I know I haven't had enough alcohol to become impaired."

"I simply cannot let you leave when you feel this way," Byron said, patting her thigh. "Come with me and you can lie down and rest for a bit until you feel better. I will escort you back to your room when you are up to it."

With Byron's hand on her back, Kim managed to stand before he encircled her waist with his arm urging her toward the bedroom.

Kim knew she was slipping further into the abyss and summoned all her strength to resist. "No. I think I'd better head back to my suite. Please, Byron, take me back," she pleaded.

A thud against the outside suite door resounded in the room and Kim saw Byron turning his head in the direction of the noise. *God, please let it be them.*

✝

Sophie and Toni burst into the suite.

Sophie narrowed her gaze at Byron, who was holding Kim upright.

"What the hell is going on? How did you get into my suite? Security," Byron screamed.

Sophie rushed to Kim's side and pulled her away from the man's grip. "What the fuck did you give her, you slimy bastard?"

Byron, caught unaware, readily let go of Kim. "Hey, she's my date."

"Not anymore." Toni turned to Sophie. "I've got her, go ahead, and take care of him."

Sophie delivered a quick, well-placed strike to Byron's carotid artery interrupting his blood supply.

Byron collapsed onto the floor.

Sophie followed Toni, leading Kim out of the suite. Kim stumbled and Toni pulled her in a tight hold, half dragging, half lifting her to safety. They only needed to get to the room where they'd stashed the new disguises.

Just a few more feet. Almost there. Shit. Thank God, Kim is such a little bitty thing, Toni thought.

While Toni was helping Kim, Sophie methodically pulled Byron's security team, who littered the floor in the hallway, into the suite. Toni was pleased by her friend's martial arts expertise. She left Sophie to finish the job. She was thankful that Byron's suite was in the section of the

18

hotel where the privacy of the guests was paramount and security cameras were magically absent.

✝

Toni managed to get Kim to the private suite at the end of the hall where they had stashed the new disguises. She pulled out the key card to enter the room quickly and without notice. Sophie had already ensured there were no security cameras, eliminating prying eyes from the transformation that was about to take place. Toni pulled Kim to a chair to prop her up and get her attention.

"Kim, honey, look at me and let me see your pupils. Come on, hon, let me see those beautiful orbs."

"Mmph, Ton, jus let me sweep, lil nap, pease. Come on, not en of worl', aft all. Jus a few mins, pease."

"Shit. If Sophie doesn't kill that bastard, I just might. Kim, I know you want to sleep now, but I need you to help me just a little bit."

Gently pulling Kim forward, Toni pushed down the zipper at the back of her dress in an attempt to remove her gown. She needed to replace it with the old lady style-pantsuit sitting in a duffel bag next to the king-sized bed.

"Mmph. No. I don wan' you to, wan' Soph. Lub Soph," Kim slurred.

"I know, hon, I know. I promise I'm not trying to take advantage of you, but Sophie is kind of busy right now, dragging those bastards' asses. I promise she will be here soon and then she can take over."

"I made mess, drink spiked, shoulda known."

Toni sighed in relief as Sophie burst through the door.

Sophie narrowed her eyes and frowned at Toni.

Toni threw up her hands in defeat and exasperation. "Hey, don't you look at me that way, you big Neanderthal. I'm just trying to help Kim into her new disguise. Get your freaking head out of the gutter and get your ass over here to help. Better yet, you get her changed."

Toni glared at Sophie, who she suspected had the good sense to realize her initial reaction was wrong, as she looked away in embarrassment.

"Sorry," Sophie mumbled to Toni's retreating form.

"Soph, you came. You my hero, I lub you," Kim slurred.

Sophie's face turned a bright shade of fuchsia as she continued to dress Kim and apply the latex face of an old woman.

Toni was quickly donning her own disguise as another old woman. As she finished with her latex mask and popped in the new contacts that would turn her eyes to the watery blue of an old woman of eighty, she sighed.

"God, I hate all these theatrics that Kim always prepares for us. This latex is so God damned itchy I want to scratch my freaking face off the entire time I have to wear it," Toni complained.

"Shut your piehole. You know as well as I do that her disguises keep our lame asses from jail and your sweet tushy from being Bertha's beeotch." Sophie was stroking Kim's hair as she put the finishing touches on her disguise.

"Fine. Whatever. You better get your ass in gear and get into your old man's outfit before those goons wake up. As soon as they do, you know they'll start doing a room-to-room search for us. How long do you think Byron will be out? He is going to wake up, right? You didn't kill the poor bastard, did you?" Toni asked.

"No, I didn't kill him but I wanted to. We have a good half hour."

"Good. That'll give us time to get that retinal scan into the computer and make the transfer of funds."

Sophie grabbed the suit and tie that was just a bit too large for her, creating the illusion that her advanced age was the cause for the ill-fitting suit. She added a hat and cane to her outfit and adjusted her posture to appear hunched. The transformation was compelling.

"Come on, grab Kim's other side and put the walker in front of her. Hopefully, we can act like she has difficulty walking and the added prop will lend some authenticity to the disguise. I'm glad Kim thought to bring that."

Toni grabbed the collapsible walker and helped Sophie place Kim's hands on the rails. Sophie and Toni each took a side and moved forward slowly creating the appearance of three people of advanced age shuffling to their next destination.

"All right. Here we go. It's show time. Do you have all the computer equipment we need in our getaway vehicle?" Sophie asked.

Toni lifted her lip in a snarl. "Why do you always do that? I'm not an imbecile. Of course everything is set up according to plan."

"I never said you were an imbecile. It's just that you sometimes get distracted with extracurricular activities. You had to take that redhead to the bathroom, didn't you? I don't think tonight was really the time or place to get distracted. Now look what's happened."

"Hey, I'm not the one who offered up Kim to go up to that prick's room and have a drink, just so we could get the retina scan. She offered because you know that Kim is the only one who could pull that off. I'm sure no actress and I'm not even going to comment on your lack of finesse. If we left it up to you, your inner Neanderthal would have surfaced and you would use toothpicks to pry his eyes open after you bashed in his head. Oh, wait, you bashed his head in after that chop to his neck. Just couldn't help yourself, could you?"

"I did not bash his head in for no reason. After I temporarily cut off his oxygen supply with a quick blow, I had to make sure he would be out for a while. Hmph. Why am I even bothering to explain myself to you? You overgrown, hormonal, oversexed, miscreant."

"Ah, ah, ah. Careful or I'll start thinking you don't love me anymore. Come on time's a wasting."

✝

Shuffling out of the suite, the three friends managed to make it to the elevator just as the door was opening. Toni waved her gnarled hand to signal to the occupants of the elevator that their entrance might be a bit slow.

"Going as fast as we can," Toni's old woman voice said.

"Lobby, please," Toni warbled out as they settled in the elevator cab. A man punched the lobby button and, in sync with acceptable elevator behavior, looked the other way, politely waiting for the elevator to reach their desired destination.

Toni reached in her pants pocket for the valet parking ticket that would bring their non-descript car around to the circular drive in front of the hotel. The parking attendant was patiently waiting as the three friends slowly made their way to him. The attendant jogged to the car and pulled up at the exact moment they reached the front of the hotel. Toni handed the attendant a five-dollar bill. She would like to have given him more, but that would have called too much attention to them and they couldn't afford to do that. He smiled at her and she suspected he was grateful for even the small amount.

"Thank you, ma'am. Do you need any assistance getting into your car?"

"No thank you, young man," Toni responded. She was almost positive the young man was working his way through college. Noting his nametag—Brian—she would find out the parking attendant's full name so an anonymous donor could provide him with a college scholarship.

"You have a great evening." Toni settled Kim into the backseat then, waving at the man, she got in on the passenger side while Sophie climbed in on the driver's side.

†

Sophie drove the car slowly away from the curb and cautiously entered traffic.

Sophie glanced at Toni. "If you stowed away the right laptop, the program is all set up for you. All you have to do is load the disc."

"Humph. I stowed the right equipment—you arrogant shithead."

Toni pulled the specially designed laptop from under the seat. Her fingers flew across the keys at a record pace. She pulled the digital photo disc from her pocket and inserted the specially designed mini CD into her laptop.

One hundred strokes later, she leaned back and smiled. "Gotcha, you bastard." The screen flashed a transaction complete message confirming the transfer of funds. "Oh, what a wonderful sight to see."

Chapter Two

Two days had passed since the fund-raiser when she got the call letting her know that the asset had surfaced. This was one mission that Char was looking forward to participating in. Her previous encounter at the fund-raiser with the witty and charming Toni had been especially pleasurable.

Char smiled to herself when she remembered how Toni had introduced herself as Camille. She was impressed at how Toni had donned not one, but two different disguises that evening. She grudgingly gave the woman props for voluntarily ingesting the drugs that would facilitate her need to leave her bartending post due to illness. Now that's dedication to a mission. No wonder she was such an important asset.

The *organization* rarely failed to achieve their missions but ever since the botched assignment two years ago, Char had something to prove and had honed her skills. Now, without fail, she always got her man—or in this case, women.

There wasn't enough time to don a disguise to make her less noticeable and it didn't really matter anyway because Char knew her undercover persona as Heather Stiles, attorney at law, was rock solid. Char knew that she stood out in a crowd—both an advantage and a disadvantage in her line of work.

Taking the chance that the trio wouldn't recognize her, she boldly entered the small café and looked around for a location with an unobstructed view of her mark. As she walked by their table, she was surprised when Toni winked at her.

She didn't hesitate to stride to the table to take the offensive and control the situation as was required of her.

"Did you just wink at me?" Char asked as the corners of her mouth lifted up in a wry smile.

"Yep," Toni answered.

"Have we met before? I think I would have remembered you if we had."

"Nope, but I bet you wish you had, right?" Toni grinned.

Char chuckled. "As a matter of fact, yes. I think you're right about that."

Char pushed back her hair and touched the emergency button on her earring. Three seconds later, her cell phone rang. "I'm sorry, will you excuse me, I need to get this."

Char took several steps away from their table and spoke brusquely into the phone. "Yes. All right… I'll be there in ten."

Char turned back around and addressed the trio of women. "I'm terribly sorry, but I suppose I'll need to take a rain check on the *getting to know you* part."

Before leaving Char stumbled into Toni and managed to attach a tracking device no larger than the head of a pin onto her jacket.

✝

25

Many had told her on more than one occasion that her emerald green eyes were a stunning contrast to her long red hair. When she smiled, it no longer reached her eyes. The innocence and warmth were no longer present—they were the eyes of a predator. She mesmerized her prey and they never recognized her cold and calculated appraisal.

Unfortunately, two years ago, her sense of security shattered. It was especially rough on her sister Dani and Char was determined to rewrite the tragic story—the ending unknown. She knew they needed to devote more agents to the mission to put closure on the situation. Unfortunately, the enemy controlled vast resources.

Char glanced quickly at her surroundings before getting into the backseat of the nondescript black vehicle. Tonight she presented a genuine smile to her mentor, Maggie, as she turned her gaze in her direction.

Maggie was a stunning woman with an air of sophistication and confidence that drew men and women to her like the female version of the Pied Piper. She had a commanding presence that created an instant veil of safety. Maggie was the only person, other than Dani that she allowed inside her inner sanctum. She owed her life to Maggie as well as the life of her younger sister. When her eyes met her mentor's, she hoped they reflected the warmth, love, and respect that she had for her savior.

Char was not naïve and knew Maggie had zero guilt about using her to further the cause. Obviously, she was the best suited for the mission because she had a personal stake in the outcome.

"Did you get visual confirmation?" Maggie broke the silence inside the vehicle.

"Yes, I did. Toni is back to her natural appearance. Kim and Sophie are also free of any disguise. I can't figure out if Toni is careless or more cunning than we thought. She actually winked at me."

"She what?"

"You heard me. She was downright cheeky and winked at me."

Maggie chuckled. "I guess her brash reputation is accurate. What did you say to her?"

"I asked her if we had met before, because I was sure if we had, I would have remembered her." Char grinned.

"You are just as cocky as she is."

"Maybe, but it did allow me to confirm the trio. Sophie usually hides her scar with makeup and clothes, but not today. I presume the third person sitting in the booth is Kim. Kim is good...she actually managed to get a picture of me." Char's voice held a hint of respect.

"Interesting. It would seem that they are just as intrigued with you as we are with them. How do you know the blonde at the fund-raiser was Toni?"

Although Maggie asked the question, it didn't fool Char, for she was like a sponge learning all of her mentor's tricks of the trade. She suspected that her mentor wanted to know about the tactics used to make this determination.

"Her lips are pretty hard to forget. Fortunately, the disguise she was wearing that night didn't alter her lips. So what do you think?"

"I think we need to see just how good Toni is before we make our move."

"Do you actually think she has any chance of identifying me?" Char hesitated then frowned.

"Doubtful, but I want to see what their next move will be. It wouldn't surprise me if Sophie at least suspects that you are not what you appear to be on the surface. Whether she remembers anything, or can put two and two together, remains to be seen," Maggie assured.

Char clearly remembered when their paths crossed—
Dani was almost a casualty. Revenge is a dish best served
cold and she would have her revenge. She knew that her
emotions weren't logical, for Sophie was as much a victim as
Natalie and Dani, but at times, even for her, feelings weren't
logical.

"We have to be prepared to get them all. I assess
them to be impossible to break apart. They would never turn
their backs on one another. I think Toni may be the weak
link, and I would personally like you to assign me to her. It
appeared to me that the other two are in love with one
another, so I have no chance with either of them. Besides, I
sense that Sophie has a vague remembrance of me, even
though I was in disguise."

"Very well. Get Toni first and the rest will follow."
Maggie paused then shook her head. "Don't underestimate
Toni for she is brilliant and may not be what she appears to
be on the surface."

"Won't happen. I believe her weakness for attractive
women will be the opening we need. I must admit to looking
forward to the chase. I planted one of Dani's tracking devices
on her jacket. I'm pretty sure that is the one she always wears
so hopefully we'll get lucky." Char smiled.

"Be careful. Her charms are legendary. I can't have
my best agent inadvertently falling in love with the target."

"Ha. I'm not like Dani. That will never happen to
me."

"My mother always told me, never say never. Not all
love is destructive and Dani survived. The same cannot be
said for Natalie." Maggie sighed. "We were so close, we
almost had her. My arrogance got in the way, and I thought
we had time. We cannot make the same mistake again."

"Dani barely survived. Love makes us stupid and careless. This is why I'm your best agent—I'll never be stupid or careless."

"Do you need Dani to work up another identity and disguise for you."

"No, I plan on taking the offensive and letting Toni think she's in control. Besides, I didn't spend eighteen months undercover as Heather Stiles, attorney at law, for nothing. We've carefully planned this out and those long months playing lawyer are about to reap the benefits."

"Very well, you are the master strategist. I defer to your expertise. I only ask that you have this wrapped up in the next month. I won't tolerate another loss. Sophie will be the hardest to get because of Natalie. The time to strike is now. After last week with them almost getting caught, they are more vulnerable and that gives us the upper hand."

Chapter Three

"What the hell were you thinking by winking at her? I swear, Toni, you are worse than a guy. You're always letting your coochie lead the way. I can just see the invisible connection between your poon and your brain," Sophie barked, sneering at her friend. "I'm totally disgusted with your antics."

Toni shrugged and directed her trademark unrepentant half grin, half smirk at her two best friends and partners in crime.

Sophie, Toni, and Kim had been best friends since their first year of college. Their recent job at the Republican fund-raiser had allowed them to emancipate fifty million dollars from Byron, a rapacious bank executive who deserved that and more.

"What? Am I the only one to recognize her total hotness?" Toni asked.

"Coochie?" Kim scrunched up her face.

"You probably prefer lady garden or nether regions." Sophie's expression softened as she smiled at Kim. "But my eighty-seven-year-old grandmother calls it her coochie. I've been hearing that slang since I was five years old."

"Really? Nana calls it her coochie? I never knew that," Toni interjected.

There she goes again trying to divert the conversation just like she always does, Sophie thought.

"Stop right there. You are not going to distract me, Toni. What you did was reckless and stupid. I'm telling you that it's no coincidence she came into this café so soon after our recent activities. Especially since she was at the fund-raiser too."

Sophie turned her penetrating gaze back to Toni. "I swear I recognize her from somewhere."

"You think she's a feebie? Maybe she was there to nail our mister BA. I'm glad we got to him first. So what if she's a feebie, there is no way she recognized us, thanks to our very own *Mission Impossible* makeup artist." Toni grinned at Kim and bumped her fist.

Kim frowned. "BA? I wish you both would stop using slang I don't know."

"Big ass, versus BS which would be big shot, or maybe bull shitter, you never know with Toni. I don't think she is a feebie—I mean—FBI agent. Sorry, Kim."

Sophie gave Kim a look of apology. "FBI agents are not that subtle. I'm pretty sure she glanced at my scar. You would have to be watching pretty close for anyone to notice but I caught her." Sophie lifted her left hand as a visual prop. "Typical spook behavior though. The way she walked in and noticed all the entry and exit points and took in all the details is classic CIA."

Toni cringed. "Okay, sorry. Do you have any ideas for mitigating the risk?"

Sophie noticed her expression and wondered if she was remembering the night that Sophie had to save her ass. She shook her head as she touched her most recent war wound that incident had caused.

"We need to find out more about her. Nice job getting a photo, Kim. I'm sure Toni will do her computer magic with face recognition."

I shouldn't have said that. Because I complimented her just now, she's going to think all is forgiven.

"Are you sure you were never a CIA agent? How did you know I got a picture?" Kim said with a broad smile.

"I pay attention."

Toni looked at Sophie and smiled.

Sophie was in love with Kim and the only person who actually knew this was Toni. She had admitted that to Toni in a momentary lapse of judgment and Toni had insisted that it was obvious that Kim shared her feelings. Sophie wasn't willing to take the chance and possibly ruin their friendship. Although she disagreed with Toni, Sophie often questioned what Kim's feelings were. It didn't matter to her that there were a mountain of unspoken words—she was definitely not ready to make an overt declaration of love.

When Kim looked away, Sophie gave Toni a subtle shake of her head in warning.

"Do you think we should have retreated back to our home base in San Francisco?" Kim asked, wringing her hands.

"No. For once, I agree with Toni. The best place to hide is right in front of their noses," Sophie said.

"Besides, what's the fun in taking all that money if you can't watch the fallout unfold?" Toni leaned back into the booth seat and crossed her long, shapely legs.

The smile on Toni's face reminded Sophie of the Cheshire cat.

"Did you see the paper this morning?" Toni asked. "These poor families have more ethics in their pinky than the whole stinking banking industry. They keep reporting to their banks about odd deposits to their accounts insisting that it wasn't their money. At least the banks are ethical enough to assure them the money is from an anonymous donor and quite legitimate. Nice work on setting the foundation up, Sophie." Toni winked at her friend. "Did you see that douchebag, Harrison, huddled with his attorneys and fellow cronies all trying to figure out how someone managed to dupe him? I bet they're still scratching their asses wondering what happened. Harrison looked like my grandpa did when his hemorrhoid was acting up."

They all laughed.

"I wanted to get some popcorn to enjoy with the entertainment, but I suppose that might shed too much light our way. Right now, no one would ever suspect that a trio of dykes from the wrong side of town could pull this kind of thing off." Toni wiggled her eyebrows.

"Stop gloating, Toni. It doesn't look good on you. Besides, we barely went undetected this time and I suspect your gal pal hottie might be leading the witch hunt. This isn't our first rodeo you know. I knew about Byron's reputation. I should never have let him get his grimy claws into her." Sophie looked at Kim and grimaced.

"It's okay, Soph, you were there and it all worked out." Kim smiled.

"Something seems off about your mystery woman. Please tell me that your final trip to the bathroom at the Republican fund-raiser last week did not result in an intimate encounter with her?" Sophie already knew the answer.

"Define intimate encounter." Toni grinned.

"Shit, Toni, how is it possible that one hundred and fifty plus IQ of yours has absolutely no effect on your decision-making ability whenever you are around a beautiful woman." Sophie shook her head.

"Ha, so you admit she is a beautiful woman. Relax, Sophie. Remember, I was a blonde, brown-eyed, voluptuous woman and not my naturally irresistible androgynous self. You can't get any more opposite of dark hair and blue eyes than the disguise Kim gave me for the fund-raiser."

"I saw a flicker of recognition, even after she denied meeting you. I'd bet my house she knows far more about us than is healthy. What I can't seem to figure out is who she's working for and why she hasn't made her move yet. Did you happen to notice anything unusual about her when the two of you got up close and personal?" Sophie asked.

Toni paused. "Hmm. I don't think so. I briefly met her in the bathroom while I was sporting my college student persona. After I changed, she kept looking in my direction before we hooked up in the bathroom. At the time, I remember thinking that she was admiring Kim's exquisite dress selection for the evening. We had an initial moment of intense eye contact from across the room. Afterward, we kinda shared the same bathroom stall, but I know I didn't let her get a good look at my eyes. I'm always careful about that when I'm wearing colored contacts. She definitely was not carrying any weapons. She's either an athlete or maybe even a martial arts expert because her body…"

"Please spare me the details," Sophie snarled.

"Um, I hate to bring this up—because you're such an insufferable know-it-all, Soph, but I believe her stumbling into me might not have been an accident. We better check my jacket for bugs or tracking devices," Toni admitted.

"All right, time to head back to the hub and try to find out who she is. Before we get there, we ought to find a way to deactivate whatever present she left behind. I don't want anyone knowing the whereabouts of our base of operations. Maybe we should find a way to send her in a new direction until we're ready to have her find you again, Toni," Sophie proposed.

"Sounds like a plan to me. Let me open my bag of tricks and I will identify where it is and how to deactivate it."

Chapter Four

The smoke-filled back room reeked of tension and anxiety. Byron Harrison started to perspire under his three thousand dollar, specially tailored Armani suit. It was never a good thing when Antonio Santori called anyone to a meeting. Antonio had every right to know what was going on, but Byron didn't have good answers for him.

He figured out a little too late that the two attractive women who broke into his room at the fund-raiser to rescue his date were somehow responsible for their losses. He and his bodyguards were knocked out making it impossible to apprehend the women—his men did an exhaustive search but the women seemed to vanish in thin air leaving him holding the proverbial bag.

Things were getting out of hand. Byron wasn't the first to lose millions, but his losses were to date the largest blow. It didn't take a rocket scientist to figure out the connection between the losses and the mysterious foundation that kept redistributing their hard-earned dollars. Unfortunately, one of the offshore accounts that he managed was Antonio's and along with Byron's personal fortune, they had wiped out all of Antonio's money too.

Rumors were flying around that there was a secret powerful society of highly intelligent people, who were succeeding in changing the distribution of power in the banking industry. Some unknown person or group was responsible for thwarting all efforts to reveal who ran the society.

If Antonio Santori was unable to find the underlying cause, what hope did Byron have of getting back his millions? Byron didn't think that it was possible for the three women to be solely behind the losses. Surely, they were just pawns in the game. If only he could have gotten to them in time, he would have been able to trace them to the power source.

Antonio entered the smoky room and Byron could feel the quiet fury hiding just beneath the man's calm exterior. His fury nearly filled the room with anticipatory doom. Byron noted how Antonio's classic Italian good looks were marred by cold black eyes. Eyes that now telegraphed his raging anger.

"Byron, it is so good you were able to join us this evening. I'm sorry I didn't get a chance to meet your lovely companion at the fund-raiser."

Byron was surprised that Antonio had waited a whole week to summon him and wondered if Antonio had discovered more information about the trio of women.

"I'm afraid she turned out to be a huge disappointment. She won't be accompanying me to any future events."

A flash of rage appeared in Antonio's eyes.

Byron knew that his tendency to add chemicals to a romantic conquest was repugnant to Antonio, but business is business and Antonio had never interfered before.

"Byron, you are an imbecilic man who has now managed to impact my business. Perhaps you deserve losing millions because of the distasteful manner in which you treat your dates—I do not. These women are like ghosts and I would like to know what you know about them," Antonio stated calmly.

Byron knew it would do no good to react to Antonio's assessment of him, so he restrained an angry retort and simply shared his knowledge. "At least one of them has advanced martial arts skills." He frowned as he unconsciously rubbed the bruise where she cut off his air supply. "I suspect all of them were in expertly designed disguises. Before they escaped, I got close enough to realize my date was wearing contacts, but I don't know her true eye color. I suspect that at least one of them is an expert with computers because somehow they were able to access our accounts through a highly sophisticated breach in our security. I can only surmise the breach was contingent on getting close to me, but I still haven't figured out how they did it. Our security has both traditional passwords and biometric access. I can understand how a talented hacker might be able to obtain the password, but the biometric access requires both my fingerprint and a retina scan."

"Is it possible that one of them is former CIA?"

"I suppose anything is possible."

"How did they slip through your physical security?"

"They must have been wearing some type of communication device, because shortly after I provided my date with a drink the other two came bursting into the suite. I dispatched my private security immediately, but there was only a trail of unconscious bodies left in their wake. The security cameras only show them entering the fund-raiser. There is no record of their exit. I suspect they utilized another disguise. There were a lot of people at the fund-raiser, so it's almost impossible to determine what disguise was used. One of the women had an interesting interaction with a fourth woman, but we weren't able to determine if she is just an innocent bystander or an integral part of their operation."

"The redhead and the blonde?" Antonio asked.

"Yes."

"They were both very striking, even with disguises it cannot be that difficult to find out who they are. Have you studied the security footage to get a clear picture?"

"Yes, of course we have, but it's like they seemed to know exactly where each camera was and we have zero clear pictures of their faces. Even the redhead managed to keep her face from the camera. We don't know if this was coincidence or specifically engineered. We could use your help and your resources with this. I don't think I need to tell you that it's starting to affect more people than just those in the banking industry."

"My connections are working on the mystery foundation angle, but the computer expert they are using has been able to move the money so quickly and so randomly we've made no headway. We cannot stop the transfer of funds without jeopardizing our own assets. By involving the masses and the media there will be too many people involved to stop the flow of funds. It seems like the meek will inherit the earth if these women have anything to say about it."

Antonio's tone lost its hard edge.

Byron suspected that he couldn't help but admire the cunning of the women. He was aware that some of the recipients of the redistributed assets were in poor working-class Italian families and suspected that they were probably reminiscent of Antonio's grandparents.

He didn't really care if the Russian mob found them first, but he wondered if Antonio would prefer to track these women down instead. He'd worked with Antonio enough to know that harming women was distasteful to him, but not to Viktor Borsky, the Russian mob boss.

"So far the redistribution of wealth is just a drop in the bucket to the whole banking industry, but to me personally, the blow was devastating," Byron lamented.

"Your personal loss is of no concern to me. Consider it payment for your stupidity and abhorrent behavior to your dates. I will expect reimbursement for my losses. Frankly, I don't care where you retrieve the money, but I do expect to see those funds back in my account by close of business two weeks from today."

Byron could almost feel his face losing all color as he realized his dire predicament. He knew there was no other way than to liquidate all his remaining personal assets. Even then, he may not quite make up for Antonio's personal losses.

Byron gritted his teeth. He was not prone to violence, but if he ever came across these women again, he'd make sure they paid. Antonio was not the only business associate he worked with. Viktor, the head of the Russian mafia, didn't have the same philosophy as Antonio regarding how to deal with the troubling women.

"I understand and I appreciate the time frame you have given me to take care of the situation," Byron acceded.

†

Antonio smiled. He had a good idea where to get information on who the women were, but he wasn't about to go out of his way to help Byron with his problem. The guy was a sleaze and the way he treated women was appalling. As long as Byron returned his funds, he was satisfied. He secretly applauded the women and thought Byron got exactly what he deserved.

Antonio let his mind wander as he reminisced about his first love. God, how he loved her. But apparently not enough to give up his new life. He grinned. Was it possible that she was behind all this? *Well, good for you that you finally found a way to finance your missions in a morally acceptable manner.*

He sent a small prayer up to his God—*may the angels watch over you, my dear sweet M.*

Chapter Five

The DC office was in a quiet neighborhood, completely removed from the normal hustle and bustle of Washington politics. Although the office was not in a questionable part of town, the office easily faded into the background and allowed the three friends to conduct business without the prying eyes of anyone who might discover their true mission.

"Bingo. We have a match. Heather Stiles, Attorney at Law. On the surface it appears that she is who she says she is." Sophie shook her head. "I don't like it. There is something familiar about this woman. Most of the information on her seems to start eighteen months ago. There's bits and pieces from prior to that time frame, but I still smell a rat here. It's almost as if someone created an identity for her—classic CIA. If her background is contrived—whoever did this is very good. Toni, can you see if you can dig a bit farther and get something else on her." Sophie leaned back in the office chair and linked her hands behind her head.

"Sophie, you are such a conspiracy theorist. If she wanted to harm us, I suspect we would already be toast—especially if she's CIA, as you suspect. I know she probably isn't what or who she says she is, but maybe she's not our enemy. I can attest to the fact that she isn't a boring corporate attorney. She was intelligent, witty, and incredibly exciting. I, for one, would not mind interacting with her again if the opportunity presents itself. Just because you haven't been laid in more than two years, doesn't mean I have to be celibate too." Toni paced the office.

"Our downfall will most definitely be related to your oversexed behavior." Sophie glared at Toni.

Toni didn't take the bait, knowing that Sophie was just trying to show her disdain for her cavalier attitude.

"I wish you two would quit bickering with one another. Have you forgotten we are a team with the same goals in mind? I do agree with Sophie. I think this woman is dangerous and I don't really know why. It's just a gut feeling I get, but I also sense that she may somehow be on our side. There does seem to be some kind of connection between Heather and our recent activities. Where that connection exists, I'm not sure. We should be cautious, but I don't think we ought to close any doors just yet." Kim touched Sophie on the arm.

"Sorry. I can't help being cautious. It's in my nature. I don't think I could survive another loss. What we do is dangerous and we are poking the hornet's nest every time we take their money. They will fight back and it won't be pretty," Sophie warned.

"I'm not saying we're invincible or anything, but you have to admit we've had a pretty good run so far. I'm not willing to hang up our spurs just yet. We've only made a small dent. A few more like our recent success and I'll feel like we have actually accomplished what we all agreed to two years ago." Toni shot her friends a wide grin.

"Spurs. What are you some kind of cowgirl now?"

"Maybe. Do cowgirls get regular action?"

"I am not even going to respond to that." Sophie looked at Kim. "See, I can behave, I'm not even going to react to the slutty cowgirl pacing the floor."

"Passive aggressive."

"Am not."

"Are too."

"Oh, for God's sake, what are you guys, five years old? We've all been best friends since college—start acting like it. You both are giving me a migraine." Kim held her head in her hands.

"Sorry," Toni and Sophie said in unison.

"Okay. I admit it—the tracking device makes it obvious that she has an unhealthy interest in me. I suppose that's kind of flattering in a creepy sort of way." Toni chuckled. "Let me do my computer magic and see if I can find anything. Soph, do you think you might be able to access your old files. You keep saying that she seems familiar to you. Do you think it might have something to do with your previous undercover work?" Toni asked.

"Maybe. Can you hack into the FBI database and cross-reference all my files with Russian drug and human trafficking. For some reason, I think there might be a link to that. Call it woman's intuition, but I get the feeling this may have something to do with my last case. If that's the situation, we are in serious, deep shit."

"Done. I'm sorry Soph. I would never jeopardize your safety or Kim's safety. We walk away if there is even a remote possibility that we will turn the Russian Mafia on our trail. I'm all for reallocating the banking industry assets, but I'm not naïve enough to think they aren't linked in some fashion to some very nasty characters. We should all agree to stop if we start poking the big bear and the mob starts taking an unusual interest in our extracurricular activities."

"Agreed," Kim and Sophie declared together.

"I think we ought to put her little tracking device to work for us. I'd like her to run into me again—on our terms." Toni smiled.

Chapter Six

Char looked around the room, assessing the authenticity of the office space. It had taken her eighteen months to establish herself as the brilliant young corporate attorney, Heather Stiles. Her sister, Dani, originally established the cover to gain Viktor's trust, but now that Toni and her friends were in her sights, her shield served a dual purpose. She was not about to let her recent encounter with Toni rattle her cage. She had a mission and she would not let her mentor down. She owed everything to Maggie. Success with her mark was imminent. She'd make her first move today. Kim may have gotten her picture, but the tracking device she'd planted on Toni would ensure another chance encounter.

Her corporate attorney persona during the past year and a half had afforded her the opportunity to get to know the DC area well. She glanced at her laptop and noted that the blinking dot settled on a popular café owned and operated by well-known lesbians. She'd been in the café before—they knew her as Heather. It was time to make another chance appearance.

I gotcha now, Toni, she thought eagerly.

✝

Char casually strolled into the quaint café where she already knew that Sophie, Toni, and Kim were having a quiet dinner. It had been three days since her planned chance meeting in the café. Char chanced a quick glance at the corner table in the back where the trio was having drinks. She winked at the waitress and asked if she could have the quiet table in the back by the three attractive women.

"Sure thing, Heather. I think two of them are a couple, but the stunning brunette is definitely single. I always see her checking out every attractive woman. Unfortunately, I must not be her type because she hasn't turned her charms on me. The other two don't seem to notice other women. "

"Good thing, because I don't think Sara would really appreciate sharing your adorable self."

"Oh, you got that right. She is a bit possessive." Candy frowned.

Char didn't miss much and Candy's reaction sent alarm bells off in her head. She liked the petite blond waitress and got the distinct impression that everything wasn't right with Candy and Sara. She'd only met Sara once and her initial impression hadn't been favorable. Sara seemed overly domineering and her mildly hostile expression toward Char radiated extreme jealously. Unfortunately, Char didn't have the time to explore this—her priorities were with the trio. She refocused her attention on her target.

"Thanks, Candy. She just looks so familiar to me. I thought so the last time I bumped into her at that little café three blocks away. She winked at me and I asked her if I met her before because she looked so familiar."

"Well, I don't really know her all that well, but I do know her name is Toni."

"Lead the way and maybe if I cross her path again, she will notice me. Another wink would certainly be welcomed by me."

"She would have to be blind not to notice you."

"You are such a doll. Please be sure to let me know if Sara ever decides to dump you." At least Char could bolster the young woman's confidence. She hoped that if Candy were in a destructive relationship, she would have enough faith in herself to leave. Char would worry about Candy later.

"Ha, such a flirt. You and Toni are a match made in heaven."

Char was happy to hear Candy's lighthearted banter return. She followed Candy to the back of the café and smiled broadly as Toni glanced up.

"Well, hello again. I think you're stalking me. You must come join us because I've never had the pleasure of having dinner with a stalker before. Since it's a full moon, I think tonight's the night to start a new tradition."

"Ah, busted. I've been stalking you for the past eighteen months and you've only just noticed me now." Char chuckled and held out her hand as an introduction. "Heather Stiles. Full-time stalker extraordinaire and part-time corporate attorney. Or is that full-time attorney and part-time stalker. I can never seem to keep those two jobs separate. I would love to join you now that you finally noticed me—if it's okay with your friends."

Char looked at Sophie and Kim.

Sophie's eyes narrowed and appeared to be scrutinizing her. The look quickly disappeared.

"Absolutely. Come join us." Sophie smiled.

"Yes, please do. Toni is a sucker for a beautiful woman, even if you are a stalker," Kim added.

†

Even though they'd engineered it so Heather would run into Toni again, Sophie was uncomfortable with the attractive redhead crashing their party. She rubbed the eight-inch scar trailing up her left wrist. She recalled that fateful evening when she'd lost her partner and everything changed for her.

Knowing that the recent reallocation of funds took a big bite out of the human slave trade coffers didn't give her the kind of comfort she desperately needed to right the wrong of losing Natalie.

Sophie couldn't shake the feeling that the woman, Heather, —if that was really her name—was somehow connected to the loss of her former partner and she was damned if she would trust her.

Sophie was careful to present her poker face. Heather seemed to be watching her closely and all the evidence to date suggested the woman was a professional. For whatever reason. Sophie wondered who sent her to do God knows what. So far, the three of them had been widely successful on their own. Even if the woman was on the right side of the equation, it didn't mean they needed her horning in on their success.

Sophie didn't like the way Toni was practically hanging on every word the newcomer said. It was almost like the woman was a new addiction that Toni couldn't kick. Sophie didn't believe in fate, but even if she did, certainly this stranger was not Toni's future.

Damn you, Toni, for letting your wants and desires get in the way of good sound judgment. You're going to get us killed one day.

Now it looked like Kim was starting to soften her view of the situation. Kim was a sucker for a good love story and Sophie just bet she had all kinds of crazy ideas running through her head about Toni and Heather. Kim did believe in fate. Sophie feared that Kim might think there was something there beyond all logic and reasoning. Kim surely was not stupid enough to ignore the fact that the woman was not who she appeared to be. The facial recognition confirmation did nothing to calm Sophie's discomfort. Sophie never threw caution to the wind. Something major was about to happen, and it just might not be what they all needed.

The foursome carefully navigated the conversation at dinner. Sophie grudgingly admitted the redhead was witty and charming and her outward appearance did not give any suggestion that she was anything but a charming corporate attorney. It was clear to Sophie that the woman's charisma overwhelmed Toni. The electricity between the two was almost palpable. Sophie was not about to let this stranger take them down and she wasn't about to let Toni's libido do it either.

†

Toni studied the stranger closely as she told another amusing story about her first couple of months in DC. When she noticed the redhead glance out the window facing the sidewalk at the front of the café and frown, she wondered what caused this reaction. Toni's eyes traveled in the direction she was looking and now it was her turn to react. She gave an almost imperceptible nod to Kim and Sophie and they both ventured a momentary glance in the same direction that Heather was looking.

Heather turned and smiled at the three women as they shifted in their seats.

"I'm sorry I must have had too much iced tea. Will you excuse me for a moment while I visit the ladies' room? I'll be back in a flash," she announced.

Toni lamented that there was not a repeat performance of witty banter followed by a steamy bathroom hookup. Kim, and especially Sophie, were scrutinizing her every move. Regardless of the woman's identity, Toni liked the fact that she could discard her sophisticated attorney persona and get down and dirty. She loved the dichotomy of her personality.

Toni sighed and admitted it was probably for the best because she needed to talk with Kim and Sophie without the woman's presence. "Don't look now, but I think our friend Byron is about to crash our little party and he's got a particularly nasty companion in tow."

"Yeah, I noticed and so did your little object of desire. Don't you find that just a little coincidental that she leaves for her bathroom break right after spying Byron and Viktor?" Sophie smirked.

"Sophie, I think we ought to wait before making up stories and going down a rabbit hole. I agree something is off with Heather, but I'm not sure exactly what that is. We still don't know whose side she's on," Kim reasoned.

"Well said, Kim. Ms. Neanderthal always jumps to conclusions before getting all the facts. I volunteer to get up close and personal with Heather. I'll get the scoop. I promise," Toni offered.

"Fine, you get up close and personal, but you'd better not get caught up so much in her wit and charm that you jeopardize everything we've worked so hard for. I am not about to put us in the line of fire just because you have an

itch that needs scratching and scratching and scratching."
Sophie glared at Toni.

"Ooh, maybe I can scratch her itch and she can scratch mine and we can combine forces or something."

"Please be careful and for once think with your head and not your...."

"Coochie?"

"Yep, that's the body part I'm worried about."

"Stop your fretting. I got this. You're such a worrywart."

✝

Char pushed open the bathroom door and scanned the room. Noting that she was alone, she quickly retrieved her phone and punched the top number on her contact list. The list did not contain real names. The unexpected presence of Byron and Victor outside of the café agitated her and messed with her plan.

"Unexpected guests... Yes, I know... No, he didn't see me sitting with them, but we know he has both Toni's and Sophie's pictures... Okay... Yes, that should work... I need a distraction so I can execute a plausible exit. I can't take the chance that he'll link me with them... I guess I'll find another way to connect with Toni... All right, I'll exit in sixty seconds."

Char closed her phone and placed it carefully back in her bag. She hit the timer on her watch and waited the sixty seconds. She smiled as she heard the sound of a loud boom just as she stood inside the bathroom door.

"Ronda must be the sweeper today," she mumbled to herself. *Gotta love a woman who enjoys a nicely placed explosive. I hope his Porsche is in tiny little pieces.*

Char glanced down at her watch. "Five, four, three, two, one…I'm outta here."

†

Char pushed open the door and carefully put on her mask of surprise and fear. She forced herself to slow her pace and approached the table where Kim, Sophie, and Toni were all grinning. Their reaction pleased Char, but she stopped herself from joining them in celebration. When they glanced up to see her approach, all three of them stopped smiling.

"You missed all the excitement. I'm surprised you didn't hear the loud boom. Some guy's Porsche just blew up into smithereens. You don't see that one every day," Toni remarked.

"I did hear it and I have to admit to being a bit frightened, so I wasn't sure if I should come out or not." Char forced her voice to tremble a little.

Sophie narrowed her gaze and Char feared maybe she was taking her act a little too far.

"Don't worry, beautiful, I'll protect you." Toni grinned.

Char toned down her reaction. "Oh, it's okay. It was just a little surprising to hear the loud noise. I need to get back to my apartment before Fred pees on the carpet in protest."

Toni raised her eyebrow.

"Fred is my golden retriever. It was nice running into you. Thanks for rescuing me from another night of eating alone."

"Why don't you consider yourself permanently rescued? Any time you need a dinner date, just call me."

Toni pulled a card from her back pocket and placed it in Char's hand.

Char pulled a business card and pen from her purse and quickly scribbled a number on the back of the card. "Here, my cell is on the back. Call me. We should get together and compare notes on the unusual event today. I just love to make up outrageous stories about things I see and this one is ripe for my imagination."

†

Toni didn't miss that Heather went in the opposite direction of the commotion outside the café.

"Tell me you gave her one of your special business cards," Sophie probed.

"Oh, yeah, definitely. Now to track where Heather Stiles, attorney at law, spends the majority of her off-duty time. I've got the phone tracking app linked to our home base computers. She won't be able to take a shit without me knowing where she's gone." Toni leaned back in the booth and smiled.

"Does she actually have to have it on her person?" Kim asked.

"Nope, it's my very sophisticated design. Once she took the card in her hand a small tracking device absorbed into her skin."

"How come it doesn't absorb into your body?" Sophie asked.

"It's kind of complicated, but basically it's a combination of biology and technology. It's programmed to ignore my DNA," Toni explained.

"How do you come up with these things?" Kim asked.

"If you can dream it, it can be done."

"Geez, you really are brilliant. Are you sure your IQ is only one hundred and fifty?" Sophie lifted her eyebrow.

"Careful, Soph, that sounded suspiciously like a compliment." Toni chuckled.

Chapter Seven

Char's high heels clicked on the hard sidewalk as she made a quick exit from the café. She turned the corner rapidly and joined an attractive blonde who was walking quickly ahead of her.

"Nice job, Ronda. Is Maggie pissed?"

"Nah, these things happen, Besides, I was more worried about their exposure. However, that does put you behind the eight ball, huh?"

"Yes and no. She doesn't trust me yet. She gave me one of her *special* business cards. So I need to drop by the office and place it on my desk where it will stay. I'm actually surprised that she would try that old trick. If she really thinks I'm some kind of spy, surely she would know I'm too smart to fall for that." Char shrugged.

"Oh, I don't know, Char. She's supposed to be brilliant—maybe it's not your run-of-the-mill tracking device."

"Hmmm, what have you heard?"

"Only that she's off-the-charts smart and has invented some really amazing things."

"Good to know. I guess I'd better be particularly cautious about where I go for the next few days until I get her to trust me."

"How will you do that?" Ronda asked.

"I plan on asking her to dinner and turning on the charm. I have to admit this mission is more fun than the last. Maybe we'll even get to be genuine friends before this is all over. Besides you, Dani, and Maggie, I don't really have anyone I can depend on."

"I'm not sure subterfuge is the best way to start a friendship. I just don't understand why Maggie didn't just approach them like she did with the rest of us."

"I'm sure she has her reasons. I would suspect Sophie is not real fond of any organization that remotely resembles the FBI or CIA and Toni—well Toni is Toni. She's always been a rogue player in everything. I don't think she does well playing with others."

"Neither do you, but Maggie got you to join." Ronda frowned.

"I had my reasons."

"Don't we all," Ronda mumbled.

Char looked up at Ronda and wondered about the strange comment from her friend. "Maggie saved our lives."

Char tried to erase the memories of her dysfunctional youth and the dirty trailer in the backwoods of Alabama.

✝

Her mother looked dead for a minute until Char heard the light snoring and noticed the cheap whiskey bottle turned on its side as the precious liquid seeped onto the filthy green carpet of the trailer. The whiskey wasn't precious to Char, but to her mother it was liquid gold.

A noise from the bedroom startled her and she looked up to see her mother's latest meal ticket. A grossly overweight man emerged from the tiny bedroom as he

57

scratched his enormous belly. He wasn't wearing much. A pair of dingy gray boxers and a wifebeater T-shirt hung haphazardly on his misshapen body.

"What the fuck are you looking at? Where's your sweet little sister?" The man leered at Char.

Char wasn't afraid of him. She could outrun the fat pig. If he ever tried to touch her again, she would kick him in the groin. She wasn't about to let him near her little sister.

Standing up to her full height of five foot ten inches tall, she hissed at the man. "You better fucking stay clear of Dani or I swear I'll bash your head in while you sleep."

The man lumbered forward. "You little bitch. I ought to teach you a lesson. Your mama has no idea how to raise you hooligans—you got no respect for your elders. I pay the bills. I make the rules."

Char easily dodged his grip and slammed the trailer door as she ran across the field of weeds to grab her sister and hide out for the night. Maybe her mama would wake up soon and put a barrier between them. When her mama wasn't drinking, she was okay. Sometimes she would even stand up for them.

✝

Char shook her head in an effort to clear those distant memories from her brain. She'd done the right thing, even if Dani had been hurt. If she hadn't, they'd probably be dead or worse by now. Dead wasn't as bad as what she imagined. It would be worse. Yeah, she had her reasons.

"Will you tell Maggie I'll contact her later with an update and that I might need a little more time?"

"Sure thing, Char. Oh, and let me know if you need anything else blown up. You know I love a good explosion now and again. Keeps my skills up. Nothing like some C-4 to get the blood flowing again. Seems that's about all I'm good for."

Char didn't really know what was going on with Ronda, but it seemed like not all was copacetic with her. She really didn't have the time now to figure it out. Besides, supportive friendships weren't really her strong point.

"Hey, I'll see you at the hub later after I take care of a few things. I might just have to give the delectable Toni a call later tonight. I don't want her forgetting me."

Char waved at Ronda and turned toward the street, looking for the next cab.

She wanted to hurry back to her office so she could analyze how Toni was able to embed a tracking chip into a business card. She'd heard about Toni's legendary inventions and wanted to check them out for herself.

Char spied a yellow cab rounding the corner and lifted her hand to get the driver's attention. The cab rolled up to Char and she folded her long body into the backseat of the cab. She leaned her head against the vinyl seat and closed her eyes after giving the cabbie the address. Ten minutes later, she arrived at her office.

The soft glow from the streetlamp flooded into the cozy office space. Char looked around the office and noted that the solid cherry desk, matching bookshelves, and soft leather chair attributed to the warmth. Otherwise, the office was devoid of intimacy. Sparse was an understatement. No personal belongings, family pictures, or other indication of the owner's personality adorned the desk.

Char walked to the high-powered desk lamp and pulled out a specially designed magnifying glass hoping to inspect Toni's business card. As she deposited her body into the soft leather, she leaned back and smiled. By all accounts, Toni was a brilliant inventor and Char needed to know how she embedded the tracking chip into the card. After a brief inspection, she detected no raised lettering or any other indication of the device.

"Hmm. How did you embed the chip you clever little minx?" It often helped her to talk aloud when she was trying to solve a problem.

She placed the card under the powerful industrial grade magnifying glass.

"Even you can't hide a slight bulge in the card when under the detection of Myra." Char had a made a game of naming her gadgets. Myra was the name of her pocket magnifying glass.

Char frowned when she found nothing raised on the card and only noted an odd shimmering glow under the magnification.

"Hmm. What do we have here? If I were a betting woman, I would say this card has a biological property attached to it. I better get this to the lab. How do I do that without revealing the lab's location? Let me think. Let me think. As Maggie always says, a problem is just an opportunity yet to be resolved."

Char leaned back in the chair and looked to the ceiling, hoping for inspiration. She absently picked up the gold pen neatly aligned perpendicular to the pad on the top of her desk and tapped it on her temple.

"Maggie's not going to like this, but I need to get some of that lab equipment transported here to the office. It's the only way."

Char chuckled as she thought about what people would think if they heard her talking to herself while all alone in her office. It's a good thing most of my colleagues leave before six, she thought.

Char pulled her cell phone from her pocket and dialed the number etched in her memory. "I need to transport some resources. No, to my office. I'm afraid there's no other option. Yes, I suspect it's biological in origin. Oh yes, she's a clever little minx. No, don't worry, I've got everything under control. Yeah, I plan to call tonight to invite her for dinner tomorrow. Okay. Thank you. Yes, tonight—I'll need it tonight."

Char pushed the button on her cell phone to end the call. She flipped the card and smiled as she punched in the numbers scribbled on the card. "Well hello, yourself. I do apologize for needing to leave so abruptly. I was hoping you might be interested in having dinner with me tomorrow night. If you give me your address, I can pick you up at say six thirty. Okay, that would work as well. Are you afraid I'll stalk you at home? Yes, me too. Goodnight, Toni."

✝

A few minutes after midnight, Char watched as Ronda parked the sleek black SUV next to her law office. She noted the emptiness in the street and breathed in the stillness of the air. Char scanned the street to make sure no prying eyes were watching the transfer of lab equipment into the secret room attached to her office.

Ronda carried the first silver box. "Hey, Char, what's with the special delivery here?"

"I think our clever little inventor may have used a biological device in her tracking card."

"No shit, I've never heard of such a thing. I thought we had the most cutting-edge technology. I'll bet that's why Maggie is so hell-bent on recruiting them."

"I can't really be sure until I check it out."

"Do you need any help with that?"

"No, thanks. I really appreciate you bringing it here, though."

"Yeah, yeah, I'm just the brawn I guess," Ronda mumbled.

"What?"

"Oh, nothing."

Char moved close to Ronda and reached out to take the box. "Here, let me take that from you and then you can get back to whatever you were doing before I so rudely interrupted you."

"No worries, it's never a problem to help you out. You know I care about you, Char. I don't know if we should trust them yet. I know Maggie thinks they'll fit right in, but I'm not so sure and Toni is an arrogant little shit. I'll bet she's planning on bedding you the first chance she gets." Ronda frowned.

"I know, Ronda, and you're a good friend, but I can take care of myself. You know my rule, once we recruit them, there won't be any additional fraternization. I have to admit that I won't mind the amount of fraternization I may have to do—all within the confines of the mission."

"You'll just be another notch on her belt, you know."

Char looked up to see Ronda scowling. *I've really got to deal with her infatuation with me soon.*

"Don't worry, personal entanglements aren't my style. You know that."

"Yeah, I do," Ronda mumbled.

Char gently set the silver box on the table in the secret back room and then walked out with Ronda to retrieve the rest of the equipment.

The back room was sparse with enhanced lighting, several large tables, and multiple outlets. The room was perfect for setting up a temporary lab.

After Char placed the rest of the silver lab boxes on the tables, she turned to Ronda to encourage her to leave. Char preferred working alone. "Thanks, Ronda, you're the best. See you tomorrow. Maybe we can grab some coffee?"

"All right, I'll call you. Don't work on this all night, okay?"

"I won't, I just want to run a few tests."

Char unpacked the expensive equipment and set up the microscopes and sensitive sample testers. She sighed as she prepared for a long night of work. She was determined to figure out how Toni managed to embed a tracking device in the card without detection. It had to be something totally unconventional.

Chapter Eight

"I'm bored. I'm bored. I'm bored. I'm bored. I'm bored," Toni chanted to herself as she spun her chair around in circles. "Whoa." Toni stopped spinning and put her head between her legs. "I guess that wasn't such a good idea."

After she braced herself on the arms of her office chair, steadying herself for a few minutes, she got up and paced her living room before plopping down on the sofa.

"What to do now for fun." She groaned. God, Heather had put her in such a tailspin that she was talking to herself.

Toni stared at her cell phone and frowned. What could she possibly be doing this late at night in her office? She leaned back against the couch and flipped the phone in her hand in a nervous gesture of frustration.

I don't suppose Kim and Sophie would object to a little stakeout tonight.

Toni jumped up, grabbed her leather jacket, and headed to her pride and joy, a Harley Davidson Softail. She knew she would have to park several blocks away from the attorney's office because a loud engine was an obvious characteristic of the famous brand.

Toni roared up to the street several blocks away from Heather's office and dismounted from her bike. She walked quickly to a location designed to give her a clear view of the building without revealing her location. The tree-lined street provided the perfect cover. Toni noticed the lights on in one of the second-floor offices.

Toni pulled out her high-powered binoculars and watched as a sleek black SUV pulled up in front of Heather's office. Toni watched as an unknown woman unloaded what appeared to be some type of equipment encased in silver cases. *Oh, Heather, what are you up to this evening?*

Toni pulled out her phone and punched in the number to Sophie's private line. She didn't really want to confirm Sophie's suspicions about the beautiful attorney, but Toni had to admit what she was seeing tonight did not bode well for her perception of Heather's trustworthiness. Something was clearly happening and without audio monitoring, Toni couldn't do anything at this point to solve this mystery.

"Hey, Soph, I hate to bother you this late at night, but something odd is happening at Heather's office and I need you to try to follow a black SUV that is currently unloading equipment. I need you to hurry, because I think she's about to leave."

Toni pushed the end button on her iPhone and watched as the unknown woman carried several more cases into the brick building. Soon after, she climbed into the SUV and pulled out onto the empty street. Damn, Sophie was gonna be pissed.

Thirty seconds later, Toni jogged off in the direction of where Sophie would approach and rounded the corner just in time to flag her down. She banged on the driver's side of the car, knowing that their window of opportunity was small. "Hurry. She's headed north down First Avenue."

Sophie rushed off into the black night.

Toni paced on the sidewalk, sending up a small prayer that Sophie would be able to catch her in time and find out a little more about the late-night activities she had just observed. After ten minutes of pacing, Toni heard a vehicle approach and turned her head to see who might be out this late in the evening. Maybe Heather was getting another nocturnal delivery. Sophie's car pulled up next to her and the driver's side window whirred as it came down. Sophie scowled.

"I can see by your pleasant expression that you just missed her. I think I'll hang around for a few more hours to see if I can find out anything more, but I suspect she may be holed up for the night and I don't want to take a chance that she'll see me."

"Why don't you just continue to track her with your phone? You'll know when she leaves the office and then you can pinpoint her new location. Maybe you can learn a few more things tomorrow at dinner. Be careful, Toni, and don't let your attraction to her blind you. I can't pinpoint it right now, but I'm sure I know her from somewhere. Call it intuition, but I think she's somehow tied to Viktor and he is someone we want to stay as far away from as possible. Someday we'll find a way to cripple his operation by liberating his funds, but we had better make damn sure we have a failsafe plan before we attempt going after the Russian mob. I don't think I could live with myself if the result is another casualty."

Toni's voice softened. "I know, Soph, I miss Natalie too, but if we go after them it won't be the same. We won't have the restrictions you had when you were with the FBI. We get to play by our rules this time, not theirs. You know I only offered my technology to them because of you. I won't make the same mistake again, even if it's for the *good guys.* I'll always be in your debt. You saved my life that night. I know I didn't deserve it because I had no business insisting on accompanying you to make sure my prototype worked the way I envisioned it. It was pure ego on my part."

"It's water under the bridge. I'd do anything for you and Kim," Sophie added.

"I know and I love you too, bud, but you know Kim *luuves* you more. Smoochy, smoochy." Toni laughed.

"Oh, shut the fuck up and just go home already. You need to be sharp for your *date* tomorrow night."

Sophie lifted her hand and waved at Toni. The electric window silently closed as she eased away with a smirk on her face.

Toni shook her head and walked to her Harley. A shiver went down her back as she relived that horrible night two years ago.

†

"I'm going with you. No arguments, Sophie. It's my invention and I'll be damned if I'll let some snot-nosed feebie test it out."

"Snot-nosed feebie? What the hell are you talking about? Natalie is young, but she's on my team and she knows what she's doing. You're the one who offered to let us test it."

"I offered to let you test it, not Natalie. I mean, I like the kid, but she's pretty green and it's a very expensive prototype."

"Natalie's the one who managed to get that snitch, Dani, to trust her. I'm only supposed to be her backup. I can't very well be the one to test it because I'm not even supposed to be there. Besides, she's spent months infiltrating the Russian mob, not me."

"Fine, then I'll hang with you as backup."

"No offense, but you're not exactly trained for this sort of mission. You'll only be a liability to us."

"It's non-negotiable. I can hang out in the van with you and monitor the recording device. If something goes wrong I can help."

"You are a stubborn little shit. I have a bad feeling about this, but you've left me no choice because my boss isn't about to pass up the opportunity for this kind of breakthrough technology. You have us over a barrel and you know it."

Toni grinned. "Well, I'm glad we got that settled."

Toni watched as Sophie waved at Natalie who was busy talking to Ted, an agent Toni had met previously through Sophie. Toni noticed that Natalie and Ted seemed to be having an animated discussion. After a few minutes, Natalie walked to where Toni and Sophie were standing outside of the nondescript white van that held the surveillance equipment. Parked parallel to the first van was the one Natalie would use.

"Hey, Toni. Thanks for letting me test your prototype. I'm impressed. I've been trained to detect bugs and recording devices and I cannot believe the camera and audio are built into this jacket. It's very stylish. Any chance I can keep it after the mission?" Natalie grinned.

"Not on your life. I plan on keeping that one for myself." Toni answered.

"Hey, what's going on with Ted?" Sophie asked. "You seemed to be having a very lively discussion."

"Oh, he's just pissed because he thinks he should be in on the action. I don't think he likes the fact that I'm the one who's been able to arrange the meeting with Dani and her two contacts. Would you believe one of them is a woman? She actually trains the poor girls to be subservient and accept whatever Viktor's customers want."

Natalie shook her head. "I just don't understand how any woman can be attached to the white slave trade. Some of those girls have barely reached puberty. Although I want to nail both that bastard and his female associate, for some reason my snitch, Dani, is rather protective of this woman and made me promise to ensure her safety while this whole operation goes down. As repulsive as it seems, maybe we can offer witness protection for this woman in exchange for her testimony. I get the impression she knows a lot about the internal workings—it might be enough to take Viktor down for good."

"Something doesn't smell right about this. You never mentioned another person. I thought the exchange was only going to involve Viktor's right-hand man and maybe a few security personnel. Paranoid bastards," Sophie grunted.

"I don't think we have to worry about this woman carrying a gun. Dani assured me there wouldn't be more than two security personnel, Dimitri, and this woman. I trust Dani. I don't think she's really had a choice in her life and the woman's circumstances have dictated what she's had to do to survive. She wants out and I want to help her. All we need to do is get them on tape and get the girls to safety before they realize anything is amiss. It's taken me a long time to gain Dani's trust," Natalie argued.

"All right. Come on, let's get a move on. We don't want to keep the bastards waiting." Sophie walked quickly to the first van. Natalie jogged to the other van, smiled and gave Sophie a thumbs-up gesture.

Toni remained quiet during the exchange, but the hairs on the back of her neck raised in alarm. She agreed with Sophie. Something just didn't seem right about the change in the operation.

Toni followed Sophie into the first van and jumped in the back. She opened her laptop to make sure the program tied to the jacket was fully functional. She knew her job was limited to monitoring the meeting from afar. Natalie's vehicle would transport the merchandise.

Toni shivered at the thought that this was how the mob viewed the young girls. The slave trade was big business. Each girl brought a price tag of more than one million dollars. Blond- haired, blue-eyed girls generated the highest price tags, but the Asian girls were also highly sought after.

Sophie slowly traversed the back streets until she rolled to an abrupt stop in a deserted area next to the unpopulated warehouse district. She was careful to keep a respectable distance from Natalie's van, but was close enough to serve as backup if needed.

Toni and Sophie placed headphones over their ears and huddled around the small laptop screen.

Toni looked at Sophie and noticed that she'd pulled her Glock 23 from its holster. Toni now had second thoughts about accompanying Sophie on this mission. Suddenly things seemed a bit more dangerous than she'd initially thought. Toni wasn't a trained agent—she was just a techno geek. Maybe she should have heeded Sophie's warnings.

Natalie scrambled out of the van and Toni watched the small screen as she approached the five dark shapes clustered around the dingy warehouse to the right of the van.

Toni saw Natalie approach one of the women who she assumed was Dani. Standing next to her was an attractive blonde. She must be the trainer.

Through the headphones, Toni heard one of the men speak. "Lift your arms and open your jacket."

Toni watched in horror as a man with a flattened nose and steely gray eyes seemed to leer as he patted Natalie down and then proceeded to unbutton her shirt as he ran his hands over her breasts and back.

"Unzip your pants," the ugly man said.

Toni glanced at Sophie who was clenching her jaw as the image on the laptop showed the man slowly running his hands over her buttocks, inner thighs, and under her panties.

"She's clear of wires."

"Good, good. Now we need to inspect the van." Another man nodded his head in the direction of the van.

The confident woman stepped in front of the man who just gave the order to inspect the van. "I want to do the inspection. My girls, my show. I've trained them, I will inspect the van while you get the money."

"You are not in charge here, Oksana. Viktor only allowed you here tonight because you have been useful to our business," the tallest man barked.

Toni surmised that this man must be Dimitri but didn't understand why the woman was so intent on inspecting the van. That thought flew out of her mind, as everything seemed to happen in slow motion after that as she watched the shitstorm unfold.

When Oksana pulled out a knife and placed it against the throat of the man, Sophie quickly exited the van and Toni followed closely behind. Natalie quickly turned around and kicked out at one of the men as he pulled his gun and shot her between the eyes.

The one Toni thought must be Dani screamed. "No, oh God, no," She cried as she knelt in front of Natalie. She gently placed Natalie's head in her lap, rocking her and sobbing over her body.

The man with the gun turned in Dani's direction and Oksana removed the knife and threw it his direction, hitting her target directly in his heart, but not before he squeezed the trigger and landed a bullet in Dani's back as she was bent over Natalie's lifeless body.

The man Toni suspected was Dimitri pulled the knife from his colleague's body and sliced Sophie's hand as she pointed her gun at the other man pulling his Beretta from his holster.

The Glock clattered to the ground, sliding next to Dimitri. He tossed aside the knife and bent down to reach for the gun just as Oksana grabbed his head and sliced his throat.

The final man standing grabbed Toni and placed the Beretta to her head.

Sophie executed a perfect roundhouse kick to his hand and the gun collided with the pavement.

Toni glanced at Oksana and was amazed at how quickly she retrieved the Beretta in her right hand while shoving the Glock into the waistband of her pants. How the hell did she do that?

Oksana peeked at Dani and frowned. She pointed the gun at the final man. "You move an inch and I'll shoot. I'm an expert shot so do not test me."

She glared at Sophie and barked an order. "The girls are in the warehouse, take them to safety and I will clean up this mess."

"You are fucking crazy if you think I'll allow that to happen," Sophie yelled.

"I don't want to shoot you, Sophie, but I will if I have to. There is nothing you can do for Natalie now and I need to attend to Dani. She's my priority." She turned her head and Toni heard Oksana speak into her shoulder. "Dani's down, send the medical team."

"Who the fuck are you?" Sophie asked.

"I'm not the enemy. Let's just leave it at that."

Toni grabbed Sophie's good arm. "Soph, come on. Your arm looks bad. Frankly, I don't care what happens to him." Toni pointed at the man the blonde was holding at gunpoint.

"We can't just leave Natalie here." A tear leaked out of Sophie's eye.

Toni looked at Oksana. "Can I please carry her to the van?"

A nod was the only answer she received.

Toni was about to remove Natalie from Dani's embrace until she realized that blood was seeping from a wound in Dani's back. When she attempted to move, Toni held her down.

"Don't move. You've been shot in the back. Wait for the medical team to arrive."

"I loved her. Will you make sure she's taken care of? Everything is not always as it seems." Dani grimaced before she collapsed on top of Natalie.

"I promise. We will take good care of her," Toni whispered.

Toni looked up as a car rapidly approached and a short brunette woman, carrying what appeared to be a medical bag and IV equipment, magically appeared. She wondered why she hadn't heard the sirens and then noticed that the vehicle was not an ambulance or aide car. Toni assumed she was the medic, but this was certainly not what she expected when she heard Oksana call for a medical team. Another woman was pulling a gurney and medical equipment out of the back of the vehicle. It looked more sophisticated than what she envisioned a normal ambulance might offer.

The medic was immediately by their side. She crouched down and assessed Dani's injuries. Dani did not appear to be moving and Toni feared for her life.

"She's been shot in the back," Toni said.

"Yeah, I can see that," the short brunette said, not looking at Toni. "We will handle it from here."

Toni looked up and watched Sophie corral six frightened girls into the van. Appraising them, she realized none looked older than twelve. The knowledge of the life the Russian mob almost forced them into made Toni physically ill.

Once Dani was secure, Toni picked up Natalie and choked back the vomit threatening to explode from her stomach as she carried the lifeless body into the van. She gently placed her in the back and attempted to reassure the young girls that they were safe. Nothing would erase the memory of this night from their traumatized brains, but at least they were not destined for the bleak life that had surely been in the cards for them prior to this fateful evening. Toni was thankful for that one bright thought.

Wordlessly, she had climbed into the driver's seat and exited the dark street. As she turned the corner, she'd heard a single gunshot.

Good, I hope the bastard rots in hell.

Chapter Nine

Char bent over the microscope as she looked at the foreign substance woven into the ink. She scraped some of the ink from the business card and placed the particles into a test tube. After she added a couple of drops of testing solution, she watched as the tube turned a bright lavender color.

"Oh, Toni, you clever, clever girl."

Char pulled out her phone and quickly pressed the numbers for headquarters.

"Hello, Maggie, I'm sorry to wake you in the middle of the night. Yes, I'm still at my office. Yes, it's as I suspected. No, I'm not sure about the impact just yet. No, I don't think so. I don't think that's what she's about. Yes, I just think she may be a bit more intrigued with me than we want at this point. No, I'll just stay here for the night... I'll call to let you know more after dinner tomorrow night."

Char shut down her phone and smiled.

"I am really going to enjoy the chase, my lovely little inventor."

Char removed her shirt and stripped down to lace underwear. She yawned and stretched her arms above her head as she ambled into the small bathroom attached to the hidden room. She scrubbed her face with her favorite lemon lavender soap and pulled the electric toothbrush from its holder.

After she crawled into the soft cotton sheets on the cot set up in the corner of the secret room she let her thoughts wander to Toni. She had to admit she was finding this mission very pleasurable. Toni intrigued her more than any other mark ever had.

Perhaps they would become friends, she thought, or maybe more. Could she possibly let someone inside the inner sanctum of her emotions? She never let that happen before, but there was something uniquely different about Toni. She'd caught her eye that very first night. What an awful way to meet someone. The terror in Toni's eyes had been unmistakable.

Thank God, it wasn't her that was a casualty. Poor Natalie, she never even saw it coming.

†

Toni looked at her phone with bleary eyes. She'd sprawled out on her couch after she decided Heather wasn't going anywhere.

It was close to three o'clock in the morning when she decided to throw the towel in and go home. Before she settled on her couch, she programmed her phone to produce an audio signal if Heather moved from her current location.

The phone glowed in the darkness of the pre-dawn— illustrating the early morning hour.

Toni rubbed her hand across her face and smacked her lips, as she tasted the cotton in her mouth. Normally, Toni would go to bed chewing a stick of gum. She hated the taste of her morning breath. She was convinced that chewing peppermint gum prevented that yucky taste on her tongue. It was just one of her many quirks.

Might as well get up and take a morning jog. Toni doubted Heather was out and about this early.

Toni grabbed a pair of sweats laying on her ultra-suede recliner and pulled them over her comfortable black Patagonia briefs. After she pulled on her matching black sports bra and bamboo T-shirt designed to wick away sweat, she headed for the Chesapeake and Ohio Canal Trail.

†

Toni set a grueling pace and was startled from her thoughts when her iPhone dinged. She glanced at the phone attached to her armband and noticed the dot moving. Hmm, another early riser.

Toni watched the dot as it moved slowly along the Rock Creek Trail. Toni wasn't prepared to meet up with Heather just yet so she veered off the trail and looked for a place to hunker down. The dot moved in her direction coming close to where Rock Creek Trail intersected with the Chesapeake and Ohio Canal Trail in Georgetown.

From her hiding place, Toni watched as Heather's long legs appeared. Heather was wearing running shorts and her muscular thighs flexed in an appealing mix of strength and femininity. Toni nearly gasped at the sight. She looked beautiful in the early morning dawn as the light reflected off her coppery hair tied back into a messy ponytail.

Toni chuckled quietly as she heard her singing to her iPod clipped to the waistband of her shorts. Her voice was a pleasant alto and surprisingly on key.

Toni was looking forward to her evening date with the alluring attorney. She knew Heather was not who she seemed, but she didn't care. She was an enigma that was worth unraveling.

Toni couldn't remember ever wanting to untangle someone's mysteries before. She had always been content with brief affairs. Something was compelling her to dig deeper this time and it wasn't just the conundrum of this woman as a possible danger to her and her friends.

After Heather had long passed the hidden spot, Toni remained with her face upturned to the sun. It was a glorious morning. Finally, she stretched and pushed out of the weeds to enter the trail and finish her run. It was a great way to start the day. Toni only hoped the end of her day would be just as pleasant.

†

Char pulled her sweaty running clothes off and stepped into the shower. Her iPad was playing one of her favorite Missy Higgins songs, *Secret*, and she sang along.

After her shower, Char transformed into her corporate attorney persona, Heather Stiles. An emerald-green silk shirt was the perfect accent to her conservative tan suit. The blouse brought out the color of her eyes.

Char glanced in the mirror and brushed invisible lint off her suit. Time to play corporate attorney.

Char hated this part of her cover. She always felt like taking another shower after meeting with her high roller clients. There wasn't one client with any redeeming qualities. Her job was to protect their assets and find every conceivable way to help them make money at the expense of those less fortunate or those unwilling to sacrifice their ethics.

It had taken her nearly a year for Viktor to notice her and several more months before he approached her after hearing of her stellar reputation. Now that this part of the mission was solid and secure, they needed the trio to help them finish their plans.

Char had personal reasons for hating Viktor and his white slave trade business, but her knowledge of the vast depravity of the business was what really fueled her efforts. She knew the human trafficking industry made an estimated thirty-two billion dollars annually. While no one really knew for sure the true scale of sex trafficking in the United States, there was an estimated three hundred thousand underage victims forced into prostitution every year. Despite the millions of dollars the federal government dedicated to fight this heinous industry, they had barely made a dent. New laws and stiffer penalties were also not making a significant impact. This is why the organization existed. They didn't have to play by the strict rules to fight this disease.

Char stepped into her office and pulled out her files for the day, glancing at her calendar to make sure she had pulled the correct documents. Her assistant was due any minute and Char wanted to make sure she was fully in character before her arrival.

Shortly after eight, Sandy knocked lightly on her door.

"Come in," Char called out.

Sandy poked her head in Char's office. "Good morning, Heather, I brought you some coffee and a muffin."

"Thanks, Sandy, you're a peach."

Sandy placed the mug and muffin on her desk as the phone starting ringing in the reception area. Sandy scurried to get the phone.

With the door open, Char overheard Sandy's portion of the conversation.

"Yes, Mr. Borsky. I'll let Heather know. Sure. We can reschedule for next week. She has an open spot on

Wednesday, will that work? Oh, okay. Why don't you call when you know your schedule," Sandy offered.

Char heard Sandy end the call and shortly thereafter, she poked her head back into Char's office.

"The Big V just canceled his appointment." Sandy grinned.

"You better not let Viktor hear you call him that." Char admonished without really meaning it.

Sandy chuckled. "Anything else I can get you before you start your day?"

"No, thanks, Sandy, I'm set. Oh, wait. Will you pick up a dozen roses for me around four o'clock? I don't want them wilting before dinner tonight. Can you just drop them off for me before you leave tonight?"

"Oooh, hot date?" Sandy asked.

"Don't act so surprised. Yes, I have a date tonight. One I am very much looking forward to."

"Is it that hot woman you met at the fundraiser?"

Char smiled to herself at the irony that it was indeed the same woman, but since Toni was in disguise, she had to play along and create the illusion that she had no clue. "No, but I guarantee this one is just as hot and witty as the one at the fundraiser."

"Well, hot damn, that's a good thing, but I really thought there was chemistry between you two. I've never seen anything quite like it before. You really ought to follow up with that one."

"Perhaps." Char smiled.

The call from Viktor was an unexpected plus because, after her refreshing run, she didn't want anything to mar the start of her day. She looked forward to her date and wanted to be in a good mood while having dinner with Toni.

Chapter Ten

Byron rolled up to the gate of the garish home of Viktor Borsky. He shook his head at the plaster statues of lions and the overly ornate gate. He hated the tawdry way Viktor flaunted his wealth, but he needed his resources.

What a disaster yesterday. He was frightened by the explosion and shivered at the thought that there was much more going on than he could possibly conceive.

Byron knew he was in way over his head. The fact that he was reaching out to the head of the Russian mob, who he was certain had their car blown up in broad daylight, left him with more than an uneasy feeling.

He didn't have much time to figure out what was going on and unfortunately, Viktor's resources were more far-reaching than Antonio's. Viktor had moles everywhere. Surely he would be able to figure out who these women worked for.

Byron pressed the intercom just outside the gate. "Byron Harrison to see Viktor. I have an appointment at ten."

The disembodied voice on the other end answered. "One moment please. The gates will open for you. Please wait in the circular drive while I send someone to meet you."

"Paranoid bastards," Byron mumbled under his breath.

Byron rolled slowly up to the circular drive, placed his Mercedes in park, and pushed the power button to turn off the vehicle. He stepped onto the circular drive as a large man with an impassive expression stepped forward and gestured at Byron.

At first, Byron didn't understand and then he realized this man's job was to check him for weapons. *Preposterous. I'm a banker for God's sake, not a thug.*

Byron lifted his arms as the thug patted him down. The man nodded and the front door opened to reveal Viktor who turned and pointed inside.

"Come. We will meet in the parlor," Viktor ordered.

Byron followed Viktor into the surprisingly cozy room. As he looked around, he noticed a photograph of a beautiful woman with long dark hair and bright blue eyes, placed prominently on a side table. Next to that picture was a photo of an equally attractive woman with short hair. The photo looked like an official portrait and her stature screamed law enforcement.

"Sit." Viktor directed Byron to an expensive leather chair.

Byron pointed to the pictures on the table. "Who are those women?"

"Do not be rude, Byron. All in good time." Viktor pointed to a decanter. "Please have a brandy with me."

"Thank you. I would be delighted to accept a drink."

Viktor poured generous amounts of brandy into two crystal glasses sitting next to the decanter. He handed one to Byron and then raised his glass in a toast.

"Cheers. To a prosperous business relationship." Viktor smirked.

"Yes, thank you for agreeing to assist with my little problem."

"It is in everyone's best interest to take care of your little problem. Although I have not been affected yet, I believe one of these women has been involved in a situation I've yet to deal with. I've waited far too long to eradicate this pest. I must avenge my dear friend Dimitri."

"Are you suggesting you know who these mysterious women are and who they work for?"

"Byron, my dear friend, you will be a great asset to me. I need a connected banker to help launder money for us, but I also have an ulterior motive to help you. I have sources that tell me these two women were responsible for a deal gone bad two years ago. I also believe they are your ghosts. We have yet to figure out what organization they report to. The dark-haired one is a technology genius that the FBI heavily attempted to recruit. The other is a former FBI agent."

"If you know who they are, why haven't you already taken care of them? Surely you know that it is only a matter of time before your business ventures are impacted," Byron inquired.

Viktor sighed. "Antonio told me you were an imbecile."

Byron stopped himself from reacting lest he fall prey to Viktor's rash response to anyone challenging his authority. He patiently waited for Viktor to continue.

"As you have learned, these women are ghosts. My moles were not able to flush out an address or any indication that they even still exist. They are technology experts and masters of disguise. I received a tip about their presence at the café we were heading to before that unfortunate instance with my car. I do not believe that was a coincidence. Unfortunately, we have to wait until they surface without their disguises. I have people under my employment keeping an eye out for them. When they resurface again we will play that American carnival game, Whack-A-Mole, and bam," Viktor smashed his fist down on the table violently, "we intend to whack them just like the moles. Unfortunately, I do not have a picture of the third woman, but I believe she was with them in the café."

"They have to be connected to some larger organization. I know you mentioned that you didn't know what organization they were connected to, but you must have heard something," Byron said as he reached for his glass of brandy and took another sip.

"My sources speak of an organization of women who are highly sought after for their expertise. I believe the President has even used their resources and I don't like what I've heard about them. Their reach is getting much wider and I believe we may be their next target."

Byron's eyes widened. "The President? Surely you are not referring to the President of the United States."

"*Durak*," Viktor mumbled. "Yes, the President of the United States. Byron, you are a stupid man."

Byron bit his tongue. He needed this man and he wasn't beneath groveling. "I don't have a lot of time to resolve our problem. In the short term, I have a cash flow problem because Antonio has only given me a brief period to replenish his lost portfolio. I'm afraid I don't have the resources to make up his losses. Not only do I need to stop these women, but I find myself in a tight spot with Antonio."

"I will lend you the money to pay Antonio, but I will expect you to support my business ventures without question. Loyalty is paramount and if I even hear one whisper that you've crossed me, you will not like my response." Viktor smiled.

To Byron the smile did not look friendly and he inwardly shivered knowing the nail in the coffin was set. Byron knew he had just made a deal with the devil.

Chapter Eleven

Char sat patiently in Taylor's Bistro waiting for her date to arrive. She carefully placed the dozen roses on the table in front of her creating an inviting display.

Earlier in the evening, she pondered why she went to the trouble of selecting, then discarding several different outfits before settling on a pair of low-rise jeans, fashionable boots, and a green tapered button-down shirt. She felt like an adolescent getting ready for her first date and finding her behavior, as it related to Toni, definitely out of character.

Char looked up as the noise from a motorcycle caught her attention. She glanced out the window and spied Toni as she dismounted gracefully from the sleek Harley Davidson. The sight prompted Char to think, *God, she is one sexy woman.*

Toni yanked off the black helmet and shook out her shiny, dark locks. She raised her hand unconsciously to her hair and finger-combed the tangled mess before striding confidently into the café. Her gaze locked on Char and she grinned, showing a row of perfect white teeth. The smile reached her eyes and Char hoped she was genuinely pleased to join her.

"Hello, beautiful. Nice touch with the roses, but I'm not really a flowers type of gal. You are looking good enough to eat tonight so maybe we should skip dinner," Toni purred as she slid into the chair across from Char.

"Such a charmer. I need sustenance for what I have planned. Food first, then we can negotiate the rest of the evening's details."

Toni chuckled. "Ah, the attorney in you comes out already."

"Hmm. You know my occupation, yet I know very little about you besides your first name. What is it you do besides full-time flirt?"

"Full-time flirt, huh? I'd say more like part-time flirt and full-time technology expert. Kind of like you are a part-time stalker and full-time attorney or is it the other way around?"

"Technology expert. Sounds fascinating. Tell me more. Also, a last name would be nice to know."

"Ah, last names are irrelevant. Besides, we could both be using aliases for all you or I know. It's remarkably easy to change one's name, you know."

"Fair enough. I really would like to know more about you. In a gesture of goodwill, I'll even tell you my middle name. Of course, that's because I use my first name with business associates and my middle name with friends and other close associates."

"Oh, close associates. I like the sound of that. How close?"

"Very close."

"Okay, I'll bite, what's your middle name?"

"Uh, uh, uh. I'll only tell you that little tidbit, if you tell me something more about yourself."

"Deal. Okay, I'm a bit of an inventor of technology."

"Fascinating. Okay, Char is my middle name. What kind of technology have you invented? Would I recognize it? Are you famous?"

Char had no idea why she decided to reveal her real name. She had an overwhelming urge for the woman to know something real about her and she wanted Toni to say her name in ecstasy, not a fake name. She craved Toni and hoped the evening would end with an intimate encounter.

"Not hardly—famous, that is. Surveillance technology is my specialty. Your turn. What other delicious tidbit can you tell me about yourself?"

"I hate being a corporate attorney and want to take a shower every time I meet with one of my rich clients. I'd rather be a full-time stalker. And now you." Char couldn't believe she blurted this out. *I'd better watch myself with Toni. I seem to want to tell her more than I should.*

Toni smiled. "Corporate attorneys do get a bad rep, sometimes. I'd like to think you're one of the good guys, but I must admit to having some preconceived notions."

Char lowered her voice and barely whispered, "I'm not the enemy, Toni. Let's just leave it at that."

Toni's eyebrow raised and she looked directly at Char with a narrowed gaze. She shook her head then smiled, but this time the smile did not reach her eyes.

"I never said you were the enemy. Hey, I think this conversation just took a decidedly serious turn and I was rather enjoying our tit for tat. So…I do believe it's my turn. Hmm, let me think. What tasty morsel shall I reveal now? Sophie and Kim, who you met the other day, are my two best friends who I went to college with. I would do just about anything for them and when I say anything, I mean anything. There is nothing off the table when it comes to protecting them from harm."

"That is an admirable trait—loyalty. I have a younger sister that I would do the same for. She had an unfortunate accident so spends a lot of time in a wheelchair. We are hopeful that she will continue to progress and that maybe one day she will be able to walk more than a few steps. Her recovery has been slow and it breaks my heart to see her like that."

"I'm sorry to hear that. I'm a lot younger than my siblings. By the time I came along both of my sisters were almost ready for college. I practically grew up as if I were an only child, and Kim and Sophie are the closest thing I'll ever have to family so I understand your feelings about your sister. Shall we flag the waitress to order?"

"Absolutely, I'm starving in more ways than one."

Toni waved at the waitress who promptly stepped up to the table.

"Good evening, ladies. Are you ready to order? Would you like to hear about this evening's specials?"

"Not for me." Toni looked at the woman across from her. "Char?"

"No, thanks, I already know what I want." Char glanced to Toni and grinned in a wolfish manner.

"I'll have the salmon with a side of house salad and your famous orange balsamic dressing." Toni waved her hand at Char. "Char?"

"The same for me and can you bring a bottle of whatever white wine is recommended with this dish."

"Perfect. I'll bring a bottle of our unoaked chardonnay. Will that work?"

"Perfect." She looked at Toni. "Unless you would like something else, Toni?"

"No, that sounds wonderful. I'm not much of a wine connoisseur, so whatever you order is fine with me."

The waitress sauntered away and Toni turned her gaze back to Char. "I do believe it's your turn again."

"Oh, nice try. Remember, I just told you about my sister, so I do believe it's your turn."

"I'd like to spend the night with you, but I don't live close and I don't want to take the time to take you to my place. How's that for honesty." Toni chuckled.

"Nice—the direct approach. I like a woman who knows what she wants and is not afraid to go for it. Unfortunately, I don't live close either. So, our choices are this nice little bed-and-breakfast a few blocks away or the Hilton located in the other direction."

The waitress approached the table with the bottle of wine and poured a small amount into Char's glass. Char took a small sip and nodded. The waitress filled both Char and Toni's glasses then placed the bottle in an ice bucket that another waitress brought to the table.

Char lifted her glass and Toni touched her glass to Char's.

"To dangerous liaisons," Char toasted.

"May the danger add to the excitement. Cheers," Toni added.

"I don't believe we've quite settled on a location for our dangerous liaison," Char remarked.

"I vote for the bed-and-breakfast. The hotel seems too sterile and casual for my taste."

"Really, I registered you as the casual type." Char raised a well-shaped eyebrow.

"Touché. Usually I am, but in this case…"

The waitress placed the salads on the table. "Here you go, ladies. Enjoy. The house salad is one of my favorites."

"Saved by the bell, or more accurately, the waitress." Char laughed.

Toni took a bite of salad. "Mmm, delicious. The dressing is a perfect pairing with the wine."

"I thought you weren't a wine connoisseur."

"I'm not, I just know what tastes good and this is heavenly."

Toni licked her lips and Char was transfixed by that small gesture. Out of the corner of her eye, Char noticed a man several tables away watching them closely.

He looked down at what appeared to be an eight-by-ten photo then up again and seemed to focus intently on Toni. She watched as he brought up his phone, aimed it in their direction, and she thought she saw him press a button appearing to take their picture. Char didn't like that one bit. The man was vaguely familiar to her and two seconds later, she remembered him as one of Viktor's lackeys. Shit. It was time to put plan B into action.

"I'm sorry, Toni, will you excuse me for a moment. I need to visit the ladies' room."

Toni grinned mischievously. "Need some assistance."

"No, not this time. Rain check on that, I promise."

Char walked quickly to the bathroom and pulled out her phone pressing the buttons quickly. "Ronda, we have problems... I think a man I recognized as one of Viktor's goons just took a picture. Yeah, I'm not sure if I'm compromised too. We now know they have Toni's picture and I'm pretty sure he just made a connection. I'm going to have to step up the timeline. I know it's not optimal. I wish I had more time to gain her trust, but I think they are going to need us as much as we need them now. I need you to help me get her to headquarters without being followed. Don't use explosives again, it's too soon. Thanks. I'll owe you again." Char chuckled at Ronda's response.

Char walked quickly to the table and joined Toni.

"Oh, good. Dinner's here. I'm anxious to finish the first part of our date and move into the next phase."

"And what is the next phase?"

"You underneath me, naked, and screaming my name in ecstasy."

"Why not you under me, begging me to let you come?"

"Oh, no worries, that's act three of our play tonight. Hurry, eat up, we've got a long night ahead of us."

"Your wish is my command." Toni picked up a forkful of salmon and placed the delicate morsel in her mouth as she moaned.

Char kept track of Viktor's man as she nearly shoveled the food down her throat. "I'll want to finish our game of tit for tat as well."

"Oh, I don't think there will be time for much talking, moaning maybe, but not talking unless it's, oh God, yes, right there."

Char laughed. "Suddenly I feel the need to get our check." Char waved to the waitress. "The dinner was wonderful, we'll take our check now."

Toni grabbed for the check, but Char was too fast and managed to pluck it from the waitress before Toni had a chance to react.

"I invited you, so I get to pay this time."

"Okay, I like the sound of this time. It means there will be another time."

"I certainly hope so," Char responded.

Char glanced at the check and slapped down cash to cover the bill along with a healthy tip of greater than twenty percent. She grabbed Toni's hand and pulled her to her feet as she shoved her to the exit.

As Char reached the front door of the bistro, she whispered in Toni's ear. "You're compromised and I think I may be too. You're going to have to trust me."

Char led Toni firmly to her silver Tesla Roadster.

"What the fuck are you talking about?"

"Remember, I'm not the enemy, but that man in the café who was closely watching you is. Three, two, one, and

92

here he comes. Come on. Please come with me, Toni. We value your life as much as you do and I've arranged for assistance. We need to hurry."

Toni yanked her arm free and looked over her shoulder. Her eyes became wide and Char noticed that her gaze focused on Viktor's goon. "Shit. Okay, you win," she hissed then quickly climbed into the passenger seat.

†

Toni glanced at Char as she put the vehicle in gear and squealed off. Char's concentration was unwavering as she handled the car like a pro and kept glancing in the rearview mirror.

Toni turned around to see a black sedan pull up close behind the Tesla.

"Come on Ronda, where the hell are you?" Char spit out.

"Who's Ronda?"

"We can play twenty questions later. Right now I need you to pull that gun out of the glove compartment for me."

"What? I don't know how to fire a weapon."

Char sighed. "I don't expect you to use it, the gun's for me. It's just a precaution. I have every confidence Ronda will be here shortly to take care of our little problem."

Toni opened the glove compartment, pulled out the gun, and placed it on her lap. "Who are you?"

"Patience. I'm sorry. I had hoped to have more time to prepare you." Char glanced at Toni and frowned.

Toni thought Char was oddly familiar to her. When she heard her say, "*I'm not the enemy. Let's just leave it at that*," she thought back to the night of Natalie's death. She wasn't ready to confront Char at that time, but now that things had seemed to escalate, she had to know.

Toni whispered, almost too low to hear, "It was you. You were there that night. Your sister is Dani."

Char looked at her and Toni saw the sadness in her eyes.

"Yes. Can we just focus on getting out of our current predicament? There will be plenty of time to explain things to you."

"Just how many names do you have? Oksana, Heather, or Char, which one is it? Or is your real name something else entirely?" Toni questioned.

"Char is my real name. Now, if you don't mind, I think twenty questions can wait until we manage to lose our unwelcome tail."

Toni looked behind her and saw a speeding black Hummer gain on the sedan following them. In one moment of horrific realization, she watched as the Hummer pulled alongside the sedan and swerved into the car. The sedan fishtailed as the Hummer crashed again into the vehicle and caused it to roll down an embankment. Toni watched as Char nodded.

"Nice job, Ronda. I hope you don't need to expend more than one bullet. He's not worth it."

Who were these people? Toni's world did not include execution-style problem solving. Toni wondered what kind of trouble she'd gotten herself into. She was never opposed to moving around a few assets, but murder was not within her repertoire.

"What exactly do you want with me? I don't think I'm in the same business as you. I appreciate you trying to help me out, but I can take care of myself. I'm a big girl and I've been doing just fine for the past twenty-eight years," Toni said bravely.

"Oh, I have no doubt you have multiple resources at your disposal and you are a clever one, but someone that is close to you and your friends has been talking to the wrong people. It's the only explanation for how they have your picture. I don't think they know where you live or where your base operations are, but they know your face and Sophie's. They might know Kim's face as well, but we don't have confirmation of that just yet."

"How do I know that it isn't someone from whatever organization you work for that is causing our current predicament? You seem to know an awful lot about me and yet I know nothing about you."

"I plan to rectify that. By the way, what did you embed into your business card? It's some kind of biological substance, right? How does it work? Would you have been able to track me to our base of operations?"

"I'm not about to tell you shit. You're so fucking brilliant, you figure it out," Toni bit out.

"I don't suppose getting naked with you is still on the table now. Damn, I was so looking forward to that." Char grinned.

"Fuck you. You're an arrogant little shit and here I thought Soph was the most arrogant woman I've ever known. Sophie will track you down and she's got a mighty short temper."

"Oh, yes, I know that about her. We'll have to work on that. It only gets in the way. She does have other talents though, and we're anxious to have her come on board."

"You ever heard of free will? Who the fuck do you think you and your *people* are?"

"We are the ones who are going to save your asses."

Toni crossed her arms across her chest and remained silent. She knew she was being ungrateful and something in her really wanted to trust Char, but she needed to take a stand on principle alone if nothing else. She was worried about Kim and Sophie. What if those goons had pictures of her friends, as well?

Toni broke her self-imposed silence. "Can you tell me if Kim and Sophie are in danger?"

Char looked at her and Toni thought she saw a hint of concern in her expression.

"I don't know, Toni. I promise we'll know more when we get to the compound. Ronda might be able to tease critical information from Viktor's lackey if he survived the crash."

Toni's eyes got wide as she heard Char mention Viktor. "Viktor Borsky?"

Char nodded.

"But why would Viktor have my picture. We haven't even targeted the Russian mob yet," Toni blurted out before she had time to censor her statement.

"As I said before, there's a mole somewhere and we need to combine forces to flush him or her out."

"You think it's someone close to us, but we really don't have many close friends. It's been the three of us for as long as I can remember. Kim and Sophie were the first friends I had that actually treated me as if I was a normal person—not some cerebral misfit. Sophie left...shit. How do you do that?"

"What?"

"Make me blurt out stuff that I know I shouldn't."

"Toni, I know you don't trust me yet, but believe me, there is very little you've said that we don't already know. I already know Sophie was an FBI agent and she left shortly after Natalie died. I can assure you there were no witnesses left that evening but you, Sophie, Dani, and me. Unfortunately, someone knew about the meeting and that someone is our mole."

"So it could just as easily be someone from your organization."

Char frowned. "Yes, I suppose that's possible. However, I'm putting my money on someone in the FBI—someone who used to work with Sophie and who knows about your special talents with surveillance technology. They did try to recruit you, didn't they?"

Toni had to admit to herself that it was more than possible. Sophie had worked with her to pull them completely off the grid after Natalie's death along with her resignation from the FBI. But, they did not go as far as allowing themselves to go under the knife to change their physical appearance—a decision she was now regretting.

"Yes, they did, but I only agreed to be an independent consultant for them. I don't play well with others," Toni acknowledged.

Char frowned.

Toni noticed her expression. *Hmm, I guess she doesn't like that little character trait. I suspect her organization only wants good little soldiers. Well, I'm not the type to follow orders blindly.*

Toni looked outside and discovered that they were in a remote part of Maryland. She didn't remember traveling this far outside of DC. Toni smiled to herself with the knowledge that the tracking program would pinpoint their exact location. She congratulated herself for insisting that Sophie put the program on her phone. It wouldn't take Sophie long to track her down when she didn't show up for their ritual coffee in the morning. No matter what Toni was doing the night before, they always got together for coffee every morning to touch base and make sure whatever plans were in motion stayed on track.

97

†

The car crunched noisily on the gravel road as they meandered farther into the wilderness. The property didn't look like much. There was a small log cabin nestled between the trees.

"This is your super-secret compound?" Toni asked incredulously.

"You sure do make hasty judgments. Come on, let me show you around." Char pushed a button and the car turned off. She exited the vehicle and looked at Toni, who remained sitting in the passenger seat with her arms crossed and a pout on her face.

"I'm not sure I'm interested in being shown around. How do I know you're not some homicidal maniac who lures unsuspecting women to your lair?" Toni inquired.

"Oh, for God's sake. If we wanted you dead, you'd be dead by now. How many times do I have to tell you, we're not the enemy?"

"Well, then you won't mind if I just keep the gun."

"I thought you didn't know how to use a gun."

"I lied." Toni smirked.

"Fine. Keep the gun if it will make you feel better, but if you accidently shoot me or any of my associates due to your inept skills with a gun, I'll hand you to the mob myself."

Toni opened the passenger door and climbed out. The gun felt foreign in her hand. Sophie had tried on numerous occasions to show Toni how to operate a handgun and she now regretted not paying more attention to those lessons. But she was damned if she'd let Char know that little factoid.

Toni followed Char into the cozy cabin.

Char headed straight for the well-crafted stone fireplace and touched a spot on one of the stones. Toni didn't see a button or any type of discoloring that would reveal the spot, but an invisible panel shifted and opened to reveal a cement set of stairs leading into some kind of basement.

Toni was shocked to discover that the long stairway preceded a cement tunnel with bright lighting leading further into the depths of the earth. The tunnel seemed to go on forever, but was probably not more than four hundred feet. At the end of the tunnel there were two separate passages— one that veered to the right and the other to the left.

Char continued down the passage to the right where two hundred feet ahead was what appeared to be a solid oak door.

On the other side of the door Toni gasped as she laid her eyes on what looked like an enormous control center complete with computers, lab equipment, and other apparatus that she couldn't readily identify. She would bet all the gadgets before her eyes were top of the line with several prototypes thrown in for good measure.

A red light was beeping above the door and Char quickly placed her hand on the biometric panel. The light turned yellow and then Char moved her eye to the crystal-shaped orb off to the side. Finally, the light turned green.

"Why don't you have the biometric panels on the outside of the door instead of the inside?" Toni asked.

Char shrugged. "Maggie is a little eccentric and didn't want to set up security in any manner that would normally be expected."

"So what happens to someone who enters and is not able to override the security?"

"Ronda's specialty is explosives. Everything is blown to smithereens."

Toni shuddered. "You people are nuts."

Toni looked around the room at the four sterile white walls creating an institutional cube, like the room where she spent the better part of her teenage years. She felt her memories bubble to the surface. Just like school. She'd be a lab rat again.

Toni turned her attention to a middle-aged woman who entered the room via a door at the far right of the control center.

Char smiled at the woman and greeted her with a hug. "Hello, Maggie. I trust that Ronda filled you in on the latest developments. Maggie, meet Toni." Char looked back at Toni. "Toni, meet Maggie."

Toni looked skeptically at Maggie, but shook the outstretched hand.

"It is a pleasure to finally meet you in person, Toni. I do apologize for how this all unraveled. We had hoped to contain things for a bit longer until Char had a chance to gain your trust."

Toni glared at Char. "You really have been stalking me," she angrily spit out.

"Guilty as charged, but I have to admit to enjoying this mission far more than any other." Char grinned.

"You can't just go around kidnapping people and expect to get away with it."

"Kidnapping? Is that what you think we've done?"

Toni thought Char looked genuinely perplexed.

"Char, why don't you take Toni to the other part of the compound so she can rest? I imagine this whole evening has been quite a shock to her system. We will have plenty of time to fill her in later. Ronda is on her way and she assures me that the little problem that surfaced this evening was resolved." Maggie bowed. "Please accept our hospitality while we regroup and decide our next course of action."

Toni noticed Maggie looking at the gun in her hand.

Maggie pointed to the gun in Toni's hand. "My dear, are you planning on shooting us? If not, I believe it might be safer if I were to take possession of Char's gun."

Toni shook her head and closed her eyes for a moment. Deep down, she did not really believe either woman would do her harm. She relinquished the gun to Maggie and smiled sheepishly.

Char grabbed Toni's hand and laced her fingers with hers.

Toni was about to protest, but it just felt right and something within her allowed the simple gesture of goodwill.

Char led her out of the control room and backtracked to the part of the tunnel where they were able to go in the other direction. The tunnel seemed to turn into a kind of tributary as the branches led in several different directions.

Char gently tugged her toward an offshoot to the right. "Come on, I'll take you to my quarters. They're actually quite nice and I even have a guest bedroom to offer, unless you'd like to bunk with me."

I would like to bunk with you, but I'm not about to admit that, Toni thought. "And then you woke up—dream on Ms. Arrogant."

"And to think I got farther on the night of the fundraiser and I didn't even have to buy you dinner. Now you play hard to get."

Toni sputtered, "You…you…knew who I was. How? Oh, never mind, I don't want to know."

"Yes, you do and I promise we'll explain everything, but Maggie is right, I think it might be a good idea to just chill for tonight. Can we do that, please? I promise I won't bite. That is unless you want me to."

Without letting go of Toni's hand, Char opened another door and directed Toni into a cozy living room with hardwood floors and a fake fireplace that looked almost real enough to burn your fingers. Fake windows were scattered about the chamber creating the illusion that both the mountains and the sea surrounded the room.

Char kicked the door shut with her foot and, without releasing Toni's hand, she pushed her up against the wall. Before Toni could guess what was happening, Char covered her mouth and kissed her like she'd never been kissed before. Toni felt herself melting into Char's embrace and was powerless to stop her reaction.

Char broke away and touched her forehead to Toni's. "I've been wanting to do that ever since I saw you enter the café. You have no idea how sexy you looked when you took off your helmet and shook out your hair."

Toni was surprised when she saw the melancholy on Char's face, but she was pissed and was not about to let this woman know how good the kiss felt. Char had kidnapped her. Maybe it was for her own good, but Toni didn't like someone else making decisions for her. Toni pushed her away and glared at her.

"I really wish we'd met under different circumstances." Char sighed.

Char led Toni to the soft leather couch, sat down, and gently pulled her down to sit.

There was a lot more to this woman than Toni imagined she revealed to others. She was desperate to figure out the person behind the mask.

"How did you get sucked into this organization?" Toni asked.

Char looked away as if the answer was somewhere else but in the room. "Maggie saved our lives. Our childhood was not exactly ideal."

A chunk of Toni's armor slid off. She believed her words were the most honest statements she'd heard Char make since they met. "Will you tell me about it?"

"Maybe someday."

The way Char's expression seemed to change in an instant fascinated Toni. As she looked into her eyes, it felt like a shield went up and a new mask was in place.

"Come on, let me show you to the guest bedroom and bath and then I've got to attend to some business. We'll explain everything tomorrow. Please just get some rest because we need that oversized brain of yours. I know you care about your friends so please just be patient and trust us. Their lives depend on all of us to be at one hundred percent. This is not a game we are playing here."

Toni nodded. Although she didn't completely trust Char, she couldn't say she mistrusted her either. She would wait for Sophie to come get her. She knew that come morning, Sophie would be on her way. In the meantime, she would not let her guard down no matter how charming Char might seem because she still considered her the enemy.

On the way to the guest bedroom Toni spied an enormous door at the end of the hallway. *Shit, I bet you could fit a small truck through that doorway.* She wondered where it led.

A few feet from the doorway, curiously, forearm crutches were propped up against the wall.

Char showed her a small bedroom furnished with a simple queen-sized bed, matching dresser, and nightstand. A homemade quilt adorned the bed. The bedroom connected to a small bathroom complete with a tiled shower and stone vanity.

"Please don't let anything happen to Sophie or Kim. I know you are expecting Sophie to come looking for me and I don't want her to get caught in the crossfire or be mistaken for the enemy."

"I give you my word—Sophie will come to no harm. We are very good at what we do and we do know who is, and who is not, the enemy."

Chapter Twelve

Viktor ended his call with Gregor. Finally, they were getting somewhere. Gregor reported seeing Toni at Taylor's Bistro. He insisted he had to go because the women were leaving and he wanted to follow them and would call back when he had more information.

He punched in Byron's phone number. "Get back here right away. I have a solid lead on our problem." Viktor could hear the excitement in Byron's voice. "Good, I'll see you shortly."

In less than ten minutes, Byron was outside his gate waiting to enter. When he arrived, a guard escorted him into the parlor where they had met earlier in the day.

"Good, you are here," Viktor said before pouring Byron a glass of Stolichnaya vodka on the rocks. "Share a drink with me." He could tell that Byron hated the taste, but the uncouth American swallowed it down without protest.

"So, I understand from your call that we've had some developments since we last met." Byron smiled.

"Yes. One of my men verified seeing Toni and a beautiful redhead having dinner at Taylor's Bistro. He took a quick photo and is currently following them." Viktor pulled his cell phone out and turned the screen to Byron. "Do you recognize either of them?"

"The dark-haired woman certainly looks like the picture you showed me earlier and the redhead is familiar to me. Let me think a minute about where I've seen her." Byron snapped his fingers. "She was at the fund-raiser sitting with a table of attorneys. The tall blonde who crashed into my suite with the one that took out my entire security team, joined her table later."

"The redhead is Heather Stiles. She is one of the attorneys I've hired to help with some of my legitimate businesses. I've been vetting her to determine whether she has the stomach for other aspects of the business. She is easy on the eyes and very intelligent. Now I am wondering whether her dinner date with Toni is pure coincidence or something more," Viktor added.

"If she was at the Republican fund-raiser I suspect I will be able to get a little more information on her."

"Don't bother. If she is an integral part of this secret network or organization, all you are likely to find is what they want you to find. Perhaps she is the third woman."

"No, definitely not—she's too tall. My date was a very small and petite woman. This woman looks like she might be nearly six feet tall," Byron clarified.

"Hmm. Then perhaps it is an unlucky coincidence for Heather that she is having dinner with Toni. Regardless, she will now be on our hit list. We cannot take a chance that she is somehow connected and, as I said before, there are more enemies besides these three women. Our source hints at a much larger association that does not hesitate to use force to eliminate any threats to their organization," Viktor added.

"It seems to be an unlikely coincidence that the tall blonde who crashed my suite with the other bitch and took out my security team, joined your attorney's table at the fund-raiser by chance." Byron frowned.

"I don't suppose you got a picture."

"Not me, personally, but there were numerous photographers at the event. None of the security cameras captured any photos of their faces. Perhaps we can find a way to collect the photos from the professional photographers. I can certainly track down the press and other public relations firms who were taking photos at the event," Byron offered.

"I am sure all three were in disguise, but we may be able to determine if there are any overlapping facial features with the photos of Toni and Sophie, who we do suspect are two out of the three women you are after. Unfortunately, our source does not know or has not yet revealed the identity of the third person."

The Russian National Anthem permeated the room and Viktor picked up the cell phone that was the origin of the music from the table. He turned away from Byron and left the room to take the call in privacy.

†

"Preveet, comrade."

Viktor ground his teeth as he listened to the voice on the other end of the cell phone.

"Where? That stupid son of a bitch. No, I want you out there sweeping that car for anything you can find. I want those women tracked down. Now. I grow weary of this little cat and mouse game. Don't call me unless you have some good news."

Viktor punched the end call icon on the phone with such fury that a small crack in the glass appeared and created a spidery pattern. Viktor growled as he spied the crack and threw it across the room. "Fucking piece of shit."

He stalked out onto the patio and waved to his guard.

The beefy Russian walked to his boss. "Yes, sir, what can I do for you?"

"Gregor had an unfortunate accident and it seems he broke his neck so he is unable to report back about what he may have found. I've already sent someone to sweep his car, but I need you to get down to the morgue and see what he may have on his body. There might be a cell phone with pictures or something else to clue me in to what he was tracking before his accident. Spread the word that any information leading to the detainment of that ex-FBI woman or her brainiac friend will result in a hefty reward of one million dollars and, of course, my sincere gratitude."

The guard nodded.

Viktor was frustrated. It seemed like at every turn something was thwarting his efforts to capture these mysterious women. They were always a step ahead. Gregor had sounded so excited when he called earlier that Viktor thought for sure the end was near and he would finally get his prize. Yet, once again, they managed to avoid capture.

Viktor had to get back to his guest—the idiot. He needed the banker and when he'd heard from Gregor, he had hoped to give Byron some good news and then secure his favor in return.

†

Viktor walked back into the parlor.

"Unfortunately, Gregor was not able to follow and detain Toni. They managed to slither away."

"Fuck. How do these women keep slipping through the cracks? I thought you had her this time. If I continue to lose money, I won't be in any position to help you with your needs," Byron spit out.

Viktor growled. "Are you threatening me?"

"No, of course not. I am very close to losing my position. If that happens, all of us are screwed. If they find out about the large sums of money diverted to that charity organization under my watch, not to mention the money I move around for my special clients in a way that does not necessarily meet banking standards, none of you will be protected. All of us are at risk here. I don't think Antonio quite understood this when he washed his hands of me, thinking that all I needed to do was tap into my own reserves to replenish his stash. Surely you do," Byron pleaded.

"Maybe it's time I had a little chat with Antonio. I don't relish doing business with that slimy little Guido, but desperate times call for desperate measures. I will not let a little *sooka* ruin my business."

Viktor turned in the direction of the doorway into the parlor as a large man with close-cropped blond hair entered. "I apologize for disturbing you, boss, but there's someone outside the gate who says they believe they have information on that ex-FBI woman you are trying to track down."

"Finally, please send our guest in." Viktor smiled at his employee, showing his even white teeth. "Byron, Ivan will show you out now. I'll be in touch."

Chapter Thirteen

Sophie looked at her watch again. She'd already left two voice messages on Toni's phone.

Kim was looking at her with an expression of deep concern. It was nine thirty in the morning and Toni hadn't joined them yet.

Sophie tapped her fingers nervously on the table. Something wasn't right. Toni was never late. She knew something was off about Heather. "God damn it. Where is she?" Sophie barked.

Kim placed her hand over Sophie's.

Sophie realized she was taking her frustration out on sweet Kim. It wasn't Kim's fault that Toni hadn't shown up yet.

"Maybe she just had a really good date last night and it spilled over until the morning," Kim offered.

"She has a fucking cell phone." Sophie was livid. She chastised herself as she noticed the hurt look on Kim's face. "I'm sorry, Kim. I'm just worried."

"I know you are. It's okay. I'm worried too. Why don't you activate that program Toni installed on your phone? At least then we can track Heather's whereabouts."

"We? If I track down Heather's location, I'm going alone. It could be dangerous and no offense, but you aren't

110

trained for this kind of thing. You have many talents, but tracking down the enemy is not one of them."

Kim jutted out her jaw. "Oh, my God, Toni is right—you are a Neanderthal. She's my friend too, and I can damn well take care of myself without your big butch ass protecting me."

"Look, Kim, I'm not saying this to be cruel, but don't you remember the last time someone who wasn't trained insisted on following me into the field—"

"You stop right there. Natalie was not killed because you or Toni did something wrong. That shitstorm had nothing to do with Toni accompanying you and you know it."

"Don't you know that I wouldn't be able to live with myself if something happened to you? I wouldn't want to go on without you. I can't go through that again."

A single tear leaked out of Sophie's eye. She knew this was as close as she was prepared to go to confess her love to Kim.

Kim placed her hand over Sophie's again and held on. "I know and I feel the same way, but that just means it's even more important that I do this with you. Please don't shut me out. I need to be with you."

"Will you do exactly as I say—no questions asked?"

"Yes."

"Even if I tell you to leave me and go for help."

Kim hesitated before she responded. "I don't know if I can make that promise, but I will do everything else you ask of me. You can't ask me to do that if you're hurt."

"What if that's the only way to ensure survival for either one of us. You have to trust me, Kim."

"I do trust you, Soph. I trust you with my life. I'm just not sure you value your own life as much as you do mine."

Sophie was frustrated. Why did she have to be so damn stubborn? "Okay. How about if I promise not to take any unnecessary chances? If I honestly think that you staying by my side will help either one of us, I won't ask you to leave. I've never broken a promise to you yet. And I think I may call Ted for some extra insurance."

"Oh, Soph, do you think that's really wise? We aren't exactly legit with what we're doing. So far, we've managed to stay under the radar of the FBI and you haven't been in contact with them for nearly two years. I'm not sure how wise it is for us to open that door. As far as they're concerned you fell off the face of the earth once you left them."

"Actually, I already made a preliminary call to him last night. I thought he might be able to provide some additional information on Heather. I just had a bad feeling. I might need his assistance and he's the only one I trust. How about if we check it out first? I'll just call and give him an update with some basic information and then put him on speed dial in case I need backup. When we get there, I'll put the coordinates in a text message ready to go just in case something goes squirrely on us. Your safety is the most important thing to me. How does that sound?"

"I suppose that is the best I can hope for. Deal." Kim offered her hand to Sophie who took it gently in her own and shook. As Sophie released her, she caressed the palm for a second before letting go.

Sophie pulled out her phone and swiped the screen to access the special program. She frowned as she looked at the small map. "It looks like Heather is two hours away in a relatively remote location. I'm not all that familiar with the area, but I know it's mostly woods. All kinds of warning bells are going off in my head. Are you sure I can't talk you out of going with me?"

"Nope, not a chance in hell."
Sophie sighed. "Okay then, we'd better get going."

Chapter Fourteen

After a restless night, Toni finally managed to close her eyes and enter dreamland. Despite her attempts to push Char out of her thoughts, she reflected on the kiss as she drifted off to sleep. She still had a smile on her face when she felt the light dance across her forehead.

Toni forced one eye open and was amazed to find a shaft of light shining above the bed. *Well, I'll be damned, that fake little window feels and looks almost as real as the early morning sunshine in my condo. How the hell do they do that?*

She peeled open her other eye and was instantly aware of the sounds of chirping birds. *They must program sights and sounds into this underground coffin to keep the natives from getting too restless. I think I'd go nuts if I had to live in a glamified bomb shelter—regardless of how luxurious they tried to make it.*

Toni jumped up in the bed after she heard a loud clatter in the hallway. Curiosity got the best of her as she scrambled to the door to try to listen to the voices outside her bedroom.

"Shush. You're going to wake her up."

Toni was sure that was Char telling someone to be quiet. She plastered her ear against the door.

114

"Are you insane? You brought someone back *here* to the compound. Does Maggie know?" the unknown voice asked.

"Of course she knows. You know there isn't much Maggie doesn't know about—especially when it involves anything to do with the compound."

"I can't imagine Maggie would be okay with you bringing one of your dates back to our little hideaway. What gives?"

"It's complicated."

"Ya think? Who is it and why didn't you take her— well, I'm assuming it's a her—to the guest accommodations?"

"It's Toni. I don't think she trusts me and I couldn't take the chance that she would try to leave and get her fine ass killed in the process."

"Ooh, beautiful Toni—the one you keep talking about. Char and Toni sitting in a tree k.i.s.s.i.n.g, first comes love—"

"Will you shut up? What are you five?"

"Do you think she'll join us?"

"I certainly hope so. It's as we suspected—they positively identified her last night. Some goon actually came after us. I'd be willing to bet the compound that it's only a matter of time before they catch up with Sophie. We're their best shot at getting out of this mess, but Maggie is convinced we can't do it without their full cooperation. I don't think that's going to be easy."

"From what I've heard, she's off-the-chart brilliant. I sure would love to pick her brain."

"Yeah, she is brilliant and sexy and—"

"Wow, I've never heard you talk like that about anyone. If I didn't know any better I'd think you were in love."

"Dani, you need to get out of here. I want to bring her some breakfast and try to explain a few things while she's still relatively compliant."

"All right, but can you bring her to the control center after breakfast? I really want to meet her before everyone else tries to monopolize her time."

In love, huh? Toni rolled that concept around in her brain. She liked thinking that someone might fall in love with her someday, but she had a hard time thinking the chameleon Char would be that person.

Toni moved away from the door and slid back into bed. She needed to pretend she was just waking up when Char came into the room.

Ten minutes later, she heard a light knock on the door.

"Come on in, because I know you're probably going to anyway whether I like it or not," Toni called out, loud enough for the person on the other side of the door to hear.

Char entered the room, carrying a tray laden with muffins, croissants, two large pots, bagels and lox, scrambled eggs, bacon, French toast and pancakes. The door remained ajar.

Toni eyed the feast and started laughing. "Where's the army? Because I certainly cannot eat all that."

Char blushed. "I didn't know what you liked, so I thought I would offer you a variety."

"You could have asked me last night, you know."

"It slipped my mind."

Toni jumped up from the bed, noticing how large and probably heavy the tray was. "Here, let me help you with that."

Toni plucked both pots from the tray and set them on the dresser.

"Thanks. I didn't know if you drank coffee or tea so one is hot water and the other is French pressed coffee in a decanter."

"What? Didn't your little spy source tell you which I preferred. You seem to know everything else about me."

Char sighed. "Damn, back to that again. Can we just sit and have a nice breakfast?"

"Where? On the bed? Why aren't we eating in the kitchen? You do have a kitchen in this little hobbit hole, don't you?"

"Yes, I have a very nice kitchen. I just thought you might appreciate me bringing you breakfast in bed."

Toni couldn't remember anyone ever being kind enough to bring her breakfast in bed. She was being a bitch and she knew it. Char was offering an olive branch and she wanted to take it.

"I'm sorry, Char. I know I'm being a bitch. Thank you. It was really sweet of you to do all of this for me." Toni sat on the bed and patted the spot next to her after crossing her legs to leave room for the tray. "Come on, join me. Clearly there's plenty."

Char put down the tray and walked to the dresser. "So, which is it, coffee or tea?"

"Coffee, please."

Char picked up the black pot, walked over, and poured coffee into both mugs on the tray. After she placed the pot back on the dresser, she seemed almost tentative when she sat down next to Toni.

Toni grabbed a croissant and took a huge bite. "Mmm, delicious." After she chewed the flaky pastry for a few seconds, she decided it was time to learn a bit more. "Okay. So, I'm not sure who is tit and who is tat, but I do believe it's your turn again. I last revealed my desire to take you to bed."

"Technically, I think I remember you saying you wanted to spend the night with me. Although this is not exactly the location we talked about—we did actually spend the night together."

"Stop trying to distract me. I want to know how you got caught up in this—organization—or whatever this is." Toni waved her hand in the air. "You said you would tell me about it someday. Well, if you really want me to trust you, someday is today."

Char took a deep breath. "I do want you to trust me, so I'm going to take a chance and tell you my pathetic little story."

Toni used her hand to gesture for Char to continue.

"I grew up in some shithole in rural Alabama." Char made a stop gesture with her hand. "I know what you're thinking. No way. She doesn't have a southern accent. Well, I've worked very hard to remove the accent and any memories of my past life. Like a surgeon with a surgical knife, I've cleanly sliced them away. Maggie gave us an education and not only did I lose my accent, but I speak seven other languages—fluently."

"Impressive, but what does living in rural Alabama have to do with a pathetic life?"

"Our mother, God bless her soul, was a raging alcoholic, and didn't really have the best discernment when it came to boyfriends. I was seventeen when it all came to a head…"

Char decided to take the shortcut home from school so when she heard voices several feet from her trailer she hid in the trees to listen in on the conversation.

That fat pig who was living in the trailer was talking with some foreign-looking man. His suit looked expensive and he had an accent that definitely wasn't from around there.

"I want the money up front and then I'll get you the girl. That hellcat sister of hers might be a problem. She's fast and strong and doesn't fight fair. Little bitch kicked me in the groin one night."

"What about the mother. Won't she miss her?"

"Nah. She's too drunk half the time to even know who's around. You need to worry about her sister."

"I will not pay you for that one, but I'll take her off your hands if you wish."

"You might have to drug her. Like I said, don't underestimate her. She's a mean one and she won't go easily. The little one is sweet as apple pie. I want a crack at her before you take her."

"We will be back in exactly one week to transport the packages. You will need to drug the sister yourself and don't damage the merchandise. You can make her suck you off, but if you damage her in any other way the deal's off."

The man in the suit walked slowly to his car and drove off.

Char wasn't stupid. She'd heard all about the underground sex slave business that was alive and well in rural Alabama. The government knew this was happening in the states, but didn't care as long as it didn't reach any of the more well-to-do areas. Poor white trash simply weren't worth saving.

She had to get Dani away from Alabama and fast. She had a week to plan their getaway. She didn't really know where she was going to get the money to flee and survive, but she didn't have a choice now. All her dreams of going to college on a scholarship and getting them both away from this shithole had just gone up in flames. She'd have to get some crap job just to survive.

Char heard the crunching of leaves and smiled as she realized her baby sister was taking the shortcut she taught her.

"Hey, Dani. Better sneak in the back window and avoid the pig. I got to get some things together so I'll be late comin' back tonight."

"Aw, Char. Ya know I don't like bein' in the trailer with just Ma and fatty. He gives me the creeps. He's always lookin' at me like I'm a big piece of fried chicken or somethin'."

"I know. I promise I won't be long. Just stay out of sight. Dani, if I was to ask ya to come run away with me, you'd do it wouldn't ya?"

"And leave Ma? We can't leave her with *him*."

"I don't want to, but Dani, I don't think we have a choice. You caught someone's eye and I don't want ya endin' up missin' like Sarah. Nobody even cared enough to go lookin' for her."

"Can we come back for her?"

"Sure, someday maybe."

"Okay, Char. I'll go with ya."

"Good girl, Dani."

Char didn't like stealing, but she had to get together some money or else they would never survive. One day she would pay it back.

On the other side of the tracks was a more affluent neighborhood. It was still rural Alabama and people trusted each other, so she knew it would be easy to sneak in and pick up a few items she could sell quickly or better yet, find some cash lying around. Most people were careless, pulled money out of their pockets and laid it on their dressers. She was counting on that.

Char had her pockets stuffed with trinkets and cash—enough to get a good start. As she approached the trailer, she heard a whimper and old fatty grunting.

Char slammed open the door and saw that disgusting pig with one hand grabbing Dani's hair and pulling her to her knees, while he fumbled with his pants.

"Come on, you sweet little apple dumpling, all you got to do is suck it hard and I promise I won't hurt you."

Char saw red and picked up the first thing she could get her hands on. A clear glass ashtray was within her grasp. After she grabbed the dirty glass weapon, she swung as hard as she could and landed a solid blow to his greasy head.

He went down in a loud thud and blood poured from his scalp.

Dani started crying and Char went to comfort her.

Dani looked at her mother's boyfriend and placed her hand over her mouth. "Is he…dead?"

"I dunno."

"Char, what are we gonna do now?"

Dani looked at their mother passed out on the couch.

Char heard rustling outside and pulled Dani to the back of the trailer. "Come on, there's somebody out there. We need to go. Now."

Dani and Char crept to the back of the trailer and silently crawled out the window. After they cleared the window, they came face-to-face with an attractive woman.

"Shh. It's okay. I'm not the enemy. I see I got here a little too late. I'm sorry about that. Let me help you. If you come with me, I promise I'll take care of everything and make sure you both get a proper education and are well cared for."

"I ain't scared of you and I'm not goin' somewhere that will get us sold off to some fat pig." Char crossed her arms.

121

The woman laughed. "I promise. We do not intend to sell you to those disgusting men. We fight those men and for the most part we win, but sometimes we lose too."

"How do I know you ain't just givin' us a line to get us to go with you peaceful like?"

"You're going to have to trust me and I know that won't be easy for you." The woman smiled.

Char didn't know why she instantly trusted this woman, but she did. Something about the way she smiled set Char at ease. She desperately needed to trust someone at this point and so she took a chance on the woman. That chance paid off.

✝

Toni listened to Char's story and although it sounded utterly incredulous, she believed every word. The second sleeve of her armor fell to the ground as her heart ached for the young girl whose foundation in life was so unstable. Her own childhood was a picnic compared to Char's. At least her parents had waited until she was in her teens to send her away to that freak school. Even the isolation she felt at the geek school was no comparison to Char's horrific teenage experience.

Although not exactly thrilled by her chosen lifestyle, her parents did manage to ignore the topic politely. At least she had been allowed to sit at the kids' table at Thanksgiving and bathe in the admiration of her nieces and nephews as the cool aunt.

Toni stopped taking home girlfriends years ago—mainly because her parents always introduced them as Toni's roommate or a close friend of the family. Girlfriends never really lasted that long anyway. She stopped taking her brief affairs home and started asking either Sophie or Kim to join her in her annual family obligation. At least she could honestly call them roommates or close friends of the family. Finally, she just stopped torturing herself and hadn't been to a family reunion in years.

"I believe that was a pretty good tat, so tit's up to you. For the record, I have very much appreciated your tits." Char chortled.

Toni raised one eyebrow. "All right. Here's something that won't be too surprising to you. I've never had a relationship last longer than three weeks."

"You got me beat—three days. Well, unless you count a mark. Some of those have lasted a month."

"I'm your mark, right?" Toni noted that Char had the decency to look remorseful. At least she hoped that was what she saw.

"Yes, I'm sorry you were my mark. You're not my mark anymore. Viktor's goon sort of forced our hand sooner than we planned for."

"Why all the energy and stalking to recruit me? Why didn't you just come out from the very beginning, explain everything and then ask me. By the way, you still haven't given me all the details. I believe you promised to explain everything to me."

"Would you have actually considered joining our effort?"

"Probably not and, for the record, I still haven't agreed to anything. I'm waiting for more details."

"I have no doubt Sophie will find her way to the compound. I'd rather wait and provide the details when she arrives. I don't want to have to explain everything more than once. If my assumptions are correct, whatever you injected in the card is attached to my body somehow. Will you always be able to track me down? Or does this biological agent expel from the body after a certain amount of time?"

"I think for now, I'll just let you wonder."

"Fair enough. I get it. You still don't trust me. If I were in your shoes, I probably would be mistrustful as well. I do hope to gain your trust in time. I'd like to be among the elite few that you care enough about to give that precious gift to."

"I must admit to being farther down the path after your personal story. I suspect you don't tell that story to many people. I admit to being honored and touched that you would share that with me."

"I hope I won't live to regret that."

"I promise I'll do everything I can to make sure I don't violate your trust."

Toni pushed away the tray, leaned into Char, and stroked her cheek as she closed the gap to place a gentle kiss on her lips. Char sighed and Toni pulled Char into a longer embrace as she gently explored the lips that had taunted her all night long in her dreams.

"I've wanted to do that all morning—actually, since you kissed me last night."

A loud clatter in the hallway interrupted the moment and Toni turned her head in the direction of the disturbance.

A young woman in a wheelchair cautiously pushed the door open and craned her neck to look inside the room.

"Hey, sis, did I give you enough time to have breakfast?"

Char sighed. "As usual, Dani, your timing is impeccable. Don't bother to knock or anything, just come on in."

Toni laughed.

"Hey, Toni. I'm Dani. You probably don't remember me."

Toni grimaced as the night Dani was shot came flooding back into her memory. "I do remember you. I'm sorry you were shot," she responded quietly.

Dani shrugged. "I'm not sorry. We got the girls to freedom and I'm working on getting back on my feet." Dani jutted her chin out. "I will get out of this wheelchair for good someday. It's just been a long road to recovery. Char helps me with my exercises and I can already walk ten steps on my own, more with my forearm crutches."

Char smiled and Toni thought she saw a fair amount of pride in the look she gave her sister.

"Yes, I'm sure you will and I'm sure Char is a great support to you. She is a woman of many talents, I'm learning."

"Oh, yes, she is, she really is, and she talks about you all the time. God, I've heard all about your brilliant inventions. I can't wait to learn about them," Dani exclaimed.

Toni couldn't help but smile at Dani's youthful exuberance. She looked at Char and noticed how red her neck and face appeared. Toni had to admit to feeling a great deal of respect for the young woman. She'd been through an awful lot in her limited years on the planet, yet she still retained a positive outlook on life. Her determination was inspiring. Many would have given up, yet she was still convinced of her recovery two long years after the injury.

"So, Dani, is there actually a reason for barging in for a second time this morning?"

"Uh, yeah. I wanted to let you know that Maggie thought it would be nice if we showed Toni around the compound, especially the technology and gadgets we have. She's interested in what Toni thinks of our resources. I'd kinda like to know her opinion on that as well," Dani divulged.

"Dani is a bit of an inventor herself and has contributed to some of our prototypes."

Dani blushed. "Nothing like what you've developed, but I'm sort of proud of a few of them."

"Who designed the simulated outside light in the window replicas?"

Dani's face lit up. "I did that. It was so depressing down here. It's like living in a cave, you know."

"It's brilliant. It really felt like dawn this morning. The simulation is spectacular. You should be proud of your accomplishment. I'm not sure I could live down here full-time, but it would be okay for long stretches because of your invention."

"It's difficult for me to be up top, but Char has another residence that she goes to a lot. She has to have somewhere to take her—"

Char interrupted, "Okay, I don't think Toni really cares about my other living space. Would you like something to eat, Dani?"

Dani winked. "Oh, yeah, sorry. I forgot she's trying to impress you. Sure, big sis, I'd love a muffin, thanks."

Dani grabbed a blueberry muffin and took a big bite.

Toni tried not to laugh out loud as she turned her head and placed her hand over her mouth.

"Go ahead. Yuk it up. When Sophie and Kim get here, I suspect comments may be made at your expense versus mine. Perhaps we should let you take a shower and get dressed. There are some clean clothes in the dresser drawers that should fit you. If you need anything, I'll be right down the hall, just holler," Char said.

Chapter Fifteen

Sophie's Toyota Tundra rolled to a stop in front of the isolated log cabin. She unbuckled her seatbelt and unsnapped her gun holster.

Kim looked at Sophie. "It doesn't look like there is anyone here, although I do see tire tracks that lead around back. Do you really think you need your gun?"

"It's always good to be prepared. Come on, let's check it out. The flashing dot is a few hundred yards or so in the direction of that cabin, but I don't see any other buildings out here. I don't like it. Something is amiss. Why don't you stay here while I check things out?"

"Nope. Not going to happen. I'm coming with you. Maybe you can check out the cabin while I follow the tire tracks."

"No. If we both get out of the truck, then we stay together. I can't protect you unless you're near me."

"Okay, that sounds fine to me."

The crunch of the gravel echoed loudly in Sophie's ears as they approached the cabin. Sophie peered into the windows, but didn't see any movement. She waved her hand and began walking around to the back of the cabin. The tire tracks seemed to go farther into the woods and she thought she saw the glint of metal several hundred feet away.

The slight rustle of leaves caught her attention and she started to pull the gun from her holster.

"Ah, ah, ah. I wouldn't do that if I were you."

Sophie turned her attention to the unknown voice.

The muscular blonde with steel-gray eyes pointed a gun at Kim's head and used her as a shield.

Sophie removed her hand from the gun and raised her hands to show they were empty. "I'm sorry. If we are trespassing on your land, we'll leave."

The woman pulled Kim along with her and approached Sophie. "Just keep your hands in the air while I liberate your gun. I don't want you getting twitchy on me."

In a movement too quick to be from an amateur, the woman removed the gun and tossed it into the woods. She kept her gun pointed at Kim's head.

"Sophie, I know you're calculating in your head how easy it will be to disarm me and get Kim to safety. I suggest you let that notion just die on the vine because I'm as much a pro as you are and I'd wager you have less than a fifty-fifty chance of success. I don't really want to shoot you or Kim, but I will if you leave me no choice."

"How...how...do you know our names?" Sophie sputtered.

"All will be revealed shortly. I need you to come this way and please don't make me shoot you. We're not the enemy, so don't force me into acting like one. I also need to forewarn you that farther into these woods, there are some rather nasty booby traps. I'm a bit of an artist with explosives and I'd hate for either of you to get your pretty little legs blown off," the blonde said.

Sophie knew the woman was right. She couldn't take the chance and would never forgive herself if something happened to Kim due to her negligence or arrogance. She'd bide her time for now and come up with a plan for escape later.

The woman waved the gun in the direction of the cabin.

Sophie took a second to slip her hand inside her jacket pocket and push the button to send the text message to Ted. She hoped for both their sakes that Ted would get the message in time.

"It's open, so go on inside. Oh, by the way, since I know your names I think it's only fair I tell you mine. I'm Ronda, explosives expert extraordinaire." Ronda chuckled.

†

Toni leaned to peer into one of the monitors and focused on the data-mining program tracking patterns in financial transactions. She was impressed with the sophistication of the program.

"So, is this how we caught your attention?"

"No, we use this program to track transactions of the shady politicians and the mob. They think they've hidden their tracks, but they haven't," Dani offered.

Char pointed to the next computer. "This computer is dedicated solely to cracking anyone's computer password that we target. We've even cracked yours."

"Impressive."

Bzzz Bzzz Beep Beep

The noise startled Toni. "What's that?"

"Someone entered the cabin and activated the tunnel entrance. If I were a betting woman, I would say your friends have arrived, although I don't think they're alone. Ronda must be escorting them here to the control center. We could probably track their progress through the security monitors there, but they'll be here shortly so it probably doesn't matter." Char pointed to a row of monitors on the far right side of the enormous room.

"Hey, Toni, come here. Let me show you something," Dani said.

Toni walked to a monitor with red dots blinking on a map of the DC area. "What's this?"

Dani beamed. "That's my tracking program on Viktor and his goons. We used his own technology to put undetectable tracking devices in every one of the cell phones that Viktor issues to his staff." Dani frowned. "Unfortunately, the dots keep multiplying like rabbits and we haven't been able to do a very good job of managing the risk. We should have known well in advance about the guy that followed you from Taylor's Bistro. I should have sent Char a message before it became a problem. I screwed up big-time."

"You've been tracking them all this time. Have you kept them from sighting us?" Toni stared wide-eyed at Dani and Char. She couldn't help being impressed. She got a warm feeling knowing that these women were somehow protecting them from afar. No one had ever done that for her except Kim and Sophie. Toni was beginning to trust the women.

"Only for about the last six months after we saw the photos they have of you and we figured out what y'all were doing. Unfortunately, his crew is getting too big for us to manage effectively anymore. I suspect he really wants to track you and your friends down. That's why Maggie wanted us to recruit you fast. She was worried we wouldn't be able to protect you for much longer," Dani divulged.

Toni was fascinated and beginning to consider what it might be like to collaborate with this mysterious organization.

Toni completely focused her attention on what Dani was showing her and was startled when Char interrupted an explanation of one of the programs running on yet another computer.

"Excellent! The gang's all here now and about time too. I was hoping we would be able to do some advance strategic planning," Char announced.

"I say we just shoot them all and be done with it."

Toni looked up when she heard the unknown voice say something about shooting someone. The gun the muscular blonde was holding jolted her into action.

Toni swiveled to Char, cocked her fist back, and landed a solid right hook to Char's cheek. "I started to trust you. Why did you bring us all here just to kill us? I don't understand." She looked at Char in confusion and with a healthy dose of sadness. She felt betrayed on the deepest level. "What's the point of gaining my trust? Is this all a big game to you?" Toni asked.

Char rubbed her cheek and glared at the muscular woman. "Are you out of your cotton-picking mind! Put that fucking gun away, Ronda. What the hell were you thinking bringing them down at gunpoint?" Char looked back at Toni. "Nice right hook, by the way. No one's killing anyone."

Ronda shrugged and placed her gun inside the holster under her jacket. "What? She's a damn feebie. You know how they are—shoot first and ask questions later. I still remember Waco. I'm quite fond of my tits, you know, and I'd rather not have them blown up."

"Give me a break. First, I am not a feebie because I left the FBI two years ago, which I'm betting you people already know. Second, Waco was like twenty years ago. I would have been a kid so I had nothing to do with that fuckup. I've only just met you and you are the most paranoid nutcase I've ever met. You would have fit in nicely with the FBI crew at Waco," Sophie snarled.

"Enough. Ronda, you will apologize to our guests. No one is shooting anyone and just to help clarify the situation, I presume you were referring to Viktor and his employees," Maggie stated in a firm, quiet voice.

Toni was surprised the woman managed to enter the room without detection until she spoke.

"Well, yeah. Who did you think I was suggesting we shoot?" Ronda's eyes grew wide. "Oh, shit. Toni, you thought I was saying we should shoot you and your pals. Sorry, my bad." Ronda turned her gaze on Maggie. "Why can't we just shoot them?"

"Ronda, there is a place for your special talents, but unfortunately shooting Viktor and his entourage will only result in another unsavory character taking his place. The mob has a very solid succession plan. In this case, cutting off the head is like cutting off the tail on a salamander. They will just regenerate a new head. Someone will step up to fill in the hole. No, we need a more permanent solution." Maggie looked squarely at Toni, Sophie, and Kim. "That is where all of you come in. We need your help to shut down Viktor and the sex slave trade for good. We need to hit them in their pocketbooks. Without the financial resources, they will not be able to operate their revolting business."

"After we put them in financial ruin, then can we shoot them?" Ronda grinned.

"Assassination is not our first option. We only use that particular choice, when all other alternatives are considered and we have no other routes to select. We cannot sink to their level or we are no better than the base animals they are," Maggie explained.

"Fine. By the way, I did not have another alternative with the goon that followed Toni and Char. Unfortunately, a car accident causes one's neck to break on occasion. I might have helped it along a little bit, but he was a loose end that I don't believe we needed to keep clipping. I found multiple photos of not only Toni, but Sophie and Char. I don't think he was able to transmit in the time he followed you, but you'd better check it out." Ronda tossed the phone to Dani.

"Char? Who is Char?" Sophie interjected.

"Oh, sorry, I'm afraid it was necessary for me to maintain my persona as Heather Stiles when we first met. I am Char," she clarified.

"I knew it." Sophie smirked.

Maggie sighed. "It is sometimes necessary to exercise a bit of caution. Ronda, I do understand your need to take care of the situation with Viktor's associate. I will not question your judgment, but please be mindful of our code."

"You have a code?" Kim spoke up.

"Yes. Killing another person is a last resort and only exercised if we believe without a doubt that keeping the person alive would jeopardize one of our agents," Maggie explained.

"Okay. Now that we've settled who is not killing whom, do you think we might be able to get back to strategic planning?" Char interrupted.

Char winced as Dani reached up to place her thumb on her cheek. "Your cheek is starting to swell and I think you might actually sport a shiner tomorrow. Why don't I get some ice for you?"

"Oh, God. I'm so sorry. I guess I jumped to the wrong conclusion." Toni looked at Char and felt genuinely remorseful for her earlier actions.

"It's okay. I probably would have done the same given the same set of circumstances," Char's voice softened as she spoke to Toni.

"No. It's not okay. Dani, if you don't mind, I'd like to take Char back to her room, get some ice, and take a closer look at the damage I caused. Why don't you stay back and show Sophie and Kim your impressive setup here. We'll be back in a little while. I want a chance to talk with Char alone if you don't mind." Toni winked.

Dani beamed. "Thanks, Toni. I'd love to show Sophie and Kim around. Maybe we can explain a few things to them and then, when you and Char get back, we can bring everyone up to speed with what we know. We've given you bits and pieces of the story, but haven't told you all of it yet. I hope after we explain everything, that you will decide to join us and together we will be a force to be reckoned with."

"Well said, Dani." Maggie turned her penetrating gaze toward Ronda. "Ronda, I think you had better move Sophie's vehicle and hide it along with the others."

†

Char wasn't sure why she had told her sad tale to Toni. It was almost as if she had just unzipped her brain and the story came tumbling out.

Toni, holding her hand, tugged Char down the corridor.

Char looked at their clasped hands and smiled. She didn't know why she let Toni have power over her. She hadn't let someone take care of her in a very long time—not since Maggie. It felt good and she let go of her need for control. For a little while at least.

Damn Ronda and her bull-in-the-china-shop mentality. Char hoped the way Ronda dragged Toni's friends into the compound hadn't set her efforts to gain Toni's trust back several steps.

When they reached the door to Char's living quarters, Toni turned her head. Char wondered if Toni was asking permission to enter the cozy room. Char nodded. If she was going to give up complete control, she might as well let Toni take the initiative.

Toni opened the door and drew Char to the couch. "Why don't you sit down while I get some ice."

Char reluctantly let go of Toni's hand as she sat down and leaned her head against the back of the couch.

Toni ambled out of the living room and Char heard rustling in the kitchen. A few minutes later Toni came into the room with a bag of ice in her left hand.

Char noticed her right hand dangling against her hip and gasped as she saw the bruising and swelling that had already started to become prominent.

Toni sat next to Char and gently placed the bag of ice on her cheek.

Char lifted Toni's right hand and raised one of her eyebrows. "Um, I'm afraid you've suffered a far greater injury than I have. I guess you're not really used to bar brawls, so we need to get some ice on your hand as well. We might need to x-ray it too."

Toni shrugged. "I'm not really known for my brawn. It seems like I'm not the only one who can claim their head is an asset. Yours is pretty hard."

Char laughed. "Yeah, well, I hope being hardheaded is not the only thing I can claim as something to be proud of. Maybe I'm not a genius like you, but hopefully I can hold an intelligent conversation or two."

"Shit, I didn't mean it like that. I find everything about you sexy and alluring, including that beautiful brain of yours. Unfortunately, having a high IQ is not really a desirable thing to possess. Most of the women I meet don't seem to want to converse with me. So we don't, you know, talk too much. May I ask you something?"

"Sure."

"How did you know I put something in the business card and even more importantly, how did you guess it contained a biological agent?"

"I suspected it when I examined the card and didn't detect any raised areas in the ink. After my initial scrutiny, I asked Ronda to bring some lab equipment to me to do further testing. I still don't know how it works, but I was pretty sure its origin was biological and that was confirmed with my testing. You never did answer my question about how long the agent will remain in my body."

"I never confirmed that anything entered your body so why are you so sure that's what occurred?" Toni asked.

"Simple, if I had the technology and knowhow, that's what I'd do. You can't assume that a business card would remain on someone, so the only way to ensure you can track a person is to inject something in them or use a biological agent. Given your brilliance with inventions, I was confident you finally developed an advanced tracking agent that somehow absorbs into the body."

"Do you know how hot that is to me for you to process information in that way?" Toni asked.

"Sure, about as hot as an inventor that designs a biological tracking agent. Your turn for some ice, although I think the ice has performed a side benefit for me. Kind of like a cold shower." Char removed the ice from her cheek and placed it on Toni's hand. "Keep that on for at least ten minutes. How's my face look?"

Toni looked into Char's eyes. "Despite the shiner you're sure to have, beautiful. You're quite beautiful, you know. I suspect you hear that all the time."

Char did hear that all the time, but for some reason, hearing it come from Toni's lips touched her in a special way. Somehow, she knew Toni's admiration went deeper than her outside appearance and she wasn't used to that.

"God, you keep distracting me and never seem to answer my questions. Although I don't think I would mind if you were able to track me down for all of eternity, I would like to know that this biological agent will work its way out of my body at some point in the future. Preferably before I have grandkids."

"You want kids?" Toni asked.

"Yes, someday I do. Please answer the question."

Toni looked sheepish as she responded. "Um, actually that's a prototype in your body and I'm not exactly sure. I think, yes, eventually it will work its way out, but I'm sorry I don't know how long it might take."

"Educated guess, please," Char pleaded.

"Not more than a year and probably not less than a week."

"Okay, your hotness level just went down a notch. I would hope you would have a better guess than between one week and a year." Char smiled.

"In that case, six months—give or take a day. Did my hotness level go back up again? I can honestly say you are the first person to acknowledge my brain as an appealing part of the whole package. It gets old when all someone sees is what's on the outside." Toni looked down.

Char thought Toni's voice had a hint of sadness to it and she made a mental note to ask more about that. In her mind, Toni was the whole package. She couldn't imagine anyone not falling desperately in love with her.

Love, shit, did I just use that four letter word in relation to Toni?

"You know, Toni, I told you everything about my sordid childhood, yet I don't really know anything about you, your family or what your life was like growing up."

"Not much to tell really. I grew up in your typical middle-class family. I'm the youngest child and I don't think my parents knew what to do with me. I got in trouble a lot— especially in school. Eventually they moved me to a special school. I hated it there and I stopped feeling normal the day they sent me away."

Char saw an expression cross Toni's beautiful face and imagined her as a teenager—scared and alone in a foreign institution away from the comfort of home. Toni didn't have to describe her experience because, written all across her face was the look Char had seen on too many occasions. All the young girls they rescued had that same frightened appearance. She absently brushed a lock of Toni's hair aside in an effort to make a connection.

Toni continued her personal revelation. "The shrink told my parents I was acting out because I was probably bored. They assumed that was why I was kissing Mary Beth Kowalski behind the bleachers. To their horror, they discovered that being a lesbian isn't actually tied to boredom. We don't talk about it now. The only one that asks me about my love life is my older sister and she and her husband never even blinked an eye when I told them. They just acted like it was the most normal thing in the world." Toni looked away. "I suppose my dad doesn't really mind either. He says he can relate because he loves women too. He's a typical male— thinks lesbians are just fine, but God forbid one of his grandsons turns out to be gay. My dad's a pig. He spent the better part of his youth chasing women behind my mom's back."

Char thought that Toni sounded bitter and perhaps this was a sore subject, so she deftly changed it. "Okay, let's take a look at your hand." Char removed the bag of ice and nodded. "Good, it looks much better. I think the swelling is down now. How does it feel? Do you think you need an x-ray? We have our own equipment here in the compound and agents who specialize in medical care."

"You do? How come I haven't seen anyone else except Dani, Ronda, and Maggie?"

"We didn't want to overwhelm you, so the other agents are lying low for now. We have about eighteen other agents who live in the compound and another twenty who we think of as independent contractors. Most of the agents are women Maggie saved from the sex slave trade business. She has an uncanny knack for picking the best. I think someone close to her was lost to the trade and she's never gotten past this overriding need to stamp out this ugly business. Since Viktor is at the top of the list, at least here in the US, she is doubly motivated to shut him down. I have my own reasons for making sure we are successful."

"Dani?"

Char nodded.

"Do you think she'll recover completely from her injury?" Toni asked.

"Yeah, I do. Well, at least eventually from her physical injury. I'm not so sure she'll recover from the emotional one," Char clarified.

"Natalie's death?"

"Yes. She fell in love with Natalie and hasn't forgiven herself for what happened."

"But that wasn't her fault. Sophie and Natalie were assigned to the case. Natalie volunteered to arrange the meeting and set everything up."

"Emotions aren't always logical. For a long time, I blamed Sophie and Natalie for Dani's injury and I admit to viewing all of you as assets to the organization. I honestly didn't view you as people. I know that's a pretty jaded view." Char looked down. She couldn't meet Toni's eyes and the look of disappointment that she was convinced would be there.

"Am I still just an asset to you?" Toni lifted Char's chin.

Char saw the hurt look in Toni's eyes.

"No, you're not just an asset. You are so much more to me than that." Char blurted out before she had a chance to censor her words.

"Good. Because I feel the same way," Toni responded.

Char shot Toni a genuine smile and stroked her face. Toni seemed to lean into the touch and Char placed a tentative kiss on her lips.

Toni grabbed both of Char's hands, lifted her from the couch, and wrapped her arms around Char's body in a gentle embrace.

Char could feel her desire begin to climb rapidly, like a thermometer placed in a pot of boiling water. This time the kiss she initiated filled her body with passion as she explored every part of Toni's lips with her mouth and tongue. Gentle nibbles increased the desire to an all-time high as she dragged Toni down the hall to her bedroom.

Char's mouth watered as she glanced at the long-legged beauty. Somehow, Toni had managed to worm her way into every one of Char's fantasies. She licked her lips as her mouth went dry.

God, Char, you're acting like some hormone-crazed teenager.

Toni was breathing hard as she reached for Char's shirt and undid the buttons slowly. As she removed the shirt, she stroked her arms down to the palms of Char's hands and gently lifted them to her lips, where she placed an almost chaste kiss to each palm.

Char removed Toni's pullover and moved her hands to the sides of Toni's body where she began stroking her belly, sending shivers down her spine. Toni thought she would come right then and there as Char's hand undid the top button on her jeans.

"I need you naked, now," Char exclaimed in a ragged voice.

Toni swiveled Char and pushed her onto the bed. "You first."

Char unbuttoned and unzipped her jeans, tugging down on her pants and quickly divesting herself from the restrictive clothing.

Toni stood wide-eyed at the foot of the bed, feasting her eyes on Char's long, lean body gift wrapped in the satin and lace of her matching green underwear. She quickly unzipped her pants, stepped out of them, climbed on top of Char before soundly kissing her. She rolled on her side and began stroking Char's collarbone until she reached the top clasp of the lacy bra. In a practiced move, the bra was undone and quickly removed, leaving Char's milky white breasts exposed.

Char's nipples quickly reacted to Toni's touch and she moaned in response. "Oh, God, that feels so good."

Toni stroked each side of her breast and then lightly rolled the nipples between her thumb and forefinger. She had an overwhelming desire to taste every inch of her body as she sucked the nipples gently letting her hand traveled down Char's body to the top of her silk panties.

Dipping her fingers just below the top band, she felt the soft hair leading to her treasure trove. Toni kissed and licked her way down, gently tugging on the silk covering her object of desire. She was anxious for her first glorious taste of the sweet nectar below. Removing the panties and flicking them to the side, Toni smiled as she caught a glimpse of her prize.

Char was a true redhead. Toni discovered fine, neatly clipped red hair and inched her way down to part the soft copper curls.

Toni's tongue snaked out as she made contact with the sensitive bud that lay beneath the coils of hair. Char's reaction was immediate as she lifted her body to meet Toni's tongue and gasped. A long low moan followed.

Char cried out. "Please, go inside."

Toni didn't need to verbalize her veneration at Char's responsiveness as she continued to lick as she gently inserted one, then two fingers, curling them up into Char's g-spot.

As Char's body moved rhythmically, Toni continued to stroke inside her vagina until she felt the first wave of orgasm. She continued to lick and suck until she felt Char's body explode and sweet juices lathered her in ecstasy.

Toni slowly crawled up Char's body, gently stroking her and feeling her body begin to relax in post-orgasmic bliss.

"Wow. Just wow. I cannot form any other intelligent thoughts just now. I hope you will forgive me, but those are the only words that come to mind at this moment," Char exclaimed.

When her breathing calmed, Char flipped Toni and grinned. "My turn and suddenly I find that I'm starving."

A sudden, loud crash sounded from the hallway.

"Shit, I forgot I put those there." A voice in the hallway cried out.

Toni laughed when she heard Dani in the hallway. Char groaned.

"Dani?" Toni asked.

"Unfortunately, yes. Little sister or not, I think I might have to kill her," Char responded.

"I suppose that knocking is not something she's inclined to do?" Toni inquired.

Bang

"Crap, this damn hallway is hard to navigate. Hey, you two. Time to get dressed. The natives are getting restless," Dani called out from the hallway.

"Don't you dare enter this bedroom. We'll be out in a minute. Toni hurt her hand with her right hook and I'm just making sure that it's not broken," Char responded.

Toni giggled. "Um, I'm pretty sure I just demonstrated how well it works."

"Shhh. If you so much as make one joke in front of Dani, I will retaliate."

"Ooh, retaliation. That could be a lot of fun." Toni smirked.

"I mean it. She's like a dog with a bone. She'll never let me live it down."

"All right. What's it worth to you?" Toni asked.

"Blackmail? Really? That's so beneath you. Where did you fling my panties? We need to get dressed."

"Well, I still kind of have some clothes on."

"Yeah, I noticed and I do believe that at a later date we will need to remedy that. It's not exactly recommended to leave me unfulfilled and I abhor the fact that I've left you dangling."

"Oh, no, we can't let that happen. No worries regarding my state of mind, I'm completely satisfied right now."

"Come on. Hurry up, you two. There's some guy topside that's making Maggie nervous. I don't like it when Maggie gets nervous," Dani called out.

Chapter Sixteen

Toni and Char walked into the control room and Toni noticed immediately the level of stress and anxiety that hovered in the air like cheap cigar smoke.

"What's all the commotion?" Toni asked.

Ronda pointed to the security monitor displaying a man peeking in the cabin's front window. "Seems our little pals here notified the FBI."

"Shit, Sophie, why did you call Ted?" Toni inquired.

"I wasn't about to go traipsing in the woods after you without some kind of backup. Besides, I trust Ted. He's one of the few people I opened up to after Natalie."

Toni looked at Dani who bent her head and swiped a hand across her eyes.

Char put a hand on Dani's shoulder.

"I suppose now is a good time to fill everyone in on our suspicion," Maggie said quietly.

Char was riveted to the monitor.

"That would be appreciated, because frankly I'm getting a bit tired of this little party," Sophie declared.

"Char, I don't think you need to worry. I don't believe he will be able to access the tunnels. All he will find is an abandoned cabin. However, I am a little worried that he might bring others to this location and that will put us all at risk. Sophie, I know you were just attempting to protect those you love, but unfortunately, you may have placed us all in grave danger. Let's wait and see what happens in the next day or two and if we need to move our base of operations, I've planned for this contingency."

"You have?" Dani lifted her tear-streaked face.

"Of course. First rule have plan B, C, and D ready to roll at a moment's notice." Maggie placed a comforting hand on her shoulder.

"You better tell us the whole story and don't leave out any details if you have any hope of our cooperation." Sophie glared.

"Very well. Let me start from the beginning," Maggie began.

"Novel place to start," Sophie added.

Kim placed a hand on Sophie's arm. "Soph, please let her tell the story without interruption. I'd like to hear what she has to say."

"Sorry, I'll try not to be rude. Please, go on." Sophie looked down.

Toni laughed to herself, noting how quickly Kim was able to get Sophie to behave.

"I suppose you could say I have a passion for ridding the world of this ghastly sex slave business. Our organization has had a fair amount of success and we've been able to free a number of girls throughout the years, before their innocent lives were ruined. However, for every girl we save, ten more are lost to us. As you are already aware, Dani was working undercover and was instrumental in helping save lives, but two years ago, we experienced a tragedy and had to regroup," Maggie explained.

"Natalie," Sophie whispered.

"Yes. We did not anticipate what transpired that evening. Later, we learned the reason for the catastrophe was due to a traitor in what we suspect is the FBI. There is a significant amount of evidence that someone from the FBI is feeding the Russian mob information. It has to be someone who knew about the meeting two years ago."

"Isn't it possible that it could be someone from your organization?" Sophie asked.

"Yes, Sophie, that is possible, but I believe unlikely. Every person who works for our organization has a passion for this work. I don't believe anything would entice them to betray us. We are like a family. Only a handful of people knew about the meeting that night."

"Can I ask who knew about the meeting?" Toni interrupted.

"Yes, certainly. Well everyone who was present of course, Natalie, Dani, Char, Sophie and you. In addition to those at the meeting, we believe at least one other FBI agent had inside information. Ronda had knowledge, and of course, I was thoroughly briefed. Sophie, I believe you would be the best person to confirm who else in the FBI knew about the meeting."

Sophie cringed and quietly revealed. "Ted had knowledge, but I've known him for ten years and I trust him with my life. More importantly, I trust him with Kim and Toni's life. Besides Ted, there were probably two or three other people, including my supervisor." Sophie narrowed her gaze at both Char and Ronda. "How do I know that your trigger happy agent here isn't the mole or how about Char? She seems to be skilled at deception."

Maggie frowned. "I suppose we cannot be one hundred percent sure of anyone, but I do think it would be prudent to be cautious around Ted. Providing him with additional information could put us all at risk. Has Ted been able to contact you since you left the FBI?"

Sophie frowned. "No, I haven't let anyone know where I reside and Toni helped to basically remove all traces of my existence. It would have been very hard for him to track me down. He was surprised to hear from me and he tried to get more details about where he could contact me."

"Sophie, I am sorry to have to tell you this, but we know for a fact that the Russian mob has your picture and a picture of Toni. Dani, would you please show them the program we created."

Dani rolled her wheelchair in front of a monitor and pointed to the display showing screen shots of various cell phones. "This is the picture that was sent to every one of Viktor's goons. It's a very good picture of you, Sophie."

Dani scrolled to a new picture. "Sorry, Char, but this is the picture we brought up today that was sent to Viktor's phone last night. It looks like that goon got a really good picture of both you and Toni. Of course, they already had a picture of Toni. It's also a really nice shot." Dani clicked a few times to show a screen shot of the picture of Toni.

"Do they have Kim's picture?" Sophie asked.

"Not that we know of." Dani rolled to another monitor.

"I showed this to Toni earlier. This program shows us where every one of Viktor's goons is located. For the past six months or so, after we learned they had your pictures, we've been playing block and tackle for you. That goon last night slipped by our web. As you can see, the red dots are multiplying at an alarming rate. They really want to catch you and word on the street is that there is a million dollar bounty on both your heads. Sorry." Dani looked down.

"I've come to the conclusion that we will not be able to stop them unless we decimate their financial resources. We've been watching, with interest, your success with creative asset management and we believe we can cripple and possibly destroy the Russian mob if we combine forces. We need your expertise and Toni's technology to pull this off. Will you consider joining forces?" Maggie asked.

Kim spoke up, "Will you give us a few minutes to talk? I'm trusting you not to listen in on our conversation with whatever fancy equipment you might have. Please give us the respect of privacy and I promise we will give your proposal serious consideration."

Maggie nodded. "Of course. Dani, please turn off any of your special devices, including the ones I probably don't know about."

Dani blushed. "Sorry. I did mean to tell you about them. I promise."

Maggie smiled and Toni thought she saw genuine affection in it.

Dani rolled out of the room and beamed at Toni.

Char winked and followed her sister.

Ronda glared and walked beside Maggie as they exited the control room.

†

Kim always trusted her gut in situations like this, but Toni and Sophie often let other factors sway them. Sophie was always so cautious and frequently let pride get in the way of making good decisions. Kim loved Toni, but she could be a handful and her weakness was beautiful women. Kim had closely watched the interaction between Toni and Char and this time she believed there was more to their chemistry than simple lust.

Kim suspected that Toni's brilliance often got in the way of lasting relationships. She'd seen the look of disappointment in Toni's eyes whenever she tried to move her liaisons beyond the initial physical attraction stage. Some of the women Toni connected with were downright cruel in their appraisal of Toni's intelligence. Whether it was jealousy or insecurity, she didn't know. She only knew that their jabs were hurtful to Toni but this time Kim was confident that Toni had met her match.

She needed both Toni and Sophie to set aside their petty differences and trust their intuition.

"All right, what does your gut say? Yes or no? I need you both to vote without analyzing everything to death." Kim gave her two partners in crime a steely gaze.

"I vote yes. I trust Char." Toni spoke up first.

"Figures you'd say that. I suppose this newfound trust came after you slept with her. I say no. My gut says there is something amiss about Ronda. For all we know she's the mole." Sophie crossed her arms.

"I vote yes. I trust Maggie, Char, and Dani. Soph, I think you're right about Ronda, but maybe not in the same way that you suspect. There is something there. I sense there is more to her story, but I don't necessarily think she's a traitor," Kim expounded.

Sophie's eyes softened as she turned to Kim. "Kim, I know I don't put much weight in intuition, but I trust you and you've not steered us wrong in the past. I can go with the majority, but I'm not about to completely let my guard down and I suggest both of you stay alert. There is still a mole out there and I, for one, plan to do everything I can to ferret out this traitor. I must admit that if they really wanted to hurt us, we'd most likely be dead already. This place is about as safe as we can get for the time being."

"Listen, Soph, I wasn't sold on Char at first, but I've spent some time with her and she's opened up about things that weren't easy for her to talk about. I care about her and I can't say that's ever happened to me before. She treats me like more than a sex object and I want what you and Kim have. Maybe I'm making the biggest mistake of my life trusting her and wanting more, but it feels right." Toni's gaze was unwavering.

"What…uh…what Kim and I have?" Sophie sputtered.

"Yeah, I'm tired of you two dancing around the issue and never telling one another how you feel. Life is too damn short to waste it on your overwhelming need to protect your fragile emotions. I've kept my mouth shut for all the wrong reasons. I always feared being odd woman out when you two finally came to your senses. Well, I'm not keeping my mouth shut anymore. Just tell her how you feel, Soph. You too, Kim."

"Toni's right. I should have told you long ago, but I just didn't want to trounce on Nat's memory. I know how much you loved her and it just got easy not to say anything as the months went by. I've loved you for a long time, long before you met Natalie." Kim looked away not knowing how Sophie would react to her confession.

"I…I…never knew that." Sophie grabbed Kim's hand and turned her so they were face-to-face. "Kim, please, look at me. I did love Natalie, but she never reciprocated that love. I came to love her in the same way I love Toni and I would do anything for her, but she ended up as my work partner, not my life partner. Shit, I've been in love with you since college, but I never thought I had a chance. We are so different and when I joined the FBI, I just thought, well—"

"Just kiss the girl and then let's get going. We have some plans to draw out. After hearing Char's story I want to nail this bastard." Toni grinned.

Sophie took Kim into her arms, gently pushed a lock of hair aside, and softly placed a kiss on her lips.

"For once, I think Toni's instructions are spot-on, and I reserve the right to continue following those orders, and perhaps add to them at a later time, in a different place." Sophie placed a soft kiss on Kim's forehead. "Okay, any ideas on how to get the spy kids back into this room?"

"I'll bet if we mosey our way to that door, they'll reappear." Toni pointed to the door on the other side of the room where they had exited earlier.

"By the way, the very first question I'd like to explore is why we don't have an audio feed in the cabin. With all this fancy technology, it seems like that would be a no-brainer. I just noticed that Ted is in the cabin and just pulled out his cell phone, and I for one would like to hear what he's saying." Sophie glanced back at the monitor and narrowed her gaze.

Toni and Kim started walking toward the door as Sophie watched the monitor.

†

The door swung open just before they reached it and Char, Maggie, Dani, and Ronda entered the control room.

All of this spy stuff was completely out of Kim's comfort zone so she decided she'd let Sophie and Toni take the lead.

"Hey, I thought you weren't monitoring us?" Sophie called over.

Dani smiled. "We weren't monitoring the audio feed, but we were looking for a sign that your discussion was over. Don't worry, none of us are expert lip readers. We do have some agents who possess that particular skill, but that's not our area of expertise."

"Good to know. I think you better turn that audio feed on pronto because Ted is on his cell phone and I'm particularly interested in hearing his conversation," Sophie advised.

"No worries, everything is taped. Whatever we don't hear live we can just run it again," Dani explained.

Toni frowned. "So you taped our conversation?"

Maggie narrowed her gaze at Dani. "I thought you disabled the audio?"

"I did, I promise. I only turned off the control room audio. I didn't disable the audio in the cabin," Dani explained quickly.

Char lifted her eyebrow. "Damn, it sounds like I need to find out more about the conversation. I have a feeling that I may have been mentioned and I'd hate to think you were disparaging me after all we've been through." Char winked at Toni.

"Can we cease the verbal fornication for right now? I'd really like to hear that audio feed," Sophie complained.

Toni mouthed *verbal fornication* and grinned at Char.

Kim placed her hand over her mouth to keep from laughing as she caught the nonverbal exchange between Toni and Char.

"It looks like Ted just finished his call. You better cue up the tape so we can listen in. Is there any way to hear the other end of the conversation besides what Ted is saying?" Sophie asked.

"Maybe, if we amplify the recording we might be able to isolate the sound coming out of the phone, but it's a longshot. This guy hasn't been on our radar, so we didn't put a tracking device on his phone. If he's the mole, he's been very careful not to make contact with Viktor through the normal channels. He certainly doesn't have one of Viktor's special cell phones." Dani's fingers typed furiously on one of the keyboards. "Done. Okay we can listen to the feed now."

"It's just some empty cabin in the middle of bum fuck Egypt.

Well, check*****report*****pleased*****

I'll send you the coordinates and maybe you and your team can find out more. So far, I haven't seen anything. The only strange thing is there seems to be multiple fresh car tracks.

****follow****

I'm not equipped to check things out thoroughly and I'm concerned about traps. I think I saw something that looks like a camouflaged trip wire. I'm not about to chance having my balls blown off.

****pay you****

Yeah, I know how important Sophie is. She called, so that's a start.

****

All right. I'll meet you there in an hour."

"I'm sorry that's the best I could do with cleaning the sound. It's not much to go on, but we should probably get Ronda to follow him."

"Why Ronda? Why not Char or one of us?" Sophie asked.

"They have pictures of Char, you, and Toni. I'm not an expert at surveillance and no offense, Dani, but that is not your area of expertise either," Maggie explained.

"You don't trust me. I get it, because I don't trust you either. Fucking government employees are all a bunch of traitors if you ask me," Ronda spit out.

153

"Can we please shelve the pissing contest? Ronda, you need to get going because our friend, Ted, is getting ready to leave," Char interjected.

"Fine, but when I return, the feebie and I are going to have it out once and for all. I'm not going to tolerate her incessant barbs," Ronda growled.

After Ronda turned to leave, Sophie flipped her the bird.

"God, you are a Neanderthal five-year-old. I'm just glad Ronda is now the recipient of your charm. I'd be willing to place a bet that you two are far more alike than either of you would admit to." Toni chuckled.

"Oh, you have no idea how right you are," Char added.

"Youth. I wonder if I was ever this...never mind, we've got a lot of work to do," Maggie said. "I hope the three of you are up to it. It's time we moved around far more assets than you've been able to accomplish during the past year and a half. We may be able to help quite a bit with Dani's financial tracking program. We've been able to isolate all of the financial resources tied to the mob. They are vast and, unfortunately, like a spider's web, they are very intricate."

Maggie walked to one of the monitors and pointed at a screen that did indeed look a bit like a spider's web to Kim.

"Look, if you don't mind, may Kim and I take a break? Although I have a certain amount of expertise with computers, this really looks like something that's more up Toni's alley. After she's had a chance to thoroughly review and evaluate your programs and technology, come and get us and we can work on brainstorming a plan of action," Sophie suggested.

"Of course. I'm sorry that, from the moment you arrived, we haven't exactly pulled out the welcome mat.

Most of our other agents are at the Virginia compound, so we have plenty of empty quarters for you to relax, rejuvenate, and maybe catch a quick nap. I'll take you myself," Maggie offered.

Toni leaned in and whispered in Kim's ear, "FYI, I think this is kind of like a college dorm and they don't always knock before entering, but go for it. I would if I were you."

Kim blushed as Toni winked at her.

Sophie raised her eyebrow. "Is there something I'm missing here?"

"No, nothing important. Toni is just being Toni. Maggie, lead the way please," Kim responded.

Chapter Seventeen

Maggie led Sophie and Kim down a long tunnel and opened the door to a cozy living space.

"I think you will find the accommodations impressive. Dani has quite a few inventions that rival those of your friend, Toni. She has unlimited untapped brilliance that will only blossom with Toni's guidance. Most of the cutting-edge technology is a result of Dani's hard work." Maggie smiled.

Sophie was impressed with the warm and inviting living area. A fireplace was nestled in the corner. She assumed it was fake, but unless you inspected the crackling logs carefully, you'd never be able to tell the difference. Even the heat from the fireplace felt real. She supposed it was another one of Dani's inventions.

Maggie pointed down the hallway. "There are two bedrooms and a master bath down there. Feel free to use one or both of the bedrooms. Help yourself to any of the T-shirts, shorts, tank tops, or sweats that are located in the drawers. I believe they will fit you nicely. Fresh towels are in the bathroom if you decide to shower or freshen up. Help yourself to any of the food in the refrigerator. I believe there is also some beer and wine. We try to keep these quarters stocked for guests. We can regroup in a few hours and talk more about our concerns about a leak. I don't think the end of the world will happen in the next few hours. Please make yourselves at home."

Maggie quietly exited the guest quarters and left Sophie and Kim alone to explore.

Kim walked down the hallway and opened the first door on the right.

Sophie didn't want to crowd Kim so she took a few steps more and opened the second door. She rummaged in the dresser drawers until she found some cotton gym shorts and a t-shirt. After she quickly donned the borrowed clothes, she looked in the mirror. The T-shirt was a little snug, but it wasn't uncomfortable. She usually wore clothes a couple of sizes too big because she hated any kind of restriction in her movements.

Her head peeked out the door and she saw Kim exit the other room and head to the couch. Leaving her room and walking toward the couch, Sophie admired Kim's toned body as she relaxed on the couch in the borrowed shorts and tight fitting T-shirt. It wasn't often she saw her friend—well, maybe more than a friend now if she got her way—in casual attire.

Sophie sat next to Kim, picked up her hand, and began caressing it.

"So what do you make of the audio playback we heard?" Kim asked.

"I don't know. In some ways, it looks bad for Ted, but I might also interpret it in another way. I never told you or Toni this, but when I left the FBI, they nearly begged me to stay. They offered a huge raise and all kinds of other perks. When I called Ted the other day, he mentioned again how much the FBI wanted me back and would reinstate me no questions asked. It's possible he was talking to someone in the bureau and they are just concerned about my safety."

"Yeah, that's possible, I guess. Do you really think Ronda could be involved?" Kim asked.

"You know, I get the feeling that Ronda is former CIA. She acts a lot like a spook. They are an especially paranoid bunch and they've never drawn inside the lines. Spooks think nothing of taking out a life. It's not like Toni has spent a great deal of time with her. It seems like she's left to her own devices quite a bit. She's probably had ample opportunity to meet with Viktor and his goons on the sly. Besides, if she is former CIA, they're known for playing both sides of the fence—as long as in their pea brains, the end justifies the means," Sophie offered.

"What do you think of Char?" Kim asked.

"I'll only admit this to you, but I think you're right. I've been watching her and I think she genuinely has feelings for Toni. Despite the initial subterfuge, I actually trust her. At first, I didn't trust Dani when she was undercover and meeting with Nat, but it's hard not to like her youthful exuberance. Have you seen how she worships Toni? She's a bright little thing. I think her inventions come damn close to the brilliance of Toni's. She has an innocence about her that I want to protect somehow. Kind of like a little sister. I can see how protective Char is and I admire that about her. I also see the sadness in Dani's eyes and I'm sure it's related to Nat. I knew that Nat was in love, but I didn't realize how much it was reciprocated."

"So either Ted or Ronda could be the traitor—what if we fed both of them different pieces of false information and see where it goes?" Kim suggested.

"Kim, you're a genius. We could also get Toni to plant one of her little biologic tracking devices on Ronda and then see where she goes. Perhaps we should pull Toni and Char together later today and float this by them," Sophie added.

"Soph, things could get crazy for us in the very near future, so maybe we should capitalize on these precious stolen moments before all hell breaks loose. I want you to know that I'm glad Toni called us out today. I was coming close to fessing up anyway. It was getting too hard not to. Life is too short and I've wasted far too much time already."

Sophie was pleased when Kim leaned in and captured her lips, gently exploring them.

Sophie responded and sought entrance with her tongue, gently sucking and increasing the intensity of the kiss. Sophie's heart raced and she questioned whether Kim was prepared to go where she desperately wanted to take her. She pulled back and looked into Kim's eyes.

Although she saw the arousal, she needed to ask. "Kim, I really want to make love to you, but if it's too soon, I understand."

"Not too soon. I'm just glad it's not too late for us. I'd like nothing better than to make love with you. I've been waiting a very long time for this," Kim responded.

Sophie had a mini meltdown in her head wondering whether she would be good enough for Kim. She wanted to make Kim sing with pleasure. One look from Kim was all it ever took to shake her to her core and leave her breathless. She decided the risk was worth it and she would do everything in her power to show Kim just how much she loved her.

"I love you," Sophie uttered those three little words.

Kim tugged gently on her hand and Sophie stood, pulling her into a warm embrace. They walked hand in hand down the hallway to the first bedroom on the right.

"I love you too, and I want this and everything that goes with what this means for me. I don't want one night with you, so if that's all this will be...well, as much as I want you, I can't go there," Kim whispered.

"Never, I'd never just want one night. I'll always want more and there will never be another for me. It's always been you and it will always be you. I want this to be for the rest of our lives and you'll break my heart if you don't want the same."

"Oh, Soph, I can't tell you how happy that makes me. Of course I want the same."

"You know, Toni is going to act like an insufferable know-it-all tomorrow." Sophie sighed.

"Oh, I wouldn't worry about that. I think if she opens that door, it's fair game for us to bring forward her blossoming relationship with Char. I'm convinced it is a relationship and not just one of her one-night stands. Teasing can go both ways."

The couple entered the bedroom and Sophie smiled as she spied the bottle of lotion on the nightstand next to the bed. She pointed to the lotion. "Hmm, I wonder if there are more presents in the drawers. Let's check it out."

"I don't need toys. I practically come every time you touch me, but I'll admit a back rub with some of that lotion would be particularly welcome right now."

"Your wish is my command. I'll need you completely undressed to do this correctly."

Kim quickly shed her shorts and T-shirt and stood naked in front of the bed.

Sophie didn't think she'd ever seen anything more beautiful. Kim's compact body was curvy in all the right places, but muscular everywhere else. Her flat stomach created a lovely path to her shock of curls, offset in a perfect triangle. Her breasts were small, but pert, and her nipple erection gave away her response to Sophie's obvious adoration of her body. It was the most erotic thing Sophie had ever seen. Sophie wanted to press her naked body against Kim's. She yanked her T-shirt above her head and pulled down her own gym shorts.

"Why don't you lie down on your stomach and I'll give you that back rub you're jonesing for," Sophie offered.

Kim climbed onto the bed and laid down with her head turned to the side. Sophie grabbed the lotion from the nightstand and straddled Kim's body as she poured lotion into her hand. Sophie didn't wish to shock Kim's body with cold lotion, so she used the friction in her hands to warm it before massaging the cream into Kim's back.

Kim moaned. "Ooh, that is sooo good. Might I also add that I can feel your hair on my ass and I think I might actually be dripping right about now."

Sophie leaned down and kissed the back of Kim's neck. Her hands traveled down Kim's back as she scooted further down to allow herself access to Kim's perfect ass. She lovingly stroked the firm behind as her thumb caressed down Kim's bottom, brushing the velvet folds beneath.

Kim arched up into Sophie's touch. "Um, I think I'd like to continue that back rub later because what you are doing right now is driving me nuts."

Sophie continued to stroke Kim—panting and bucking was her reward. Sophie moved to the side and gently turned Kim and continued her loving touch. Using a teasing approach, she brought Kim to the edge and then covered her naked body with her own.

Kim whimpered at the loss of Sophie's fingers, but quickly adjusted to the new sensation of Sophie's body grinding on top of her. Sophie felt Kim's hand reach across to her ass and begin to stroke her from behind.

Both women began panting wildly as they reached climax at the same time, each calling out the other's name.

As Sophie's breathing calmed, she rolled to the side and began caressing Kim's breasts and stomach with utter devotion. "I've never experienced that before."

Kim's expression showed astonishment. "You've never had an orgasm before?"

Sophie blushed. "No, I've had sex before and yes I've experienced release, but I've never had a simultaneous orgasm with anyone. That was the most beautiful experience I've ever had. I guess it really does make a difference when you're in love with the person you're intimate with."

"Yes, it does and yes, that was damn near a religious experience for me too. That's my first time too—you know together like that."

Sophie closed her eyes and let out a sigh. "I wish we could stay right here like this forever."

"Me too," Kim caressed Sophie's cheek. "But we both know we can't."

Sophie nodded. "One day we will."

"Count on it."

"I am." After kissing Kim once more, Sophie shook her head. "I hate to switch gears, but I'm worried about how we're going to possibly move those vast resources without getting caught. I have total faith in Toni's inventions, but we barely made it out last time without collateral damage. I don't have the foggiest idea how we're going to pull this off," Sophie admitted.

"I get the sense that Char is a master strategist, so maybe she has an idea. I'd let Char, Toni, and Dani work out the details and I'm sure they will involve us in a way that will capitalize on our unique talents. It will be kind of nice having more people watching our backs."

"I'll volunteer to watch your back any day of the week. It's such a lovely backside." Sophie leered at Kim.

Chapter Eighteen

Char, Dani, and Toni leaned over a table, pushing around reports, maps, papers, and other diagrams. Coffee cups and empty Coke cans littered the table, along with open bags of chips and crumbs from devoured sandwiches.

"No, that won't work." Toni pushed her hand through her hair in frustration. "We can all assume that Viktor is wise as to how we obtained Byron's retinal access. Besides, his weakness is not beautiful women."

"Unfortunately, Toni is correct. That bastard's taste is more along the lines of his business. He always picks from his own group of new girls and tosses them aside like a piece of garbage when they get too old," Char spit out.

"Then how are we going to obtain access without getting the retinal scan?" Dani asked.

"I say we shoot him, dig out his eye, whack off his hand, and, voilà, two birds with one stone," Ronda offered.

Char turned to Ronda. "When did you get back? I didn't even hear you enter. So what's the update?"

"It was hard to follow him from out here in the boons and I think I might have spooked him because he went back to his residence, or at least I think it was his residence. He didn't meet anyone that I could see."

"Fuck," Dani said.

"Since when did you start swearing?" Char chastised.

"I'm not three, you know. I can swear if I want." Dani jutted out her chin.

"Um, can we get back to our plans please?" Toni suggested.

"So what do we know so far, Dani?"

"Well, it seems like Viktor is getting a little nervous because, even though we hit Byron, he's made contact with him and we can assume he needs Byron's banking influence—probably money laundering. I think that means something went wrong with his previous connection," Dani explained.

"I was almost to the point of learning more about his connections when he approached me to handle some of his more legitimate businesses, but then he canceled our meeting and unfortunately everything went to shit after that. Eighteen months of work down the drain." Char shook her head.

"Maybe not. I think his previous connection may have been that other banker who we ruined. They fired his ass after we managed to redistribute thirty percent of his clients' assets. Do you think we might be able to dig through those old records and discover something of use?" Toni asked.

Dani clapped her hands together. "Oh, goody. I have just the program to use." Dani looked up at Toni. "It's a new program that I'd love you to take a look at."

Toni smiled at Dani. She liked the young woman. "I would be honored to check it out. I'm sure I can learn quite a few tricks from you."

Dani beamed and Char whispered in Toni's ear. "Thank you. She's brightened more around you than in the entire two years since Natalie's death."

Toni grabbed Char's hand and gave it a little squeeze. "Do you mind checking on the lovebirds while I look at Dani's program?"

"Sure, I can do that. Besides I understand Sophie has her own expertise with computers that I think we might need right now."

†

Sophie was sprawled out on the bed, with Kim wrapped in her arms, when she heard the light knocking sound.

"Just a minute," Sophie called out.

Kim scrambled off the bed and looked around the room.

Sophie picked up a pair of gym shorts and grinned at Kim while she held them out by her forefinger. "Looking for these?"

"Gimme those. I'd worry about getting your clothes on, if I were you. I hear they aren't too shy about entering without knocking," Kim teased.

Sophie spotted her discarded T-shirt and shorts and dressed quickly. She glanced back at Kim and noted her sitting on the bed tugging on her shirt.

"Come on in," Sophie shouted out.

Sophie could hear someone in the living room area and a few seconds later, she heard a crisp knock on the bedroom door. Sophie opened the door and waved Char inside.

Char sat on a chair in the corner, while Sophie joined Kim on the bed.

"So, did we give you two enough time to rejuvenate your brains? We could use your help," Char inquired.

Kim blushed. "Yeah, we're ready to join you. Thanks for the break."

Char smiled at Kim. "You're very welcome. Dani is showing Toni a new program she's designed that may shed some light on how we will be able to penetrate Viktor's financial holdings. While we still haven't quite figured out how to get the retinal scan, I believe Toni and Dani might have a way to uncover where all his holdings are. I'm pretty sure he has some of those holdings under different names and different corporations that only he has access to."

"Is there any way we can use Byron's choice of date enhancement to drug Viktor and then pry open his eyes to get the scan?" Sophie asked.

"I don't think so. He's always surrounded by guards. I don't know how we could get the drugs in his system. We don't have any agents who can pass for twelve or thirteen." Char shuddered. "That's his preferred age range."

"You mentioned that you have about forty agents, correct? What if we planned a major siege on his residence, drugged him, and then got the scan and handprints?" Kim asked.

"It's risky. Ronda would be the most qualified to lead the assault if we choose that route. I don't know if Maggie is willing to take the risk but I'm pretty talented with that kind of offensive. I would be willing to volunteer my services and I know of at least three others that would join us," Char offered.

"I think I could be helpful if we decide to go that route. I can take out at least ten guards without firing a single bullet," Sophie chimed in.

"I respectfully withdraw the idea. Soph, I don't want you involved in something that risky and I'm sorry, I didn't realize what a shitty and selfish idea it was. I shouldn't have been so cavalier with the lives of the other agents." Kim looked down.

"Don't apologize, Kim. It's actually a viable option," Char commented.

"Char, Kim and I were talking." Sophie paused. "We wanted to run something by you and Toni."

Char smiled. "Careful, it almost sounds like you might be starting to trust me."

"God, you are a perfect match for Toni. You're even starting to sound like her. In all seriousness, we have a major pest problem and all our planning could go up in smoke unless we rid ourselves of the mole. We've narrowed down our top two choices to Ronda or Ted." Sophie held up her hand. "Stop, I know you don't think it could be Ronda, but we can't be absolutely sure of that. It seems like she operates on her own quite a bit and you don't really know where she goes or who she talks with. I get the sense she is the lone cowboy type. She could easily be playing both sides and then advocate for Viktor's disposal as a means of ensuring that her activities are buried," Sophie explained.

"All right. After we do some initial planning, let's meet in my quarters. I'd like to bring Dani and Maggie in on the planning. Would that be okay?" Char asked.

"Sure, she might have some additional ideas. How about if Kim and I put on some sweats and join everyone in the control room. Maybe with all our heads together we can add to the shared pool of knowledge and come up with a brilliant plan that minimizes the risk to everyone." Sophie stood up and kissed the top of Kim's head.

"Sounds good to me. I'll leave you two to it and meet you in the living room." Char stood and left the bedroom.

Sophie smiled at Kim and held out her hand. "To be continued."

†

Char, Sophie, and Kim strolled into the control room. Char noticed how animated Dani was around Toni.

"That's incredible, Dani. Your program is genius," Toni exclaimed.

"You really think so?" Dani asked.

"Absolutely. You've found a way to not only track every single person's accounts, but you've managed to crack all the account numbers and passwords. Now all we need is Viktor's retina scan and handprint and we'll be able to decimate his resources." Toni smiled down at Dani.

"I'm afraid that is where we're now stuck. Kim came up with an idea, but it's risky," Char added.

"Do tell, what's the idea?" Toni asked.

"Well, we could do a major siege on Viktor's residence and drug him to obtain the needed biometric access," Char explained.

"Now we're talking. I'm in. Can we take them all out in the process?" Ronda asked.

"Maggie will never agree to that. Assassinations are only done as a last resort," Dani interjected.

"I think we may be at that point," Maggie spoke quietly as she slipped into the room.

Char was surprised that Maggie would agree to an assassination.

Ronda pumped her fist in the air. "Yes. Finally, I get to utilize the skills they trained me to do. We don't even need to risk a siege on the house. I can take him out and all we need is a retrieval team to obtain the body."

"You're a trained assassin? I'm surprised this organization provided that type of training." Sophie narrowed her gaze at Ronda.

"That training was not provided here, but we have made use of Ronda's skills on occasion. That option is never completely off the table, but it remains a last-resort alternative," Maggie clarified.

Ronda looked away. "Where I was trained is of no concern to you. All you need to know is that I remain one of the best in the business."

Sophie opened her mouth and Kim touched her arm.

"Well, I'd like to consider some other alternatives before we revert to cold-blooded murder," Toni remarked.

"What are you, some kind a pacifist?" Ronda asked.

"No, but as a computer geek, this is all the way outside my comfort zone," Toni answered.

"There's got to be some way to draw him out. I mean he must do normal things like go out to dinner or have meetings with other business associates. He had a meeting scheduled with me. Let's find out where he goes and who he sees and maybe we can find some way to get him alone, even if we do have to drug him and his bodyguards," Char proposed.

"I agree. I don't think I can live with myself if I'm a party to premeditated murder. That makes us no better than him," Kim added.

"Fuck. That's what we get for hooking up with a bunch of pansy-assed, do-gooder civilians," Ronda growled.

"Shut up, Ronda. Brute force isn't always the answer." Dani looked at Char. "It's not going to be easy, because from what we've learned so far, he has most of his meetings at his residence."

"All we need is one meeting where we can isolate him," Char advised.

"Hey, Kim, I just had an idea. What if we arranged a meeting with someone he already does business with and you developed a latex mask to match their face. Could you do that?" Toni asked.

"Maybe. I might need some technology assistance and a high-quality picture. I'll also need voice recordings to match their voice if we're going to pull this off. You and Dani are the most ingenious inventors I know, I'm sure we could make that work," Kim responded.

A loud boom sounded and the walls inside the control room shook. Small particles of cement rained down on their heads.

"Shit, what the hell was that?" Toni asked.

Char glanced at one of the monitors. "I'm afraid we have visitors. It looks like one of Viktor's goons tripped one of Ronda's special welcome mats. I only see one guy running back to a black SUV. I'm assuming whoever was with him didn't make it. Ronda, you better check things out and sweep the area."

"I'm on it." Ronda rushed out of the room.

"I guess that answers the mystery of who the mole is. I don't think it's a coincidence that Ted was just here this morning," Dani posed.

"Not necessarily." Sophie nodded in the direction of where Ronda just left. "She had ample opportunity to make contact with Viktor while she was supposedly following Ted. If she's supposed to be such a professional, how come she wasn't able to follow him without detection?" Sophie inquired.

"Ted is FBI. They're professionals too and surely they would notice a tail. It's not necessarily that farfetched that he would be nervous. Besides, I can't imagine you would have put your trust in some second-rate agent. I just have a really hard time believing that Ronda would betray us," Char explained.

"Money is a powerful motivator and now that she has all three of us in one location, she'll get triple the reward. She probably waited until we all entered this compound before making her move," Sophie insisted.

"I don't think we're going to solve anything right now about who the mole is. Char, remember when Sophie and I told you we had something we wanted to talk to you about?" Kim asked.

"Yeah."

"I'm sure Ronda will be back any minute. Can we find a secure location? We'd like to run something by you, Maggie, Dani, and Toni. We have an idea about how to smoke the mole out," Kim said.

"I'm concerned that this location is now compromised. I think we'd better move to another hub. Dani, will you be able to ensure that our Virginia hub is free of any monitoring devices? I don't want to believe that one of my agents is a traitor, but I need to ensure the safety of everyone and frankly, you three are key to this mission. I will send Ronda on a mission that will keep her occupied for the next day. That should give us plenty of time to consider your proposal," Maggie said.

Char was uncomfortable with the notion that her fellow agent might be the mole, but she trusted Maggie to do the right thing, no matter what the outcome.

Toni frowned. "How far away is the new hub and is it equipped as well as this control room? I'm duly impressed with everything here and I would hate to lose access to all this technology."

"No worries. This is actually our second hub. The Virginia hub is even more advanced, but right now, there's a bunch of other agents crawling all over that location. It could get a little cozy. Any chance we can move them somewhere else for a few weeks while we work this all out?" Dani asked.

"I think that can be arranged. We should probably take as much equipment as we can just in case one of Ronda's bombs is triggered by someone hitting just the right place on the fireplace and they manage to find the control room." Maggie sighed. "I'd hoped we wouldn't have to abandon this location."

Char immediately took charge. She quickly shut down several computers, unplugged the cords, and wrapped them up as she tossed them on the table. "Dani, can you grab the duffel bags and we can toss these cords and other small items into them?"

Dani rolled toward the door. "Yeah, sure. Toni, would you mind coming with me to help me grab Char's to-go bag and then we can get mine."

Toni touched Char on the arm and Char felt reassured by her touch.

"Since we don't really have travel bags, how about if I help Dani and, Sophie, you and Kim help Char grab as much equipment as you can," Toni suggested.

"We should plan to leave in thirty minutes. Anything we aren't able to salvage in that time will be considered the cost of doing business." Maggie shrugged.

Chapter Nineteen

Viktor relaxed in his Jacuzzi while a young Asian girl whimpered in the corner. A cigar dangled from his mouth like a flaccid penis. The symbolism didn't register with him even though his frustration with the whole fucking mess had left him feeling impotent.

He was tired and angry that every effort to rid himself of the meddling women ended in another dead end. He had no doubt there was a connection to the stolen money and interruptions to his business.

He'd already spent millions and was prepared to spend more. One girl brought a million or more in revenue so the cost was negligible compared to his continued loss of merchandise.

Viktor usually preferred blond, blue-eyed girls, but it was increasingly more difficult to obtain that particular variety of human flesh. The Asian market was still flowing, so he compromised. After all, he had needs and it was days since his last conquest.

"Girl, bring me that robe."

Viktor watched as the young trembling girl retrieved the robe and held it out for him. Seeing her fear increased his state of arousal.

He slipped on the robe and left the tie undone. "You should be thankful I chose you to service me. Get on your knees…"

"Excuse me, sir." A beefy guard interrupted.

Viktor looked up and growled. "What the fuck is it now?"

"Sir, I'm sorry to disturb your leisure time, but I didn't think you would want me to wait to provide an update."

Viktor waved his arm at the girl and she scrambled back to the corner. "Don't move a muscle, I'll be back, my little flower blossom." Viktor gestured to the man. "Come with me."

"Vladmir is in the parlor waiting for you. He has the update."

Viktor closed the robe and tied it shut as he walked into his mansion and down the hallway to the parlor.

†

A middle-aged man with thinning hair was pacing in the parlor as Viktor flung open the door.

"This better be important. You are interrupting my leisure time," Viktor snarled.

"Two of my men are dead. I was lucky to escape unharmed. The area surrounding the cabin contains numerous traps—both trip wires and land mines. As far as I could tell, a professional designed the perimeter protection. Whoever set the traps is an expert with explosives. Oddly, the cabin itself did not contain any snares, but it didn't reveal anything useful either. I recommend sending an expert to defuse the rest of the bombs before we attempt to examine the cabin or the surrounding area."

"I work with a bunch of imbeciles," Viktor complained. "I told you to be careful. The source warned us about the explosives. Find me that expert and get your ass back to that cabin. I want answers. If I don't hear good news by midnight, I will be very unhappy. No more fuckups or I'll be forced to make an example of someone."

The man bowed and quickly exited the room.

Furious, Viktor stalked to the coffee table and grabbed his phone. He punched a number saved in his speed dial list. "Two of my men are dead."

Viktor's frustration grew when he heard the voice on the other end respond, "Don't try to pin this cluster fuck on me. I warned you about the trip wires."

"I'm warning you. Don't fuck with me. I've paid you well. I want a location for those *sookas*. I don't give a rat's ass about the risk of exposure. We are too close to lose the momentum now. Call me when you have the information I need."

Viktor ended the call and threw the phone against the wall, smashing it into several large pieces.

"Dirk," Viktor shouted out. "Get your ass in here and get me a new phone."

Dirk hurried into the room and handed Viktor a phone.

"I don't care if the whole country blows up. Do not disturb me again during my leisure time tonight. Bring the girl to me."

"Yes, sir. I apologize for the earlier interruption. It won't happen again."

Viktor untied his robe and flopped onto the couch.

A few minutes later Dirk arrived, dragging the shivering girl into the room.

Viktor waved his hand and Dirk disappeared.

"I apologize for the interruption earlier," Viktor said without emotion. Upon seeing the frightened girl, Viktor had an immediate erection. He liked it when they trembled.

Viktor pointed to the space on the floor in front of his opened legs. "Kneel there." He placed each arm on top of the couch and leaned back. "I bet you've never seen such a magnificent sight…"

Three hours later, in a remote location, an explosion sent tremors in the earth and lit up the sky for miles. Five of Viktor's employees died in the blast and not a single scrap of evidence remained. Mother Earth closed off the tunnels with rock and debris. Authorities scratched their heads for days wondering why a remote cabin in the woods was completely demolished. Remnants of other smaller detonations littered the surrounding property, making it resemble a war zone.

Chapter Twenty

Toni was tired, hungry, and grumpy—not necessarily in that order. A lot had happened in the past few days and they still hadn't talked about Sophie and Kim's idea about how to smoke the mole out.

The new hub was almost an exact replica of the one they'd just abandoned.

After lugging the equipment into the new control room, Toni had tossed Char's to-go bag on the floor and sat down in one of the rolling desk chairs.

"I need food." Toni pouted. "If you want this brain to work, you need to feed me."

Dani grinned. "I could eat too."

"I think we all deserve a well-earned break. Would anyone like to rustle up some food from one of the quarters? They should all be fully stocked." Maggie looked at Char.

"Fine. I'll go, but if you are expecting some kind of gourmet meal, you're going to have to join me while I cook. I'm not lugging it back to the control room."

Toni looked at her watch. "It's kinda late for a gourmet meal. I'd settle for a bag of chips or some ice cream." Toni grinned and winked at Char. "If you're some kind of master chef in your spare time, Char, I reserve the right to a rain check—without the presence of all these other bozos."

"Do you think that after Toni's appetite is satisfied we can talk about our thoughts on smoking out the mole?" Sophie asked.

"I vote for ice cream." Kim smiled.

"Ice cream's good." Dani made the thumbs-up gesture.

"Junk food, it is. Toni, want to come with me to forage through the tunnels for strategy sustenance?" Char grabbed Toni's arm and looped her own arm through it, leading her out of the control room.

"And then we can talk about the mole, right?" Sophie called out to a departing Char and Toni.

"Yeah, yeah, after food, we'll have a powwow." Toni chuckled. Sophie was always such a worrywart.

"Hey, don't get caught up in any other extracurricular activities while you're getting food." Toni heard Sophie mutter as the door shut.

†

The corners of Char's mouth turned up as she spied the treasure in the freezer. "Bingo, we hit the mother lode. I knew I could depend on Val to keep this stocked with Ben and Jerry's. She usually crashes here unless she's on assignment or relocated. She has a terrible sweet tooth. So how does chocolate chip cookie dough, cherry Garcia, and vanilla toffee bar crunch sound?"

Char pulled out the three pints of ice cream and handed one to Toni.

"So, six spoons? Not that I'm jealous or anything, but who is Val?" Toni asked.

"Oh, yeah. Maggie won't really admit it, but she loves ice cream. She eats it right from the container just like the rest of us." Char waved her hand in the air. "Val's just another agent. We're barely friends. Besides sharing a love of all things sweet, our paths don't really cross that often."

"Good. I'd hate to think I'm competing for your affections."

Char looked directly into Toni's eyes. "There is no competition because I've never let anyone get remotely close before. It's one of my rules. Don't fall in love and don't date fellow agents. It's probably a really bad idea, but somehow I feel the need to change my rules."

"I never liked rules unless I could bend or break them." Toni leaned in and kissed Char. The two pints of ice cream in Char's hands created a barrier to a full-fledged embrace and Toni growled. "I suppose it's a good thing the ice cream is in the way. Sophie will have a shit fit if we take too long."

"To be continued. Come on, let's find the spoons and head back. You're the one who started this little scavenger hunt, or was that your way to get me alone?" Char asked.

"Clever girl."

✝

Sophie was trying to exercise patience, but it wasn't exactly her strong suit. She wanted Char and Toni to hurry up and get their asses back to the hub. They were probably playing kissy face right now.

Just at that moment, Char and Toni strolled into the control room carrying their treasure.

"About fucking time," Sophie groused.

"Soph, you are such a sourpuss." Toni grinned. "So where should we put the treats?"

"Let's put them all on the table and everyone can just dig in. I hope you like our choices." Char set her two pints down.

"Good choices, sis. Hand me a spoon please." Dani rolled closer to the ice cream.

"I know this isn't the most pleasant topic, but are we ready now to talk about our problem with the mole?" Maggie asked.

"Kim and I were talking and believe me, I get it, because, although I'm not the most trusting sort—to think that someone you trust and depend on could be betraying you—well, let's just say it doesn't feel too good. I know you don't think Ronda is a traitor and I hate wondering if Ted could be responsible either, but the only way to find out is to set a trap. Our plan has two parts because it's always good to have contingencies. Maggie, I know you understand that because you're probably a former girl scout like me, huh? Always be prepared."

Sophie held up three fingers. "Part one is to feed both Ronda and Ted false information about where we're holed up. Part two is to use Toni's brilliant biologic tracking prototype and track both Ted and Ronda. That's the part that might take some advance planning," Sophie explained.

"Ronda probably won't be as easy as Ted. She already knows about your business card, Toni, because she brought all the lab equipment when I suspected you had planted a biological agent in it," Char noted.

Toni glanced at Maggie. "Maggie, I think you'd be the best person to make sure she comes in contact with a material that will transmit the agent because she trusts you more than me now. I don't think she's all that thrilled with our new colleagues and it's clear how I feel."

Sophie was surprised to see the look that passed between Char and Toni.

"I have an idea about how we can assure that Ted absorbs the agent." Dani dug into the ice cream container and shoveled a huge spoonful of chocolate chip cookie dough into her mouth before she continued. "Sophie can call him up and say she needs his help and then arrange a meeting in a public location. She can allude to where she's holed up. I can go instead of Sophie and hand him the card with the false location written in Sophie's handwriting."

"No way am I letting you do that," Char bristled. "Kim, you're a master with disguises. Do you think you could create one for me? I can hand him the card and since I've already got the tracking device in my system, it can't transfer to me."

Char caught Toni's eye. "Toni, would that work?"

"Yeah, I can make it work. How will we know if either of them takes the bait? Just because Ted shows up at the false location, doesn't mean he's the mole. He could be trying to help Sophie." Toni looked perplexed.

"Toni, I know your place has a panic room. I think we should give that location to Ted, wait in your safe room, and see who shows. I know you have all kinds of surveillance equipment in there. If only Ted shows, I agree that doesn't help us. However, if some of Viktor's men show, then we know Ted is the mole. I'm sorry, I know that compromises your place because at this point only Kim and I know where you live when we come to DC," Sophie explained.

Toni blew out a puff of air and looked up at the ceiling. "Okay, I'm willing to sacrifice my privacy for the greater good, but I want to be waiting in that room to see for myself if Ted is as big a bastard as we suspect."

"You're not going there alone. I'm coming with and if Ted is the mole, God help him because I think I might actually want to kill him for placing you and Kim in danger."

"Well, I'm sure not going to leave the two of you to all that fun. I'm coming with." Kim shot out her hand and put it in front of Sophie's face. "Don't even think of saying no, Sophie."

Sophie sighed. "I know. You're a big girl and you don't need me acting like a Neanderthal."

"You guys are like the three musketeers. All for one and one for all. As much as I would love to join you, someone has to be at the other location in case Ronda is the mole. Can we all have the tracking app and a way to communicate with one another, in case the other group needs backup?" Char inquired.

"Hey, you're not planning on manning the other location all by yourself, are you?" Toni frowned.

Maggie shook her head. "No, I'll send at least three other agents as backup. I have just the location to suggest. We have a safe house that is equipped with surveillance equipment and they will see trouble coming well in advance. It should provide them adequate time to prepare for any possible threat. Do whatever you feel is necessary to protect yourselves, even if that requires elimination."

Maggie looked at Kim and Toni. "I'm sorry. I know that neither of you were in favor of that option, but if forced to act, we will do whatever is necessary to protect our own. The protection extends to all of you now."

Dani set the spoon down and folded her hands in her lap. "What can I do? I want to help."

Toni put a hand on Dani's shoulder. "You can help with the overall surveillance and communication. If you see something odd with anything, you need to let us all know. I trust your instincts. You'll be the only one who will see everything from the thirty thousand foot perspective. Sometimes when you're in the weeds, it's hard to see the whole picture."

Char set down her spoon and kissed Toni on the cheek.

Toni blushed.

Sophie was pleased the group considered their scheme viable and everyone seemed to jump in and embrace their part of the plan.

"Char, unfortunately all of my disguises are back at our hub in DC. I have the perfect disguise for you, but someone will have to retrieve it. Since I appear to be the only one who has escaped their scrutiny, I think it would be best if I went," Kim offered.

"I don't think we should let you go without an escort. Maggie, can we send someone like Val to go with her?" Char asked.

"Of course. I'll call her right now and maybe she can get a few bites of her stash of ice cream." Maggie winked at Char.

"I know it's kind of late, but maybe I should go tonight and then Sophie can make the call tomorrow and we can place the ball in motion. That should make it even less risky because we'll have the veil of darkness as cover. I doubt they know the location of our hub." Kim stretched and touched Sophie on the cheek. "Don't worry. I'll be perfectly safe."

"Ronda is still out on the assignment I gave to her, but she is due back tomorrow afternoon. Toni, can you provide me with the biologic tracking device by then?" Maggie asked.

"I assume you have a fully functioning lab?"

"Yes, we do. Char can show you."

"Yeah, I think I can manage to create a card for Ted and something else for you to give Ronda." Toni scratched her head. "Any ideas on what we should use with Ronda. What could you give her that wouldn't seem odd?"

"She loves new gadgets. Could you do something with that? Or with a new weapon? She kinda likes her weapons," Dani offered.

"Perfect. Dani, whatever you have, I can make work. I'll need to get your DNA, Maggie, so that the tracking device transfers to Ronda and not you. You should come with us to the lab right now. I have several hours of work before tomorrow morning." Toni massaged the back of her neck.

"Why don't we all plan to meet back here at eight o'clock tomorrow morning and then we can make sure everything is set up. Maggie, have you assigned our quarters yet?" Sophie asked.

"Char and Toni can take the quarters where they liberated Val's stockpile of ice cream. Dani can take the adjoining rooms and I'll show you to your quarters. Toni, let me show Sophie to her quarters and then I'll come to the lab." Maggie turned to Sophie. "I assume you want Kim to join you when she returns."

Sophie nodded.

"Can I go with Char and Toni? I'd like to see her tracking prototype and maybe even learn a little more about biological technology." Dani looked hopeful.

"If Toni does not object, I don't see why not." Maggie smiled.

"That would actually be great. I could use Dani's help." Toni grabbed the chocolate chip cookie dough ice cream and headed to the control room exit.

Char grabbed her spoon and followed Toni.

Dani tossed the cherry Garcia in her lap, picked up her spoon and rolled along behind Char.

"Before I show you to your quarters, Sophie, let me call Val to escort Kim to your hub." Maggie pulled her cell phone out and quickly punched in a number. "Hello, Val, yes, a quick errand is necessary. I apologize for the late call, but it is important to accomplish the run this evening. Yes, please come back to the Virginia hub and fortunately for you, there is still some vanilla toffee bar crunch left. Yes, that would be Char. Okay see you in ten." Maggie touched Kim on the shoulder. "You might as well come with us and that way you will know which quarters you've been assigned to."

Maggie, Kim, and Sophie exited the control room and headed for the tunnel leading to the other part of the underground web.

Chapter Twenty-one

The false sunlight peeked through the fake window as Toni groaned and tossed her forearm across her eyes. "Shit, I just got to sleep." She glanced at the clock on the nightstand. "Two hours ago." She grunted and shut her eyes as she tried to go back to sleep.

The chirping of the birds caused her to pry one eye open and her lips curved up as she remembered she wasn't alone. She turned to a very naked Char and noticed the arm casually placed across her stomach. She thought how nice it was to wake up next to a beautiful woman. *I could get used to this.*

Toni watched the sleeping woman. God, she was so damn beautiful, she took her breath away. The depth of her feelings scared her. She couldn't remember ever feeling this way in the morning. Normally she couldn't wait to get away. Her hand traveled Char's body and she felt the first stirrings of life.

"Good morning." Char grinned at her. "Dani's little inventions can be a bit irritating sometimes, huh? Birds wake you up? I should have turned them off."

"It's okay. We need to get up pretty soon anyway. Although, I wouldn't mind a few more moments of cuddling." Toni groaned as she realized she just admitted to wanting to cuddle.

"Cuddling?" Char raised an eyebrow. "Didn't take you for the cuddling type."

"Can you just erase the last few moments from your brain? I haven't had my coffee yet."

"Oh no. I think what you said is sweet and I'd love to spend a few more moments tangled in your arms. Of course if it turns into something a bit more, shall we say, active, I wouldn't mind that either." Char stretched and placed a gentle kiss on Toni's nose.

Toni lamented the fact that they didn't really have time to make love again if either one wanted a shower. Of course, they could take a shower together and see where that led. She shook her head. Shit, not much time for that either.

"You're not in favor of something more active?" Char questioned.

"No, sorry. I was just thinking that we should shower together and maybe something will evolve and then I realized we have less than an hour to get ready and head to the control room."

"An hour is more than enough time for what I have in mind. I don't really have much to do to get ready, considering that Kim will need to prepare me for my errand today." Char groaned. "God, I hate that sticky mess of makeup combined with hot latex. I saw that gleam in her eye last night. I wonder what disguise she's chosen for me."

"Probably the old man—it's one of her favorites."

Char jumped out of bed and pulled the covers off Toni. "Come on, time's a wasting and I for one, would like to take advantage of the few extra minutes we have this morning."

†

From outside the shower Toni leered at the very delicious backside of her girlfriend. *Wait, did I just think of her as my girlfriend? Yeah, I guess I did and I like it.* She'd showered with other women before, but there was just something uniquely alluring about this woman. Char had a sexiness about her that was unparalleled. Toni's mouth literally watered at the prospect of running her soapy hands up and down Char's toned body. She planned to spend extra time on her breasts and coochie. Toni chuckled to herself as she remembered Sophie talking about how her grandmother always referred to someone's vagina as their coochie.

Toni was startled from her daydream as Char purred, "Hey, what are you waiting for? It's cold and lonely in here without you."

Toni obediently stepped into the steamy shower. She grabbed the bar of soap and rubbed it until generous heaps of lather filled her hands. With slow deliberate strokes, Toni ran her hands across Char's body, not missing an inch of skin. When the soap comingled with the shower water and the moisture of Char's arousal, Toni shuddered. The smell was a magical fusion of pure hedonistic essence of who Char was. *They should sell this stuff. God, what a turn-on.*

Char pressed both hands against the wall and pushed back against Toni. Her groan echoed against the four glass walls, amplifying the sound.

Toni's accompanying moan added to the symphony as their voices came together in perfect harmony.

"Oh, my God, Toni, that feels positively sinful." Char panted as her hips moved in rhythm with Toni's caresses.

Toni pressed hard against Char's ass and reached around to stroke her clit with the soapy mixture. "Do you like how that feels?"

Char moaned louder.

"I'll take that as a yes." Toni moved in the same rhythm with Char and felt her arousal climb. She rubbed against Char like a cat in heat.

"God, I need to have you inside of me now," Char managed to gasp out.

Toni expertly thrust two fingers inside Char and began slow, deliberate strokes.

Char moved with the rhythm of Toni's fingers, moaning trying to gain a deeper purchase of the fingers.

"You want more," Toni whispered the statement. She tongued Char's ear before caressing her neck.

"Yes," Char whimpered.

"Then you shall have more."

Toni slipped a third finger inside and increased the movement while holding their bodies together in her iron grip. She pumped vigorously, their bodies merging as they moved as one. Toni could feel the first tremors of Char's orgasm begin along with her own building arousal.

"Please, don't stop," Char begged.

"Not on your life."

Their bodies stiffened and they punctuated their mutual release by each calling out the other's name.

With water cascading over her body, Char sucked in a deep breath, turned in Toni's arms, and pulled her into a tight embrace. "I'm never taking another shower alone again. I don't think I do a good enough job getting clean."

"Always at your service, ma'am." Toni grinned and mimicked tipping an invisible hat. She leaned into Char and closed her eyes. "I wish we had more time."

Char's hand slid between their bodies and she slowly stroked Toni. "We have time," she cooed. Her long slender fingers entered Toni and they began again.

†

Ronda pinched the bridge of her nose. A headache was coming on. It had been a long and boring assignment and she was glad to be back at the Virginia home base. She wanted to sneak in a shower and a quick bite to eat before checking in with Maggie and the rest.

As she reached out to open the door to the control room, Maggie called out to her. "Ah good, you're back. Why don't you follow me to the lab? Dani has a new weapon for you to try out. She's quite pleased with herself. It looks like a pen, but discharges tiny darts with enough tranquilizer in them to disarm a three-hundred-pound man. The effects are nearly instantaneous and the propulsion can penetrate fabric as tough as leather. The best part is the range of this weapon can be as great as four hundred feet. Just point and click at any part of the body. It's no longer necessary to be up close and personal to disable a target—a viable alternative to termination."

"Nice, but you know I don't have a problem taking out these bastards. My personal value system differs a bit from yours. No offense, Maggie, but sometimes y'all are a bit too soft. However, this could come in handy when I need to take out several people in a matter of seconds without causing too much ruckus. So what's the downside to this miracle gadget?" Ronda asked.

"It can only hold up to three darts and there's not an easy way to reload. It's almost better to carry more than one, versus trying to reload," Maggie answered.

"So, can I have more than one?"

"Since this is a prototype to test, we only have one available. If it works well, we can develop more. We moved Sophie, Kim, and Toni to our safe house on Charles Avenue. We may have to keep them there until everything is resolved with Viktor."

"That sounds like a good idea. Do you need me to go there and provide protection detail?"

"No, Char and Val have volunteered. You can feel free to relax and enjoy the rest of your day. Go out and have some fun. Just check in sometime tomorrow and we can bring you up to speed if there are any more developments you need to know about."

✝

Char shuffled to her seat and watched the door, waiting for Ted's arrival.

The waitress, Candy, arrived at her table and lobbed a bright smile at her. "What can I get you, sir?"

Char noticed the bruise on Candy's cheek and frowned. "Did you hurt yourself?" She pointed to Candy's cheek.

Candy looked down. "Oh, I just ran into a wall going to the bathroom in the middle of the night. Clumsy me. Biscuits and gravy are on special today. Kind of heavy for me, but everyone seems to love it. We serve breakfast until one, but if you would prefer lunch, the grilled chicken is good and much lighter."

Char didn't like seeing the bruise and made a mental note to find out the real story.

The front door of the café opened and Ted walked in.

"Oh dear, I left my wallet in my car." Char patted her crumpled jacket. "Will you excuse me while I get it?"

Char shuffled to Ted and bumped into him as he looked around the café.

"Excuse me." Ted looked briefly at the old man.

Char placed the card in Ted's hand and shuffled out the door. After she left the café, she looked in the window, noticing Ted looking at the card in his hand before he turned it over.

Sophie had quickly scribbled Toni's address on the *special* card this morning and it looked as if Ted had taken the bait.

Char hurried to her car and got in. It wouldn't be long now if he was the one. With the car running, she peeled away from the curb, needing to get to the other safe house quickly in case Ronda was actually the mole.

†

It was a dreary day in DC as the rain misted the dingy streets. Ronda's mood was as foul as the weather. She hated when the weather wouldn't make its mind up. Either rain or clear up—the infuriating drizzle added to her irritation. What the hell, it wasn't as if they lived in Seattle.

She skulked around the corner, a block away from the café, where she watched Ted look around before entering. At least the drizzle encouraged people to move quickly through the streets and no one seemed to pay too much attention to her observant eyes as she loitered against a brick wall.

A few minutes later, she studied the shuffling old man. He was moving too quickly for a man of his advanced age. When he jumped into the expensive Tesla and drove off, Ronda hissed. "Char, what are you up to now?"

They were all playing a game of cat and mouse and Ronda was damned if she would be the mouse. It was time to make contact with Ted.

An evil snicker erupted from her lips.

✝

Char pressed the button on her hands-free console and made the call to Dani. "Everything went as planned. Can you confirm the tracking device absorbed into his skin?... What?... Well, that's very interesting... Yeah, I'll be careful... Does Maggie know this?... Okay, better keep me informed on both their locations. I think you'd better update Toni and the rest of them with this new development.... The day should prove very enlightening, indeed... Let's not jump to conclusions just yet—we need to see how this all plays out... Yeah, I'm glad we thought of the tracking devices too... Okay, talk to you later."

Char touched the screen and ended the call. The makeup started to itch so she pressed harder on the gas pedal. She was anxious to get to the Charles Avenue safe house. She didn't want to think about how this day would end. Someone was going to get hurt and she wanted to make damn sure it wasn't Toni. She'd just found her and she wasn't about to let her go.

Toni had assured her that the panic room at her place was impenetrable—no one could breach the fortress. She had to trust Sophie's martial arts skills and although she was impressive, it had not been enough to save Natalie. That thought gnawed at her sense of reasoning. She would be glad when all this was finished and they could focus on the next stage of their plan to decimate the Russian slave trade business.

Char was distracted and almost missed the turnoff as she slowed the car but took the corner a little too fast. The tires screeched as she regained control. *Damn, I need to pay attention and keep my head in the game.*

There was a lot at stake and people she cared a great deal for were making themselves the bait. If there was a better way, she would have proposed it, but the plan was as solid as they could hope for.

She'd made good time, she realized, as she hopped out of her car and entered the safe house. Maybe Val and the rest of the agents were already set up. She knew they would see any threat a mile away. Stopping inside the door, Char finally had time to look at the tracking app and creased her brow as she confirmed what Dani already told her. Shit, that didn't look good. *Ronda, what are you involved in?*

Char blew out a big breath. At least the dots were not heading in her direction.

☦

Viktor was lounging in his bedroom watching an American football game. It was one of his guilty pleasures.

His new cell phone buzzed on the nightstand and he eagerly picked it up.

"Hello... Finally... I will have four of my best men meet you there... Yes, you need to go because we need you to get Sophie to open the door... No, you imbecile, I don't want to attract unwanted attention... Just get your ass over there now before they move to a new location... I don't care—dead or alive—it makes no difference to me."

Viktor ended the call and smiled. He could almost taste the resolution to his problem. It would be worth the three million dollars he would pay to the informant. This time those *sookas* would not wriggle free.

Viktor turned his attention back to the game. Everything was going as planned. He could relax and enjoy his football game in peace. Perhaps he would celebrate and take a stroll in the city and visit his favorite restaurant tonight. He would call Byron later to tell him the good news and then Byron would owe him a great favor—one he intended to collect on.

The year had been a total cluster fuck and he intended to make up for lost time, lost revenue, and lost merchandise.

Chapter Twenty-two

The hum of the equipment and corresponding heat that permeated throughout the compact space almost encouraged the complacency that Toni felt. Toni felt her eyes begin to close as she relaxed in the room. That was the last thing she needed—a nap at this time was definitely ill advised.

Sophie looked around the spacious room and whistled. "Damn, Toni, you've added quite a few new toys since the last time I was here. I see you've fully stocked the bar, pantry, and refrigerator. I don't suppose you have a stash of weapons I might want to use?"

Toni shook her head. "No, sorry, but I did manage to snatch Dani's latest invention." Toni pulled out a gold-plated pen from her back pocket. "This little baby shoots poison darts—well, actually they're darts filled with heavy-duty tranquilizers. They can stop a professional wrestler in a matter of seconds."

"Impressive. I'm kinda glad they don't have poison in them. You and I are definitely not wired to do permanent damage to anyone."

Kim looked around the room. "God, I've never seen so many monitors. You have practically every possible angle covered with your surveillance," she remarked.

Toni brushed her fingers against her chest. "Yep, no one steps one hundred feet within the perimeter without me seeing or hearing them," Toni bragged.

Sophie pulled her Glock from her holster and set it on one of the tables. "Just in case. I don't want to shoot anyone but I will if I have to. Sorry, Kim, I know violence is not in your DNA, but I will use whatever force is necessary to protect you."

Toni wanted to change the subject and not focus on the possible danger or violence they might face. "So, shall I break out the junk food while we wait?" Toni asked.

Kim turned her wrist upright and glanced at her watch. "Hey, can we just take a quick look at the tracking apps? I think Char and Maggie should have planted both seeds by now."

Toni's stomach growled. "Sorry, I guess I'll just have to tell Sally to wait a few minutes longer while I pull out my cell phone."

"Sally?" Kim quirked her eyebrow.

"Yeah, I name my body parts. Sally's my stomach, Tonya's my tits and Virginia's my—"

"You are positively infantile," Sophie growled.

"I am going to ignore that jab because I know you're just a little stressed right now." Toni pulled her cell phone from her back pocket and pressed the button with fingerprint access. After she swiped the cover and selected the app she exclaimed excitedly. "Bingo. Hmm, now that's fascinating."

Sophie leaned to look at the phone. "Is that what I think it is?"

"What? What are you guys talking about? Clue me in please." Kim approached and peered over Toni's other shoulder.

Toni pointed to the screen. "See those two dots. Both of them are on the same trajectory. They're damn near on top of one another and the dots seem to be heading our way."

"Does that mean that both Ted and Ronda are the moles? Do you think they're working together?" Kim asked.

"I don't really like to jump to conclusions. At this point, all we know is the dots are heading this way. If Viktor's goons show up—that's another piece of information that would be hard to ignore. Toni, can you make sure the audio is sensitive enough to pick up everything." Sophie glanced at the monitors.

Toni followed Sophie's gaze. "Um, I think we have company. Those four guys approaching the building don't really look much like Jehovah's Witnesses. I'm not sure I'm all that interested in buying what they might be selling."

Sophie frowned. "How far away are the dots?"

"Oh, I would estimate we will have contact in less than five."

"Sophie, you're not going to answer the door are you. I know you want to catch Ted red-handed, but isn't it enough that we see him with those goons?" Kim's voice wavered as she asked the question.

"Toni, can you tape any conversation that occurs on the perimeter?" Sophie asked.

"Yeah, I can do that. I'll start both the audio and video feed."

"Good. Then let's hope he says something incriminating so I can use that as evidence of his betrayal," Sophie responded.

Toni switched on the audio and video feed and pressed the record button.

She watched as one of the men approaching the building held up his hand. "Viktor told us to wait for the pencil neck. He'll get us inside and then we can take care of those *sookas*."

"Maybe we can have some fun with them before delivering them to Viktor." Another male voice filled the compact space pinging off the walls as the audio feed produced a crystal clear sound in the panic room.

"Bastards," Sophie hissed.

The third man looked over his shoulder and the approaching vehicle loomed large in the last monitor to the right of where Toni was sitting.

Ted climbed out of his car and looked right then left before he approached the building. His eyes traveled to the four men hovering around the door. "Get the fuck back while I knock on the door. I don't want any one of you in the remote vicinity of the peephole. God, why are the big ones always so stupid," Ted spit out.

Ted knocked loudly on the door. "Soph, it's me, Ted."

Kim turned to Sophie. "Do you think that will be enough?"

"Maybe," Sophie responded.

"Come on, Sophie. It's safe. Open up the door and let me help you. I don't know what kind of trouble you've gotten yourself involved in, but I promise I'll do whatever I can to assist you." Ted's voice filtered into the room.

Toni caught movement on one of the monitors and gasped as she saw one of the men topple like a wilting flower. Ronda's body looked large as Toni noticed one of Dani's tranquilizer pens in her hand and another goon fell to the ground.

Thunk Clink

Ted swirled around just in time to see a third man crumple and hit the pavement. In one fluid motion, he pulled out his gun and shot at Ronda. The pen dropped to the concrete as Ted hit his target.

"Fuck, she set me up. I should have known Sophie would put the pieces together." Ted waved at the fourth man. "What the fuck are you waiting for, go after her. I am working with a bunch of morons," he growled.

Toni's senses went on high alert as once again she witnessed everything unfold in a matter of minutes. It was déjà vu.

Ronda rolled, took cover, and used her uninjured hand to retrieve her gun. She crawled around the corner in an attempt to avoid the fourth man who was now shooting at her. She fired back and managed to clip him in his knee.

He screamed in pain.

"Sophie, you have to help her. If Ted joins the firefight, she's a sitting duck out there," Toni screamed.

"No, Sophie, he's got a gun. Please don't get yourself killed," Kim pleaded.

Sophie grinned at Kim, "Yeah, but my gun's bigger and I'm a much better shot."

Ted shot at the lock on the door and began kicking it in.

Sophie barreled out of the panic room and leveled her gun on Ted as he busted through the door. "Game over, Ted."

Wild-eyed, Ted raised his gun and pulled the trigger.

Bullets danced in the air as they simultaneously left their point of origin. Each bullet met its intended target.

Sophie's bullet landed between Ted's eyes.

Toni watched in horror as blood oozed from Sophie's shoulder. Out of the corner of her eye, she saw movement on one of the monitors. Shit. Char. What the hell was she doing here?

Char bolted into the middle of the firefight between the remaining mobster and Ronda.

Kim rushed out of the confined space and cried out when Sophie stumbled and collapsed onto the floor.

Toni couldn't seem to get her body to move. She froze—living out the nightmare in panic mode—she observed everything unfold in brilliant Technicolor. Finally, she witnessed the fourth man go down and breathed a sigh of relief.

Char burst into Toni's living room with her gun sweeping right and left.

"Sophie's been shot and I think Ronda has too. Kim and I are fine. I'm pretty sure the threat is neutralized." Toni cautiously approached Char.

Char pulled Toni into a fierce embrace and that's when Toni felt the sticky wet substance against her shirt.

Toni pulled back and looked down at Char's abdomen. "Char, you've been shot too. We need to call 911."

"No. Val's on her way. She's the sweeper today. She'll take care of all of this and I'll get Maggie to send the medical unit right away. Don't worry, it's just a scratch. I've had worse." Char turned her head toward Kim. "Kim, how's Sophie?"

"I…I…don't know," Kim stuttered as tears ran down her cheeks.

"Sophie's just fine. You worry about that hole in your stomach. It's just a shoulder wound. I've had worse too," Sophie grunted.

Ronda limped into the room. "Now, that was fun. Val on her way?" she asked.

"Yep, and because I saw your dot moving along with Ted's I figured I better have medical follow our sweeper. Trouble always seems to follow you, Ronda." Char chuckled then placed on hand on her wound. "Damn, that hurts."

"You put a tracking device on me? God, Char, that hurts worse than this tiny little bullet. How could you possibly think I would betray you or the agency?" Ronda sounded indignant.

"You people are crazy," Toni remarked.

"You put a tracking device on Ted, didn't you? Then your crazy ass followed him. Right?" Char asked.

Ronda grinned. "I sure did. I knew that motherfucker was the mole and I was gonna catch the bastard red-handed. When I got here, I figured the three musketeers were in danger so I used Dani's new weapon to take out the first three, I didn't figure Ted would be as good as he was and then the last guy started shooting. Nice timing, Char. I owe you."

"Nah, you've done the same for me a million times."

Toni looked from Ronda to Char and shook her head. The sound of clattering metal garnered her attention as she witnessed several strange women spill into the room carrying medical bags and rolling in stretchers.

A tall commanding brunette tossed out an order. "Char, Ronda, get your butts on those stretchers while they start the IVs." She tossed her head in the direction of Sophie. "I presume that one there is Sophie. Bunch of idiot cowboys," she muttered.

"We love you too, Cindy." Ronda grinned.

"Can I please ride with Char?" Toni asked.

"I want to go with Sophie," Kim chimed in.

"Sure, why not. How about you, Ronda? Don't you have someone just dying to accompany you to the medical hub?"

"Yeah, you, Cindy. 'Cause I know you love me, right?" Ronda batted her lashes at Cindy.

Cindy laughed. "Come on, stud, time for me to start an IV and give you some even better drugs than whatever you took earlier this evening to be so misinformed."

Ronda placed her good hand over her heart. "Oh that hurt, that really hurt."

Cindy kissed Ronda's cheek and gently led her to the gurney.

Chapter Twenty-three

Char opened one eye, then the other and slowly became aware of her surroundings. Infirmary. Oh yeah, she remembered. She was shot last night. She attempted to shake the cobwebs from her head.

Someone stirred next to her. She smiled when she noticed Toni's dark hair splayed across the bed sheets covering her legs. She felt her hand entwined with Toni's and noticed how Toni was bent over, sitting in a chair beside the bed, her head twisted in an awkward angle as she lightly snored. She had to be uncomfortable in that position.

Char brushed her fingers against Toni's forehead and the black head popped up.

"How are you feeling?" Toni asked.

"Like I've been shot," Char responded glibly.

Toni frowned. "Are you in any pain?"

"No, I'm sure they broke out the good drugs. How are Sophie and Ronda?"

"Sophie kept bitching the whole way—insisting she just needed a few stitches and she was good to go. Ronda kept flirting with Cindy and seemed to be in good spirits. In fact, I think she was in her element last night. The surgeon, on the other hand—I can't remember her name—was grumbling about how you damn macho agents ought to give them forewarning when you're going to get more than one of you shot up. She had to triage the three of you. Yours was by far the worst injury—so you win. The other two got pawned off to someone I assume has less experience," Toni explained.

Char turned her head and noted the occupants in the two beds next to hers. Sophie seemed to have an appendage attached to her bed in the form of Kim, and Cindy was gently brushing the hair from Ronda's face. "I see that we all have a fan base."

"Oh, yeah, but you really scored because, up until a few minutes ago, when Dani was called away, your fan base totaled two." Toni chuckled. "Ronda winked at me a few minutes ago. So she's awake, but pretending to be asleep—probably enjoying the tender loving care of Cindy."

Char started to laugh then coughed. "Damn, that hurts. If I know Cindy, she's pretending not to notice that Ronda is awake."

"Ooh, I'll have to remember that trick."

"Shit, what time is it?"

"Eight thirty."

"I assume that's eight thirty in the morning. Damn, I need to call the office. My cover is probably compromised, but just in case, we need to come up with something plausible to tell my assistant, Sandy, why I won't be in for several weeks." Char raised herself up from her current position.

Toni gently pushed Char back down. "Whoa, lay your ass back down. Dani told me she planned to take care of that first thing this morning. She probably already called Sandy and told her about your burst appendix."

"Nice. Good cover story. Was that her idea or yours?" Char asked.

"Hers. Your little sister is very clever."

"She is, but she's so innocent sometimes that I worry about her. She's more fragile than she lets on. So, am I minus any particular internal organ?" Char flinched when she touched her side.

"No, all organs intact. She did have to remove a portion of one of your intestines. The surgery took four hours. I was getting worried. I've gotten accustomed to hanging out with you."

Char squeezed Toni's hand. "Ditto."

Char wasn't ready to admit it yet, but what Maggie had warned her about was happening to her—whether she liked it or not. She was falling in love with Toni.

"Dani and Maggie are off somewhere, plotting and planning. When all of you are fully recovered, we can talk about phase two. Ted is dead, but we let three of Viktor's men live. I'm thinking he isn't going to be too happy with us when they return and let him know the results of their little assault."

"I'm surprised Ronda let any of them live. She must be getting soft in her old age." Char shifted in the bed and then winced.

"Oh, I don't think Ronda is getting soft. Cindy wouldn't let her off the gurney. If it was anyone else besides Cindy, I think she would have eliminated them." Toni shuddered.

"You really are a gentle soul, huh? Does it bother you that I've been forced to make the choice to kill an enemy?" Char held her breath, afraid of Toni's response.

"No. I don't think I could do it myself, but I understand. I don't think any less of you. Besides, it would be hard to judge the woman I seem to be falling in love with," Toni responded.

"You...you...love me?" Char sputtered.

"It's okay. You don't have to feel the same way. I just wanted to be totally honest with you and put that out there on the off chance we have any kind of future together."

A single tear rolled down Char's face. "I do feel the same way. It's just that my life is here with the agency and Dani, and well—you have options. I don't want to presume that after all this is through, you'd want to join us. Two months ago, I might have tried to use every trick in the book including professing my love to you, just to get you to join. I swear on the life of my sister, I'm not feeding you a line."

"I believe you." Toni leaned down and brushed her lips on Char's. "I've been having a lot of fun collaborating with Dani on new inventions. Maybe the agency is my destiny."

"Cindy, you better get me some more anti-nausea medicine. The sweetness of those two is making me sick," Ronda called out.

"I knew you were awake, you little faker." Cindy smacked Ronda's arm.

"Ow. What was that for? Injured warrior here." Ronda winked.

"Just like a regular hospital—you can't get any rest. Would you all shut the hell up? I'm trying to nap here," Sophie complained.

†

Viktor was pacing in his parlor. He was furious. He couldn't ever remember being this angry. He was tempted to kill all three of them for their incompetence, but at this rate, he couldn't afford to lose any more valuable employees. Something didn't feel right about any of this. There was no way possible for three women to evade him like this—they had to have the support of a much bigger network. Viktor stroked his chin with his enormous hand. Perhaps the rumor of a secret agency was true. Well, they were fucking with the wrong person.

I will personally make sure each and every one of them are sent to a permanent resting place, he vowed mentally.

"Where is that imbecile, Ted?" Viktor asked.

A large man with a buzz cut looked at the ground. "I don't know. We woke up outside of the residence just as the place exploded. I suspect someone is an explosives expert because there was nothing left to figure out what happened. Ted was at the door and screamed at us to back away while he made contact. That's the last thing I remember." The man pulled a small dart from his jacket. "I found this in my shoulder. I don't know what happened to Boris, but the others found the same thing."

Viktor grabbed the dart from his hand and stomped on it. "Fucking *sookas*."

The man whispered, "I thought you might want to have them analyzed. Shall I retrieve the other two darts for you?"

Viktor nodded. "Send out word that the bounty has doubled. If something happened to Ted, we've lost our inside advantage. I want every single man scouring the city for those women."

"Done. Is there anything you'd like me to do?"

"*Da.* I need every scrap of information you can obtain about one of my attorneys, Heather Stiles. I had an appointment with her several weeks ago. I don't believe it's a coincidence that not only was she sitting at the same table with that blonde at the Republican fund-raiser, but she also had dinner with that other *sooka* the night of her disappearance. I want to know every last detail, including the brand of toilet paper she uses. Understand?"

"Yes, sir."

✝

Dani was nervous as she and Maggie hovered around one of the monitors in the control room. She was glad that Sophie, Kim, and Toni agreed to work with them to take Viktor down. She pointed at the screen. "Do you see this?"

"Yes," Maggie responded.

"I think that may be our opening. All his meetings with these particular attorneys are at their offices. I think he chooses them for his more reputable business lines. He had a meeting scheduled with Char, but then canceled the second meeting the day she brought Toni to the compound. Unfortunately, his meetings are not very predictable. It's not ideal, but if I can improve on the range of the darts, I think we have a good chance. He usually has three guards with him, but I think I can get four darts into the pen. We still need a second person to disable anyone else in the office. It will be hard to determine how many darts we'll need. Too bad Char's cover is probably blown. That would be perfect because we could control everything."

"We need to wait until Ronda recovers. She seems to be quite proficient with this new weapon. We can't afford to waste any of the darts. By the way, is there any chance he will be able to produce the same results with the darts we left behind. I failed to mention that to Val so her team didn't know to recover them in the sweep." Maggie knitted her brows.

"No, I don't think so. They are scheduled to disintegrate in forty-eight hours. They would need to get

209

them to a lab and perform all kinds of tests before they discovered anything noteworthy. Frankly, I don't even think forty-eight hours would be enough time to figure out anything significant about them."

"Dani, you are every bit as brilliant as Toni. You two will make a remarkable team."

Dani blushed. "I'm learning a lot from her, but the best thing is that I think Char's in love with her."

Maggie raised her eyebrows toward the ceiling. "I did tell Char—never say never and that not all love is destructive. I believe they will be good for one another. I do hope Toni chooses to remain with our agency after we are through with this nasty business."

Dani turned her attention to the clanking at the control room door.

Ronda struggled inside hobbling in with forearm crutches. "God, Dani, how do you maneuver so well with these damn things? Of course it doesn't help when you've also got an injured hand."

"I don't, which is why I'm in my wheelchair way too much to build my endurance. I need to get back on my regimen after this whole mess is resolved. Why aren't you still in the infirmary? I can't imagine Cindy just let you leave." Dani smirked.

"Cindy is not the boss of me."

The control room door burst open and Cindy glared at Ronda. "Yes, I most certainly am the boss of you—you ungrateful little shit. Get your ass back to the infirmary."

Ronda touched her middle and index fingers to her head and saluted Cindy. "Yes, ma'am. Do I get a treat if I comply without complaint?"

The corners of Cindy's mouth turned up. "Maybe."

Ronda walked toward Cindy as she turned her head and tossed out a parting comment, "I'd like to be involved in phase two and, if you don't mind, I'd like to be privy to all the important facts."

Dani grinned. "You'll be our star agent, I promise. You'll have top clearance for every piece of information you need to be successful. We'll wait until next week to set up a strategy session so, in the meantime, if I were you, I would take whatever Cindy is offering. Cindy gives the best leg massages."

Ronda leered at Cindy. "Can I have a massage, please? Pretty please, with sugar on top. I promise to be good. And you even have my permission to massage more than my legs."

Cindy glared at Ronda, but Dani saw one corner of her lips lift up.

†

Char sighed. She was tired of the same argument. There was no way she was going to let Ronda do this without backup. This was important to her. It was personal and Toni knew that. "Why are you being so stubborn? Val is good, but I'm better."

"You just had major surgery two weeks ago. Why can't you let Ronda and Val handle this?" Toni pleaded.

"You know why, so I don't want to fight about this. I am perfectly capable of handling myself."

"The surgeon told you not to do anything strenuous for at least another month. You were shot in the stomach for fuck's sake. You could have died so I have to ask, do you have some kind of death wish?" Toni huffed.

A clatter at the door distracted Char from the argument.

Dani lurched forward, awkwardly navigating the entryway with her forearm crutches.

"Don't you ever knock?" Char griped.

Dani's reaction was immediate and she blanched.

Toni glared at Char and rushed to the door to hold it open while Dani entered. "She doesn't mean it. She's just pissed at me and unfortunately you caught the brunt of her anger," Toni whispered.

"I'm sorry, Dani. Toni's right. I'm just angry that she's fighting me on something so important to me. You know how I feel about the slave trade. I want to be the one to shut that bastard down—or at least play a key role."

"You've already played a key role and your reward was a slug in your gut. How much more do they expect you to sacrifice? No, I won't allow it," Toni asserted.

Char didn't want to make the situation worse. She loved Toni, but she had to establish her independence. No matter what, no one had the right to control her. "You don't get a vote in this. My life, my body, my choice. Please, don't ever forget that."

Toni slumped into a chair and began crying. "I'm sorry, I'm just really scared of losing you. I love you and I just found you so please don't do anything to jeopardize that."

Char sat down next to Toni and pulled her into her arms. "Shh, I'm not going anywhere. Please trust me. Besides Ronda, I'm the best choice."

"I know. I'd suggest Sophie, but with her shoulder still healing I know that's just selfish of me to even think of that alternative."

Dani cleared her throat. "I actually came in here for a reason. I'm sorry I didn't knock, but there have been some recent developments that might actually shed a new light on our plans."

"No. I really am sorry, little sis, you don't ever need to knock." Char laughed. "Wait, let me rephrase that. You do need to knock on our bedroom door, but I think you already know that. So what's the new scoop?"

"It seems Viktor is insisting on having a meeting with you and you alone. He called Sandy to set up an appointment. Just in case, we bugged the office phones. It was a long shot because I thought for sure your cover was blown. We have evidence that Gregor transmitted a picture of you when you were having dinner together. It's definitely a trap, but I still think we'll have the upper hand since the meeting will take place in our territory versus his," Dani revealed.

"Hmm, I like it. Our odds are getting better by the minute. So what did Sandy say?" Char asked.

"Well, that's where it gets a little complicated. She told Viktor that you were recovering from surgery and were not expected back for at least a month. She offered to set him up with one of the other attorneys. He refused to see anyone else. He insisted that an appointment be scheduled the minute you return. Maggie thinks you should call Sandy and tell her you're coming back a little earlier than anticipated." Dani shifted in her crutches. "Sorry, Toni, but I agree. I think we've got Viktor running scared. When someone's angry and off kilter, they make grave errors in judgment. The sooner you return and schedule this meeting, the better." Dani's brow furrowed.

"It's okay. I understand. May I at least be at central control? I want to see everything that's happening real time—otherwise I'll start chomping on my toenails because my fingernails are already down to the nub. Although…it has been rather convenient in other ways." Toni raised her eyebrows up and down in a Groucho Marx expression.

Char blushed.

Dani bumped her fist with Toni's.

Char was relieved that Toni could so easily add levity to the situation despite her concern. It was one of the things she loved most about Toni.

†

Viktor was eating dinner when his private security guard handed him the phone.

"It's that assistant of Stiles on the phone for you. I believe you have been waiting for this call," the guard said.

Viktor smiled and patted his napkin to his mouth. "*Da*, yes, you can go now."

"Hello. Yes, that would work with my schedule. Thank you, I appreciate you arranging for an earlier appointment. I do hope Ms. Stiles has recovered fully from her surgery."

Viktor ended the call and leaned back in his chair.

I will find out what I want to know and you will pray for a quick death before I am done with you, Ms. Stiles.

"Ivan, get back in here," Viktor hollered. "I need you to prepare our vests. We will not go unprepared. I smell a trap, but this time I will be the cat and they will be the mice."

"Yes, sir. The lightweight Kevlar should go undetected."

"Pity. Such a beautiful woman. I have clients who might pay well for her, but I don't think they will want her after I am through with her."

"Who would you like to accompany you to the meeting?" the guard asked.

"I will give the three who disappointed me earlier one more chance. You can summon them and I believe you should also accompany us."

214

"Thank you, sir. I am honored to be chosen."

Chapter Twenty-four

The quiet knock on the door woke Sophie from a particularly nice dream of enjoying a picnic lunch with Kim in a field of daises. A peaceful feeling always engulfed her when she thought of Kim.

Kim stirred, but thankfully did not wake up.

Sophie carefully disengaged herself from Kim as she slipped out of the bed to answer the door.

Dani stood on the other side leaning heavily on her forearm crutches.

"Hi, Dani. What can I do for you? It's kinda late and Kim's asleep."

"Can I just talk to you for a few minutes?" Dani asked.

Sophie liked the kid and she looked so forlorn, she didn't have the heart to turn her away. "Sure. Come on in."

Dani tried to navigate the room carefully, but one of her crutches banged against the table.

Sophie cringed when she heard the noise and looked back over her shoulder. She groaned when she saw Kim yawning as she came out of the bedroom.

"Hey, Dani."

"I'm sorry. I didn't mean to wake you up too." Dani looked down.

"Don't worry about it. It must be important for you to come see us so late." Kim gestured to the couch.

Dani sat down.

"Coffee?" Kim asked.

Dani shook her head.

Sophie sat across from Dani. "Go ahead, spit it out, Dani. You obviously came here to ask me something. What is it?" Sophie asked.

Kim sat next to Dani and patted her hand. "It's okay. I'm sure whatever it is, it's not the end of the world."

"I want Sophie to be at the meeting tomorrow," Dani blurted out. "Well, not exactly at the meeting, but in Char's secret room next to her office."

Kim frowned. "I thought it was decided that because of Sophie's shoulder, she wouldn't be the best choice as backup."

"Char's all I have left. I saw you in action the night of Nat's death..." Dani swiped at her tears. "I...I...can't lose her. I'm worried and I want a contingency in case something goes wrong. Nobody even needs to know you're there. You can monitor things from the room because she has security cameras and audio already set up. You only have to act if you see something go wrong. Will you do it?" Dani looked up—her eyes wet with unshed tears.

Sophie didn't want to refuse this young woman and honestly, she wanted to be a part of the action. Dani had just given her the perfect opening. "I may not be able to use a gun just yet, but I've gotten pretty good with your little pen darts. If you make sure I'm equipped with one of those you got yourself a deal." Sophie glanced at a scowling Kim.

Dani struggled to her feet without her crutches and awkwardly hugged Sophie. "Thanks, Sophie. You have no idea how much your help means to me."

Dani picked up her crutches and hobbled out the door, smiling as she nodded goodbye.

Kim sighed. "I don't suppose I can say anything to keep you from being the backup."

Sophie caressed Kim's cheek and brushed her lips. "Nope. Come on, let's go back to bed. It sounds like it's going to be a long boring day for me. I'm sure I'll have to get there at o'dark hundred to slip inside the room unnoticed. I better take one of your romance novels with me to pass the time until the meeting at five thirty."

Before they reached the bedroom door Sophie heard a more insistent knock on the door. "Oh, for Christ's sake— what is this grand central fucking station?" Sophie grumbled.

Sophie opened the door to a serious-looking Ronda.

"May I come in?"

"Why the hell not?" Sophie opened the door wider and gestured for Ronda to enter.

"No offense, but do you think I could talk to you alone?" Ronda asked.

Kim looked perplexed, but offered, "I'll just head off to bed."

Sophie pointed at the couch and Ronda sat down.

"Look, I don't often say this and if you ever tell anyone else about our talk tonight I'm gonna have to hurt you."

Sophie glared at Ronda. "Just spit it out, Ronda. I'm tired and I'd like to get *some* sleep tonight."

"I wanted to say I'm sorry. I misjudged you but I have my reasons for hating government employees." Ronda held up her hand. "I know you're not a feebie anymore. I...uh...I...wanted to thank you for saving my ass. You didn't have to do that, especially since you thought I was the mole and all. I owe you."

Sophie shrugged. "Well, you didn't have to risk your life either. You weren't exactly sitting on your ass watching us get attacked. I appreciate you following Ted and providing back-up."

"Yeah, well, I hate fucking traitors."

"Former CIA?"

Ronda looked surprised. "Yeah. How did you know?"

"Oh, I've been around enough spooks to know the telltale signs. So, why did you get out?" Sophie asked.

"It got to a point where I thought I might be selling my soul to the devil. I wasn't sure I could tell anymore whether I was still working for the good guys. I was part of a special team. Our job was to eliminate risk permanently. I got too good at it and it started eating on my conscious."

Sophie raised an eyebrow in surprise. "Wow. I didn't ever peg you for someone with a conscious. You're good though and not just at assassinations. I'm just glad you're part of our team."

"Thanks. So, we're good?"

Sophie stuck out her hand. "Yeah, we're good. For the record—we're even—you don't owe me anything."

"Hey, Sophie."

"Yeah?"

Ronda looked at the ground. "Um, do you think Toni is in love with Char?"

"Yes, I'm pretty sure she is," Sophie responded.

"And do you think Char loves her back?"

Sophie looked at Ronda and she thought she recognized the same kind of feelings she once had for Natalie. She felt sorry for Ronda and surmised there was a lot more to her than she allowed others to see. Beneath that tough exterior was just another human being looking for connection. She hoped that maybe Ronda would look for that with someone else.

"Yeah, Ronda, I think she does."

"Good, Char deserves to have someone love her," Ronda whispered.

†

"Sit still. I have to make sure the seams on this mask are hidden," Kim scolded.

"But it's itchy. I've never had to wear a disguise before. How the hell do you people do this?" Ronda squirmed in her chair.

"We only have a few more minutes to get you ready." Kim chuckled. "I can't wait to hear all about your day as Char's assistant. Remember, you have to *politely* answer the phone. You can't be your normal charming self."

"Hardy, har, har. I can playact just as good as the rest of you. Just because I excel at guns and explosives, doesn't mean I don't possess other skills." Ronda folded her arms across her chest.

"By the way, what did you guys do to ensure Sandy won't be showing up for work today?"

"Such a shitty business we're in." Ronda laughed. "Val went this morning and poor Sandy is going to have a mess on her hands with a broken sewage line. Literally, shit all over the place."

Kim crinkled up her nose. "Ew. Couldn't you think of something less disgusting?"

"Anything less revolting and she might choose to just call the repairman and come into work. No, this guarantees that she'll stay home to make sure it's taken care of."

"We are going to use the foundation dollars to make up for any loss, aren't we?" Kim asked.

Ronda nodded.

"I think we should give Sandy a hefty bonus for any pain and suffering."

"Oh, we will. Once we liberate Viktor's millions, we should have plenty of money to rebuild the Maryland hub and take care of Sandy and numerous others more deserving of his wealth."

Kim smoothed out the last part of the mask and patted Ronda's shoulder. "Okay, you're all set. Off you go, *Sandy*. Have a nice day." Kim laughed.

✝

Toni placed her hand on Kim's shoulder as she noticed her eyes glued to the monitor. The gesture was an attempt to reassure her. "Kim, honey, I don't think anything important is going to happen for at least another hour. It's only four o'clock," she said softly.

Kim blew out a breath. "I know. I'm just worried about them. Aren't you the least bit concerned?"

"Of course I am, but they're all competent women who are capable of handling themselves."

"We all know Viktor is leading them into a trap. I just haven't quite figured out what he has up his sleeve. He has to know Char is dangerous. I mean, my God, how many men has he already lost."

"That's why we have to be the eyes and ears from afar. If we notice anything out of place, we can warn them. The three of them are the best there are for this sort of thing. We have our talents—but let's face it, in a crisis like this we suck."

Toni moved away from the monitors and sent up a silent prayer. She didn't really believe in God *per se*—but a prayer to the universe couldn't hurt.

Dani rolled into the control room with two pints of Ben and Jerry's ice cream and four spoons on her lap. "I've got comfort food."

"How come you have four spoons?" Kim asked.

"I met Maggie in the tunnel and she mentioned she would be joining us in a few minutes. She had something she wanted to take care of first," Dani explained.

"Hmm, I wonder what that sly fox is up to now," Toni said.

Dani placed the containers of ice cream on the table and handed out the spoons.

Kim pulled open the container of chocolate chip cookie dough and dug in.

"Dani, do you think the disguise we created for Ronda was good enough?" she asked around a mouthful of ice cream. "You know what Sandy looks like in person but I only had a picture to work with."

Toni noted the look of insecurity on Kim's face.

"Aw, Kim, it was perfect. I know Sandy and I couldn't tell the difference. You did good," Dani assured.

"So now we wait." Toni dug into the container of cherry Garcia. "And eat ice cream."

"Yes, ice cream is always good for the soul. You did get me a spoon, Dani?" Maggie entered the control room and smiled.

"Of course," Dani replied.

†

"Contact in less than a minute." Char heard in her comm link. She assumed Ronda heard the communication as well. She hoped that Ronda would also turn on her link when

Viktor entered the office so she could hear the conversation just outside her office and know what to expect.

"Good evening. Sandy, is it?"

"Yes, Mr. Borsky. Heather is expecting you. Can I get anything for you or your associates? Coffee or tea perhaps?" Ronda's voice rang clear in Char's ear.

"No, but perhaps you can find places for two of my men to wait, while Ivan, Andrei, and I conduct our business with Ms. Stiles."

"Of course, come with me, gentlemen. The rest of you can go right in."

Char heard rustling as Viktor and his two men entered her office.

"Shit, Kevlar," Ronda hissed into the comm link.

Thunk

"Aim for the neck…" Char heard this last piece of advice from Ronda.

Ronda's comm link went silent.

"Char, they're wearing Kevlar vests and pants. Ronda's down. They used one of the darts that bounced off his vest," the voice screamed in the comm link.

Char looked up into the barrel of Viktor's gun.

"Hello, Ms. Stiles. Or, shall I call you something else? If you do not wish for an unfortunate accident to happen to your colleague, Sandy, you will come peacefully with me and we can discuss business at my home. I am particularly intrigued by a few things and need your clarification."

Char narrowed her gaze at Viktor and slowly rose. She picked up the gold pen and placed it in her jacket pocket. She was confident they were monitoring her and the cavalry would be on the way soon enough. "No need for the weapon in my face. I'm unarmed. I'll come with you." Char lifted her arms in a gesture of surrender.

As Char exited her office, she noticed Ronda slumped on the desk and one of Viktor's men crumpled on the floor in a heap. *Good girl, Ronda, one less man for me to take care of.*

"Come. We will retrieve him later," Viktor ordered.

"What do we do with the receptionist?" Ivan asked.

"Leave her. After all, I promised Ms. Stiles here that she would come to no harm if she submitted peacefully. I think a principled man should honor his promise." Viktor laughed.

Your days are numbered, you bastard.

†

Sophie calmly watched the events unfold. Nice move with the pen, Char. She carefully calculated her next move. It would be important to follow quickly and act. She hoped the surprise would be an asset for Char and she would be able to take out at least two of the men before Viktor registered what was happening.

Sophie slipped off her shoes and quietly exited the room. The group was just now leaving the office and Sophie thought she saw a glint off the rooftop as the late evening sun reflected off the building across the street. When she was ten feet behind the group, she heard a voice in the comm link. "Backup behind you, Char."

Sophie aimed her pen and managed to hit two of her targets before Viktor registered what was happening and placed his gun against Char's temple.

Viktor grabbed Char and turned her around, placing her body in front of his. "Take another step and she gets a one-way ticket to hell."

Sophie took a step back and heard a new voice in the comm link. "Duck."

A second later Viktor crumpled to the ground, his eyes open in surprise as blood poured out of the wound in the back of his head.

Sophie capitalized on the momentary distraction and aimed the pen at the final target. The dart landed squarely on his neck and his demise was nearly instantaneous.

Char scrambled out from under Viktor and grinned at Sophie. "Nice job, but who took out Viktor?" She reached into her ear and removed the comm link. "Ew, Goon blood."

Sophie shaded her eyes with her hand and squinted up at the rooftop. "I suspect Maggie prepared for contingency number four."

"Who sucked you into being backup?" Char asked.

"Your sister's big green eyes are pretty hard to resist. I can't stand it when a woman cries."

The comm link crackled to life. "Val's on her way down and we sent another sweeper to help, but you better get them inside the office before you garner too much attention. We've blocked off the street. You know how DC is, they're always doing construction somewhere in the city." The voice in the comm link chuckled.

"Don't forget to get a high-quality picture of Viktor's retina and his handprint before you return to the compound. I would prefer that you not cut off his hand and rip out his eyeball like Ronda suggested." Sophie recognized Toni's voice in the comm link.

"Not to be too morbid or anything, but if you didn't already get a picture of Viktor's retina, you better get one soon before it changes with the loss of blood flow to the eyes." Sophie shrugged. "At least that's what your brainiac girlfriend told me."

"Okay, it should only take me a couple of seconds." Char leaned over the body and touched the nearly invisible button on the lapel of her jacket six times. That should give Toni enough images to choose from.

Char shivered as she turned away from Viktor's lifeless body.

"I'll get Viktor's body." Sophie pulled off her jacket and wrapped it around Viktor's head before dragging him into the office. Her shoulder started to ache.

"I hate moving the big ones. I'm always afraid they'll make my back go out," Char complained as she hauled one of Viktor's men inside the office.

Sophie deposited Viktor in the front reception area and met Val at the door as she was lugging another goon into the office.

"Nice shot, Val. Ronda is going to be so pissed that you got to take him out. By the way does anyone know how long Ronda will be in dreamland?" Char asked.

"About four hours give or take a few minutes," a voice in the comm link answered.

"Char had to remove her comm link," Sophie said into the link, she turned to Char. "They said the tranquilizer lasts about four hours."

"Sophie, why don't you sit this out? I can get the last guy," Val offered.

"Thanks, my shoulder is killing me."

"Goddammit, Soph, I told you not to overextend yourself," Kim said in her ear.

"Hey, baby. By the way, thanks for all the updates. They really helped us coordinate our efforts." Sophie grinned.

"Yeah, you all were a lifesaver for us," Char added and gave a thumbs-up to the cameras.

"Good job, Char. Thanks for putting your ass on the line for all of us. As the bait, you had the hardest job." Sophie held up her fist for Char to bump.

"I'm just damned glad I had the best for backup." Char glanced at Val then turned her gaze to Sophie.

†

Toni's fingers flew over the keyboard as she hummed the tune, "We're In the Money."

"Done," she exclaimed.

The screen flashed *Transaction Complete*.

"What a beautiful sight. Nine hundred and fifty-seven million dollars." Toni whistled. "Holy shit, just think of the good we'll do with all that money."

"Can we send a hefty check to Sandy, please? I feel really bad about her house. I know we were just trying to protect her, but she was an innocent in all this. I'd like to make sure she can actually just buy a brand-new house rather than trying to get that smell out." Char crinkled her nose in disgust.

"I also have a request. There's a young gentleman I'd like to do something for as well," Toni added.

"Ladies, you all deserve a nice long vacation. I propose we take a hiatus from the asset management business for the next three months," Maggie chimed in.

"Ice cream celebration?" Dani asked.

"Absolutely." Everyone answered at once.

†

The sweeper team descended on Viktor's mansion and they dropped off the trash.

It appeared deserted as the bodies—one dead, the rest alive—were unceremoniously left in Viktor's beloved parlor.

Out of the corner of her eye, Val noticed movement. She quickly pulled her gun and pointed it at the small shadow in the corner.

"Don't move a fucking muscle," Val called out.

The shadow moved and Val heard a whimper. Val took another step forward and spied a young Asian girl trembling in the corner.

"Shit, it's only a girl." Val put her gun away and slowly approached the frightened girl. "Sorry, we're not here to hurt you." Val used her softest, calmest voice.

The girl took a timid step forward and looked at Viktor's lifeless body. When the girl spit on his body, Val laughed.

"Kimiko." The girl pointed to her chest.

"Val." Val pointed to herself. "Do you speak English?"

Kimiko shook her head.

Val offered her hand.

Kimiko blinked twice and put her tiny hand in Val's.

"Come on, little one. I'm gonna take you somewhere safe where no one can hurt you again. I sure hope Char has some time for English lessons." Val smiled at the young girl and they walked out of Viktor's chamber of horrors. Val ordered the team to sweep the entire mansion for any other young girls.

Val knew that intelligence on Viktor's operation revealed that his greed overrode his desire and at any one time, there was only one young girl at the mansion, but she had hopes they would find others. However, as expected, they didn't. Val swore she would do everything in her power to track down as many of the other girls Viktor already managed to sell into slavery. It was a disappointment not to find anyone else, but at least Kimiko was safe now.

Just before she ushered Kimiko outside, Val turned to one of the sweepers. "Make sure you secure all his computers and files. We need to find where he stashes the girls and where the ones he sold went."

Chapter Twenty-five

Four months later…

Taking a three-month sabbatical was a surprisingly common occurrence in corporate law, affording Char the opportunity to spend quality time with Toni and deepen their relationship.

Dani remained at the hub for a few weeks, monitoring surveillance activity that might reveal if their last mission resulted in a blown cover for Char—it had not.

Maggie believed that Heather Stiles could continue to play a key role with future missions due to her hard-won connections with the corrupt Washington politicians.

Relieved that her persona was still intact, Char decided to distance herself from those politicians and take on more responsibility with the foundation. Fortunately, the subtle shift in her work had not yet raised any alarm bells with anyone the organization had in their crosshairs.

Char leaned back on her desk. Her stomach grumbled and a buzzer from reception alerted her to something needing her attention.

"Tall, dark, and sexy is here with your lunch," Sandy said over the intercom.

"Perfect timing," Char responded.

"Oh, and sorry to tell you this because I know it will interrupt your titillating lunch, but a Antonio Santori insists that he needs to speak with you right away," Sandy added.

"Interesting," Char said to herself.

She pushed the intercom button. "Can you ask Mr. Santori to wait a few minutes while I shovel down lunch and enjoy a few minutes with tall, dark, and sexy."

"Sure thing," Sandy said, then chuckled.

Toni strolled into the office and plopped down a paper bag. The aroma of Char's favorite Italian meatball sandwich wafted to her nostrils.

"Oh, God, you are an angel. I'm starving."

"I'm not really an angel, but I'll take a kiss in return for my delivery." Toni leaned in and pulled Char into a passionate embrace.

"Oh, forget the meatball sandwich. I think I'll spend my precious minutes devouring your lips."

"I think that's the highest praise I've ever heard. What do you think Mr. Santori wants? I saw him in the reception area before I came in," Toni inquired.

"I don't know. It's odd though. I've actually not had any dealings with him and to be honest, as gangsters go, he's actually one of the better ones. We've made an informed decision to let him be. Hmm, come to think of it, Maggie made a point of steering us clear of Antonio and I never questioned her about it."

"He was never on our radar too much. I think Byron managed his accounts. When we liberated those funds on the night of the fund-raiser, I'm sure he was affected. Do you want me to hang around while you meet with him?" Toni asked.

"Oh, honey, that's really sweet of you. You are brilliant, but your assets don't exactly include master protector." Char laughed.

"Fine, but I think I'll call Ronda just in case you need some support." Toni waved her hand. "Later."

A few seconds after Toni left, Char heard a knock on her door.

"Come in."

Sandy poked her head inside. "Is it okay to send Mr. Santori in now?"

Char looked longingly at her lunch and sighed. "Sure, go ahead."

Antonio was dressed in an impeccable Armani suit and his handsome face bore a smile for Char. "Ms. Stiles, it is a pleasure to finally meet you."

"Please sit. Can I get you anything to drink?"

"No, thank you. Let me get right to the point. It has come to my attention that you were the last person Viktor Borsky visited before his demise. You and your colleagues have done me a great service."

Char raised her eyebrow. "Excuse me? I have no idea what your point is. Mr. Borsky was my client. Other than that, I know nothing of his murder."

"I know better." Santori winked at Char. "You and your cohorts managed to eliminate a rather distasteful human being. In my business, men like Viktor give us all a bad name. I assure you, I am not your enemy. While I was less than pleased that my funds were affected along with Byron's, I don't hold you or your colleagues responsible. I'd like us to come to an agreement that I believe will be in the best interest of both our organizations. Will you listen to my proposal before deciding?"

Char shook her head. "You are drawing false conclusions, Mr. Santori, but I must say, I'm intrigued by your little scenario. Please go on."

"I do not and have never supported the sex slave trade. I do admit to dabbling in the drug business. Nasty business. I recently had an epiphany when my oldest son got involved with drugs. Perhaps your organization can see fit to leave my business alone if I agree to remain uninvolved in the drug or sex slave businesses. I may even lend a hand now and again with those who tinker in those repulsive ventures."

Char remained silent.

"Have I surprised you?"

"By your outlandish claims? Yes. I'm not sure where you are going with your suppositions."

"If it matters at all to you, I applaud your redistribution of the wealth. Some of my people have benefited. Think about my offer. I would prefer not to have you and your colleagues as an enemy. Perhaps we will not be friends, but rather polite acquaintances. You may be astonished to learn that our history, training, and values are more alike than they are different. Perhaps I have taken a different path, but I am not entirely your enemy."

Char raised an eyebrow. She'd used those words herself but could not allow him to know how close to the truth he was. "Mr. Santori, I am a corporate lawyer and my clients look to me for advice about their finances. Whatever your suppositions are, I can assure you they are wrong. If you need a lawyer for your finances I will consider taking you on as a client but other than that I cannot help you."

"Very well. I would like to be your client."

"Okay. Ask Sandy to set you up with an appointment and we can discuss your finances."

Antonio Santori stood and held out his hand. "Thank you for taking the time to see me when I didn't have an appointment. I will make that appointment now and see you hopefully later this week."

Char took his hand and shook it. "I will look forward to our next meeting."

"Have a nice day, Ms. Stiles, and give my regards to Maggie—she is a remarkable woman."

She watched as the man went out the door and let out the breath she'd been holding. "That was interesting. I think Maggie has a bit of explaining to do about Mr. Santori."

Char retrieved her cell phone and accessed her contact for Maggie's private line.

"Hello, Char, is something wrong?"

"I don't know. You tell me. Antonio Santori just sent you his regards." Char let the statement hang in the air like smoke from a cigarette. She could hear Maggie sigh.

"I see. I was afraid this might come up. Secrets sometimes have a way of rearing their ugly head at the most inopportune times. Although this is not the kind of conversation we should be having on the phone, I will tell you that Antonio and I have history. Unfortunately, the road I traveled is not the same road he ultimately chose to take. I had hoped that one day Antonio would find his way back. Perhaps this is a precursor for him to decide to revisit his former choice. Char, you must understand that no one is all good or all evil. We all have the capacity to either do great things or cause terrible destruction. It is the balance or percentage of good versus evil that is important to keep in perspective."

Maggie paused.

Char wondered if that was all the information she would get, but then Maggie continued.

"Char, hate and revenge are very powerful emotions that sometimes tend to alter the balance and create a higher percentage of malevolence within a person."

"I'm not sure I buy that, Maggie. Everyone has choices and you can let the events in your life control you or you can choose to react in a righteous manner. I'd like to think I didn't let hate or revenge tip the scales."

"Love and forgiveness are also powerful emotions that influence who we are and who we become. Your love for Dani helped mold you so that your percentage of virtue tipped those scales and the outcome was a much higher percentage of decency within. I believe Antonio still has an acceptable balance with his nobility still in the lead. I promise to reveal everything to you and the team. Let me have a day to think about this new development and then we can set a meeting for tomorrow. You deserve to hear the whole truth. Don't worry—if Antonio wanted to destroy us, we would already be finished. He and I made a pact a long time ago to leave one another alone unless either of us crossed the line. So far, he has not crossed my line and I feel confident we have not crossed his. Please arrange for the rest of the team to meet at the Maryland hub tomorrow at one o'clock sharp."

"All right. You've never steered me wrong before and I still trust you and the work we are doing. I'll see you tomorrow." Char touched the end button and turned to see Ronda bursting through her office door.

"Your girl just called me to check up on you. Is everything copacetic here?" Ronda asked.

"Yeah, I just had a very interesting conversation with Maggie about Antonio Santori. She's scheduled a meeting for tomorrow at one o'clock at the Maryland compound."

"Santori? Interesting. So…details?"

"Maggie was kind of cryptic with me, but promised to fill us all in tomorrow. You know Maggie, she gave me some philosophical mumbo jumbo about good and evil and acceptable balances," Char responded.

"And? What does that have to do with Santori?"

"They have *history*."

"History? That's sounds fascinating. Did she share anything else?" Ronda asked.

"Nope. You're just going to have to hear about it along with the rest of us tomorrow. By the way, I don't need you to come rescue me. Toni is such a worrywart."

"That's cause she *luuves* you." Ronda chuckled. "Well, if everything is okay I better get going. I got places to be, people to see, and explosives to set."

Char chuckled. "Gotta love a woman who can create interesting fireworks."

"Yep, that's me—your year around Fourth of July expert." Ronda waved at Char as she walked out of the office.

†

Char plopped down in the booth and set her head on Toni's shoulder as she looked at the newspaper Toni seemed engrossed in.

Parking attendant hits the foundation lottery.

Brian Moore, a medical student at John Hopkin's University is the latest recipient of the secret philanthropic foundation that has been funding deserving young students.

All across the country, the mysterious foundation hands out checks in a seemingly random fashion. Recipients feel as if they've just won the lottery without ever having to buy a ticket.

Critics point to the startling parallels with the famous Eva Peron Foundation and wonder about the origin of the funds as well as how those funds are distributed. There is very little information on the inner workings of the Foundation. However, for those who benefit from the funds there is nothing but praise.

Brian tells all about his good fortune. "Wow, it's hard for people like me to afford school, especially since I won't be getting any kind of loan forgiveness offers like the practicing physicians. I've always known I wanted to do regenerative research. They don't exactly hand out money to research physicians after you're done with school. You have to prove yourself. I thought I would be in debt until I died and then this lawyer, Ms. Stiles, gave me a check that more than covers the costs of my schooling. She was smokin' hot too."

"Oh, hey, babe." Toni kissed Char on the cheek. "Did you see you made the paper, my smokin' hot lover girl."

"Ha, ha, very funny. How come this kid was so important to you?" Char asked.

"He just made an impression. When I gave him a measly five at the fund-raiser, he was genuinely grateful. His response touched me, that's all. Besides, he's wants to do regenerative research. Did Dani tell you about our recent breakthrough?"

"Oh, honey, you are a genuinely nice person. I'm glad Maggie assigned you to me. Hopefully your niceness is rubbing off." Char brushed a lock of hair away from Toni's face. "So what's this about a breakthrough? Are you talking about the recent nanobot injection that you and Dani have been working on? I swear the stuff you two think up is right out of a sci-fi movie. Speaking of which, I think there was an episode about nanobots on the new *Outer Limits*." Char shuddered. "I sure hope Dani doesn't have the same side effects. The guy literally developed another set of eyes in the back of his head."

"Nope. To my knowledge, there aren't any unintended results from the injections. I never took you for a sci-fi fan. I love the new *Outer Limits*. In fact, that's where I get a lot of my ideas. I figure whatever some Hollywood writer can think up, I can invent—minus the dire consequences of science gone amok."

"Just be careful. I know Dani is anxious to run again and insists on playing guinea pig, but I worry sometimes," Char warned.

"You've gotta trust me. I would never put Dani in harm's way," Toni insisted.

"I know. I do trust you."

Toni looked up and Char followed her gaze.

Dani limped into the café. Her forearm crutches were noticeably absent. A big grin was on her face.

"A quarter of a mile." Dani's smile was as wide as the Grand Canyon.

"That's awesome, Dani. Are you feeling any side effects at all?" Toni asked.

"Nope. I think this is it. I can almost feel the nerves repairing. I still feel a bit of pain, especially after a long session, but it keeps getting less and less. I might have overdone it just a tad today, which is why I was kinda limping a little. I'm anxious to continue the treatment and see how far I can go without pain."

"Just don't push yourself too much. Pain is the way our body tells us it's time to slow down," Toni warned.

Dani slid into the booth directly facing Char and Toni. "Anything interesting in the paper?"

"Yeah, your sister is smokin' hot and Brian finally got his check."

"Oh, let me see." Dani grabbed the paper.

"I can't believe how far you've come with the research. God, it's only been three months and already Dani is walking without her crutches. You are so gonna get lucky tonight," Char whispered in Toni's ear.

Char's breath sent shivers down her spine. After four months, they were still going strong and Toni couldn't remember a time in her life when she'd been so happy.

"Hey, I almost forgot to ask you about your meeting with the infamous Mr. Santori. I have to admit to being concerned when I saw him in your waiting room."

"It was quite interesting."

"Really? In what way."

"Well, apparently Maggie and Santori have *history*."

Toni arched her eyebrow. "Really?"

"Yeah. I had a very interesting conversation with Maggie on the phone after he left." Char raised an eyebrow. "You know, you didn't have to send Ronda. I can take care of myself."

Toni looked down. "Sorry, I know you're a bad ass. I just don't want to see you hurt again. So tell me about the conversation."

"I get the distinct impression that Maggie and Antonio worked together a long time ago, but I'm just guessing. It seems they took divergent paths. It felt like Maggie was trying to provide some kind of justification for Antonio's business dealings. She scheduled a meeting with the team and I think you should tell Kim and Sophie about it. Although we've come a long way in the trust department, I still sense Sophie's hesitation with me at times. I think the news about this recent development and the upcoming meeting will come better from you."

"Okay. Where and when?" Toni asked.

"One o'clock tomorrow at the Maryland hub."

"So, honestly, what is your assessment of the situation?"

"Good question. I trust Maggie and she's about as shrewd as they come. If she has some kind of history with Antonio and made a deliberate decision to leave him be, I'm sure she had her reasons. I don't think he's exactly an ally, but perhaps he's not an enemy either. I'm not a super patient person, but Maggie assured me that she would reveal all tomorrow. Hey, enough business talk. What have you been up to today?" Char asked.

"Oh, a little of this and a little of that. I'm like a kid in a candy store in the control room lab. You guys have every little toy a geek like me could ever wish for. By the way, Kimiko wanted to come with us. I think she has a huge crush on you, honey. She cornered me and asked, *Ms. Char, where she*, in that cute little accent of hers," Toni teased.

"She's like twelve. Twelve-year-olds are far too young to get crushes."

"Ah, contraire. I was literally drooling for my grade school English teacher. She was almost as hot as you are. It must be the hot English teacher thing. Of course, whenever you're not around she follows Dani like a little puppy dog. Maggie says she's doing much better and her nightmares seem to be less and less. Poor thing. I'm glad Val found her. Do you think we should try to reunite her with her family?"

"No, I don't think so. They're probably the ones who sold her in the first place. No, she's probably better under Maggie's care. I'm glad you're there to teach her the science stuff. Don't think I haven't noticed how she seems to idolize you. I think it's more likely that she has a crush on you, Ms. Tall, Dark, and Sexy—that's what Sandy calls you. I'm just glad you're mine."

Everything seemed to be falling in place for Char and she hoped this new development with Antonio Santori wouldn't interfere with all the positive changes during the past four months. Char wasn't sure she should completely trust Antonio, and Maggie was circumspect but didn't seem worried.

Maybe I should just let my concerns go by the wayside. She shook her head. *He is still a mobster and I have a problem with that.*

She supposed that as mobsters go, he was probably the least offensive, if that was possible. His primary business was gambling and she didn't have a huge issue with that. She'd heard he also dabbled in the legalized escort business in Las Vegas but as long as all the women were there by choice, she didn't feel the need to override Maggie's directives. She supposed time would tell whether Antonio would prove to be a problem for the agency or not. Knowing Maggie as she did, she would already have a plan B in her back pocket.

†

Kim and Sophie had decided to take up residence at the Virginia compound after their one-month vacation to the Fiji Islands. As a former FBI agent, regiment and structure were comfortable notions for Sophie and she believed in what the organization was trying to accomplish. However, her mistrustful nature of authority kept Sophie from complete and utter devotion to anyone but her two best friends. Dani and Char were slowly worming their way into Sophie's circle of trust, but for some reason she still held Maggie at arm's length.

Lounging in their quarters one evening, Sophie was surprised when Kim confronted her. "I know you believe in the work we're doing for Maggie, but I get the sense that you're holding back."

Sophie smiled and looked Kim in the eyes. "You know, love, I think people underestimate you sometimes. Although you probably know me better than anyone, I still get the sense that you don't miss too much when it comes to people's true feelings about things."

Kim chuckled. "Well, I certainly missed the boat when I didn't recognize your feelings."

Sophie waved her hand. "That was a case of being deeply embedded in the weeds with your own feelings and not being able to see the situation clearly."

"You, my love, are a master at changing the topic of discussion. Why don't you trust Maggie?" Kim asked.

"Oh, I don't know. It's not exactly that I don't trust her or believe in what we're doing. I've even grown comfortable living at the compound, especially now that I have you by my side. It feels safe here and that's important to me. You're important to me. I just get this niggling feeling that there is much more to Maggie than she shares and that bothers me. You and Toni have been an open book. Dani's been incredibly open and almost naively trusting as well. Even Char is starting to open up to us—undoubtedly due to her relationship with Toni, but she still seems much more open and honest than Maggie."

"That's true, I also sense there is something more to learn about Maggie, but I think we should assume she has good intentions."

Sophie chuckled. "Babe, you are such an optimist and that is what I love about you."

"Yes, I am and that optimism extends to believing a certain talented agent will bless me with her very capable hands."

†

At first, Toni lamented the loss of her condominium after the sweepers blew everything up. Before Char had come along, Toni had valued her independence and privacy, but now it didn't seem to matter. Even Dani's frequent interruptions didn't bother her anymore. Dani was like the little sister she never had.

Living with Char in the Virginia compound had been great. The Maryland compound was near completion and they had to make a decision about where they wanted to live. Some days she wanted to stay at the Virginia compound with Kim, Sophie, and Dani. Other days she wanted to be free of their menagerie of friends. Time would tell whether she would be able to live in these tight quarters permanently or whether she would need her own place again for some amount of regained independence. She hoped Char wouldn't take offense and would understand. Char might even have her own need for independence. They were still learning about one another, all their idiosyncrasies and little habits.

Toni took the chance and brought Char home to meet her family. This was a big step for her. Her oldest sister, Tracy, was thrilled. Her other sister, Karen—not so much. Yet Toni harbored hope that it would just take Karen a little more time to get used to the fact that her sister actually had a steady partner.

The biggest surprise was her mom. Char poured on the charm and completely blew her mom's stereotypic views of lesbians out of the water.

"She's so beautiful," her mom said in astonishment. At first, it pissed Toni off. Toni had met some incredibly handsome butch women and she cringed at her mom's judgmental attitude and perceptions about what is and is not attractive. Eventually she let it go because, after all, her mom had grown up in a different era. Her mom also explained her reticence had more to do with the fact that Toni wouldn't ever have children or a family.

Char promptly corrected that misconception. "I have every intention of having kids," she innocently proclaimed.

Toni's mom beamed at that declaration but Toni nearly spit out her coffee when she heard it. She loved Char, but she wasn't quite sure she was ready for that level of commitment yet. She needed a little more time before she could seriously consider bringing a new life into the world and sharing the immense responsibility that went along with raising a child together. Maybe they should start with a cat or a dog.

†

It felt a little like déjà vu because Candy was their waitress again, but this time Dani had joined their group at the café. She thought back to when she'd engineered that first meeting with the trio and when Toni had so brazenly winked at her.

Char watched as a myriad of expressions crossed Toni's face. She wondered what deep thoughts her lover rolled around in that big brain of hers.

Never in a million years did she think she would fall in love, but that's exactly what had happened. She was thrilled that Toni had decided to stay with the agency. Despite her personal desire to have Toni close, Dani and Toni made an unbeatable research team and the agency definitely benefited from Toni's brilliance. Yeah, her lover was a genius.

As Candy approached the table with a smile, Dani whispered, "Do you know her?"

Char nodded.

"Hey, Char, Toni, how's it going?"

Toni looked puzzled.

Char figured she was surprised that Candy knew her real name. She whispered in her ear, "I'll tell you later."

Char had taken an instant liking to Candy and had sensed something was amiss with her relationship with her girlfriend, Sara. She thought back to that evening when she'd had a serious conversation with the petite blonde.

†

"It's probably none of my business, but I have to ask. Did Sara do that to you?" Char pointed at the bruise on Candy's cheek.

Candy looked away. "She just had a hard day. Her job is really stressful and I wasn't very sympathetic. I can be kinda sarcastic at times."

Char scowled. "Candy, look at me."

Candy met Char's eyes.

"No one ever deserves to be hit. Do you hear me? If you need help getting out of a bad situation, please give me a call. I promise I can help you."

Candy's eyes welled up with tears. "I don't have anyplace to go. She owns our house and I don't make enough to rent my own apartment, especially with the cost of tuition these days."

"Why don't you let me worry about the money? I have an inside track to a foundation that I'm sure will help you. Just promise me you will call if it gets to a point where you're ready to move on." Char scribbled her cell phone number on the back of her business card and pressed the card into Candy's hand.

"Thanks, Heather."

"Listen. Now that we're friends, you should know I go by my middle name, Char. Heather is the name I give to my business associates." Char gave Candy a reassuring smile.

Candy nodded and scurried off when another waitress called out to her.

Less than a week later, Candy had called in tears and Char quickly arranged for her to get a bequest from the foundation. Candy seemed better lately, but the sadness in her eyes still lingered.

✝

"Hey, Candy." Char gestured to her sister and grinned. "I don't think you've met my little sister, Dani."

Candy looked at Dani and gave her a shy smile. "I can definitely see the resemblance. You're every bit as beautiful as your sister, Char."

Dani blushed and stuck out her hand. "Thank you. It's really nice to meet you."

Char looked from Dani to Candy.

Well, I'll be darned. After two years, I think my little sister has finally taken notice of someone.

"So, Candy, what time do you get off tonight?" Char asked.

"Oh, I have the short shift. I'm off at nine."

"Excellent. Do you think you might want to join us for a drink later tonight? We wanted to see this new female singer/songwriter at the lesbian bar down the street," Char said.

"Oh, I don't want to impose or anything."

"You're not imposing. I'd really like you to come," Dani blurted out. "You'd be doing me a favor. Right now I'm a third wheel and the two of them can be downright sickening with their lovey-dovey looks." Dani pointed at Char and Toni.

"Okay, if you're sure," Candy responded with a tremulous smile.

"We're sure," all three women said in unison.

"I'll come back and get you around nine, okay?" Dani smiled.

"It's a date." Candy smacked her hand against her mouth. "Oh, I didn't mean it like that."

"No, it's okay, it can be a date if that's all right with you," Dani proclaimed boldly.

"Okay." Candy blushed and looked directly at Dani.

Kim and Sophie came barreling into the café.

Sophie looked from Candy to Dani. "Hey, what did we miss?"

"Later," all three voices blended into one.

†

Maggie paced the control room at the Maryland hub. It was ten minutes before one and she still didn't know how she would explain her ties with Antonio. She struggled with how much information to give her primary team. Did they deserve to know all of her history? Could she justifiably keep some of the more private information to herself?

Maggie had once been deeply in love with Antonio and she wasn't sure she ever really got over him. At one time, they had shared the same values, the same passion for what she considered right and wrong. How did it all get so complicated? She looked up when she heard the door open.

Char and Toni were the first to arrive. Char stepped into the room, made a beeline for her and touched her on the arm. Looking into Char's eyes, she thought she saw understanding and acceptance, but she wasn't sure. Char was always very intuitive.

Maggie was pleased when Dani came limping into the room without her crutches. This one bright spot to her day helped generate the confidence she needed to reveal her history.

Kim and Sophie followed.

Maggie imagined that Sophie, with her natural skepticism, would be the harshest critic but she hoped that Kim would temper her response.

A few minutes later Ronda, Cindy, and Val joined the small group of senior level operatives.

Maggie cleared her throat and watched as all eyes turned in her direction. Most of the team had already taken seats in the control room but Sophie stood with her arms crossed. "I'm sorry to disturb your busy day, but it was critical that I bring you all together to brief you on a recent development that was unanticipated."

Char nodded.

"Char had a visit yesterday from Antonio Santori."

"Are we compromised?" Sophie asked.

Sophie's cold detached tone shook Maggie. "No. Antonio has known about us for a long time."

"What the fuck? And you're just telling us this now," Ronda bellowed.

"Shut up, Ronda, let her talk," Char interjected.

"Antonio and I go way back. He and I worked for the same agency twenty years ago. We were practically kids and both of us were recruited at the same time. We became very close. That agency was very similar to our organization, but after a few years I questioned some of the orders I was given. Politics played a major role in who was marked for destruction or ruin and our missions ceased making sense.

Antonio had the same questions I did and we decided to leave the agency and strike out on our own.

"At first things went really well for us and we managed to break apart some of the smaller human trafficking rings, but financial resources were limited and Antonio started to make independent decisions about where we would get the money to continue our operation. I didn't agree with his tactics and we parted ways. It was an amicable split and we both set rules.

"As long as Antonio did not enter into the more unsavory business ventures, I would not intercede. Although he danced on the line a few years ago, when I learned of his involvement in the drug business, I chose not to interfere, determining that I wanted to focus all my energies on busting up Viktor's slave trade business. Fortunately, Antonio came to the realization on his own that the drug business was not for him.

"When Toni, Sophie, and Kim liberated those funds from Byron that were attached to Antonio, I believe his interest was sparked and he thought I violated our agreement. I needed to recruit you not only to assist us with Viktor, but also to insure you would stay away from Antonio. I believe his visit to Char's office was a gentle reminder."

"You used us so you could protect your lover?" Sophie glared at Maggie. "I always thought you were underhanded in your dealings with Toni, Kim and me and now this proves it."

"That's not true," Maggie replied.

Char shot her hand up palm first. "Let her finish before you go off halfcocked, Sophie."

"She's brought him down on us. What more is there to know? I won't allow our lives to be compromised. We were doing just fine before the lot of you came along."

"Let her speak," Kim said. "Please, for me."

"Fine."

"Thank you, Kim. I am being as honest as I can in this matter. And for the record, I did not set any of you up."

Char nodded. "Maggie, it might be a little more than that. He did request that we leave his business alone, but also suggested that he might help us out with busting up any human trafficking rings. Thinking back on the conversation, I sensed his sincerity when he spoke about the repulsiveness of the sex slave business. He also indicated his approval of our redistribution of funds. I don't think him telling me to give you his regards was a random comment. It seemed like he was giving me a deliberate message," Char explained.

"Nothing Antonio does is random. I suspect you are correct. He was sending me a very personal signal that he is interested in joining forces—"

"And, just how do you know that? Have you been in contact with him all along?" Sophie sneered.

"Let her speak." Kim patted Sophie's hand.

Maggie closed her eyes briefly and shook her head. "As I was saying, I'm just not sure we should be doing that. There are still some areas of disagreement, although I will admit to seeing more shades of gray today than my more idealistic view of the world so many years ago."

Maggie looked around the room trying to get a sense of what her top agents felt about her explanation. She didn't think she detected any open hostility from anyone other than Sophie.

"Dani has been doing some digging lately because, unfortunately, as soon as we created the void by taking Viktor down, others have been positioning themselves to fill it. If you thought Viktor was the devil, compared to Leonid Petrov, he was a saint. Leonid is a very rich psychopath and he has decided to expand his business into the United States. I do not make this recommendation lightly, but I think it's time to consider Antonio's veiled offer of assistance. I know for a fact that Leonid will be a common enemy."

Maggie watched as the group split into smaller groups of twos and threes and whispered to one another. Kim seemed to be a calming influence on Sophie, but Maggie knew if she was to convince them to join forces with Antonio, she needed the woman on board.

Char was the first to speak up. "He was rather charming and it's not like we're always squeaky clean with our tactics. I support your recommendation, Maggie."

"You know my background, Maggie, and I'm the first to acknowledge that I have no business teaching morality to others. I support you too," Ronda added.

Dani held her thumb up.

Val gave Maggie a subtle nod.

Cindy smiled. "I'll be there to patch up all their lame asses."

"Well, what the hell are we waiting for, let's start managing those vast assets of Leonid's and invite Antonio to the party," Toni shouted.

Kim smiled and nodded.

"Until it is unanimous, we won't do anything." Maggie looked at Sophie. "Are you in?"

"You have not completely convinced me and if it were up to me, we'd be walking out right now. But, Kim and Toni are on board, so I will go along with including Santori in our plans. Just know that if I see any type of subterfuge on your part, I will walk away, even if it is alone."

"You won't," Maggie said forcibly. "No one, I repeat, no one is important enough for me to betray any of you and that includes you, Sophie."

Sophie nodded her head. "Then let's get to work." She grinned. "Leonid does not stand a chance against us."

†

Later that night, wrapped in Toni's arms, Char sighed. "You do know I love you, right?"

"Yes. I love you too." Toni searched her lover's face. "What's up?"

"Leonid is going to make Viktor seem tame in comparison."

"I think that is an accurate assessment."

"I couldn't stand it if I lost you."

Toni leaned in and kissed Char soundly. "You're stuck with me. Nothing will happen to me, or you, because we will have each other's back."

"We will, won't we?" Char pulled Toni closer. "Come here. I need to check out that back of yours."

About the Author

Annette Mori

Annette is a health care executive living in the beautiful Pacific Northwest with her new wife (got to love Washington state) and their three furry kids. Well actually, it might be more than three, but they do not count the ones they only feed. Annette is fifty-five years old and believes it is not too late to try something new. As an avid reader, she is pleased there are thousands of good books to choose from, and hopes that one day hers will be one of the many for readers to consider. She reads at least three to four books a week, so please keep them coming. She has a habit to feed after all.

No matter if you loved it or hated it, I would love your comments. Feel free to e-mail me at annettemori0859@gmail.com. I will always be a WIP (work in progress—just learned that) so feedback is a gift.

Other Books from Affinity eBook Press

Do Dreams Come True—JM Dragon Laurel Rogers was unceremoniously dumped by her long-time lover, painter Ronnie Lancaster, finding her belongings outside the apartment they shared. To add to her misery, the next day she loses her job, fired by the Dragon of Finance, Christen Jamison. What else can go wrong? Oh yes, her best friend becomes engaged to the brother of the Dragon. For ten years, Christen Jamison has never forgiven her partner for walking out on her. She's given up on love, making her work her life as the accountant for the family business. After she is directed to fire a woman who should never have been on the redundancy list—Laurel Rogers—Christen begins to doubt her commitment to the store's management and policies. How do two people who really shouldn't get on end up in a relationship? Find out in this deliciously ordinary romance.

Return to Me—Erin O'Reilly Renowned microbiologist Sydney Tanner left work as normal for her trip home but never arrived. Ellie Scott her wife of ten years frantically, to the point of obsession, attempts to find her—the only evidence there is something amiss is Syd's crashed truck, then the clues go cold. Ellie refuses to believe that she will never see Syd again but realizes many months later with nothing solid to go on, it's time to attempt to move forward with a life without Syd. Leaving her hometown she accepts a new job at Salvation, aptly named for Ellie's predicament. There Ellie meets beautiful Maya Rojas who is the director of Salvation—a rehabilitation hospital. Although she hasn't given up on finding Syd, Ellie finds herself increasingly drawn to Maya. Will Salvation bring just that to Ellie, allowing her to find peace and happiness again, or will it have her questioning all that she believes in? A wonderful romance cloaked within an intriguing mystery.

Terminal Event—Ali Spooner Tally Rainwater was born with the gift of second sight, something she never understood. A near-fatal accident, at age twelve, makes her visions clearer, but not the reason for them. As she matures, Lisa, a spirit, enters her visions to guide her in using her gift, but still not the reason why. After Tally's gift helps locate the body of a murdered teen, she realizes her gift is to help lost souls find their peace. When it's discovered a serial killer murdered a teen, Blair "Spooky" Cooper is the Agent in Charge assigned to the case. A task force of local detectives and FBI forms to track the killer. Blair enlists the aid of Tally, and together with the team, Tally helps them piece together the puzzle of murders spanning twenty years throughout the Deep South. Even with the complication of the case, Blair and Tally have an undeniable attraction to each other. As they close in on the killer, the killer focuses on Tally, jeopardizing her bond with Blair and everyone around her. For the sake of the case, they put their attraction on the back burner until the killer is caught. Will the killer be caught or continue to evade authorities? Can Tally and Blair's budding romance survive the possibility? Read this intense murder mystery romance and find out.

Arc Over Time—Jen Silver Dr Kathryn Moss has job offers flowing in after her exciting archaeological discoveries at Starling Hill the previous year. Now she has choices to make that could jeopardise her relationship with Denise Sullivan, the fiery journalist, who has become her lover. For Denise the choice seems obvious. She thinks they have moved beyond the casual sex stage to something more like a true relationship. However, she's not sure how to handle Kathryn's continuing infatuation with Ellie Winters. Ellie's new career as a promising artist proves to be a catalyst for the simmering tensions in relations between her wife Robin, Kathryn, and Denise. Will Denise persevere in her pursuit of the reluctant professor? Does Ellie have anything to fear from Kathryn's fascination with her art, or is there another motive behind the professor's obsessive interest? This wonderful romantic continuation with the characters from *Starting Over* ties up loose ends. But the question is—does everyone have a happy ending? A must read.

The Presence—Charlene Neal After catching her husband red-handed in bed with his secretary, Kayleigh Gibbs takes her daughter and her Jeep and flees across the country. She opens up her own veterinarian practice, and they move into an old, secluded farmhouse in Hoekwil, South Africa. At her best friend's housewarming party Kayleigh meets the beautiful and enchanting Rebecca Steward. Rebecca is instantly drawn to Kayleigh, but is still recovering from a breakup—her girlfriend left her for a man. She's afraid of a repeat performance with Kayleigh, and won't pursue a romantic relationship with her, preferring instead to develop a platonic friendship. When odd, inexplicable things start happening on the farmhouse, a terrified Kayleigh turns to Rebecca for comfort, only to find herself developing unexplainable feelings for her new friend. Rebecca, despite her best intentions, is falling in love with Kayleigh. But when Rebecca moves in with Kayleigh to help her get to the bottom of the haunting, she finds more than she bargained for. Can Rebecca and Kayleigh overcome ghosts from the past and their own insecurities, or will a presence from the past tear them apart?

A Walk Away—Lacey Schmidt   Kat and Rand's daily worlds are 2,100 miles apart, but something about their meeting on the magical shores of the nation's oldest national park east of the Mississippi sparks questions that neither woman can just walk away without answering. Sometimes chance brings you to the right person to help you resolve some of your baggage, and you learn to like yourself a little more. Kat and Rand are smart enough to recognize this chance in each other, but they also find that there is a catch to every opportunity—walking toward something is always walking away from something else.

Love Forever, Live Forever—Annette Mori   No one forgets their first love. For Nicky, that's Sara, who abruptly disappears one day, leaving only a cryptic letter. That day scarred her soul. When the pain starts to diminish, Nicky begins to get her life back on track until it is derailed once again by an unimaginable twist. Changed forever, Nicky becomes a careless, womanizing nomad known as the Little Wild One, until she meets Annie. Thirteen years later, Nicky's finally settled and happy. Fate intervenes and puts her directly back into the path of her first love, Sara, and the corresponding events send her into a tailspin. Now she must decide—who will be the person she ends up living with and loving forever?

Possessing Morgan—Erica Lawson New York City, in the height of summer. Crime seems to have taken a holiday, and Detective Morgan O'Callaghan is bored, bored, bored. Paperwork is mating and multiplying on her desk, and even a jaywalker is starting to look good. Anything to get her out from behind her desk! Enter Andrea Worthington, Charleston socialite and all-around rich girl, right down to the wealthy fiancé. She's also the new Assistant District Attorney assigned to Morgan's precinct. Their first meeting is like two freight trains crashing head-on. Then a high profile, career make-or-break murder case throws them together again. The investigation has barely begun when Andrea becomes the target of a nearly fatal hit-and-run. But was it really aimed at her? Can she and Morgan find the common ground they need to solve the case and stop the attacks, or are the gaps just too wide to bridge?

Twenty-three Miles—Renee MacKenzie Talia Lisher has a long family history of lying, about anything and everything. With her father dead, and her mom gone on a quest to start a new life, Talia struggles to keep in touch with her only remaining family, her incarcerated brother. When Talia sets her sights on Officer Shay Eliot, she vows to stop lying. She starts watching Shay, waiting for just the right circumstances and amount of courage to talk to her. Talia might be watching Shay, but someone in a dark van is watching Talia. Is the mystery driver a dangerous part of her family's past, or is it all just a coincidence? Shay Eliot has left the police force because of what she perceives as a hostile work environment. When a brutal double-murder on the 23-mile-long Colonial Parkway puts the FBI's magnifying glass squarely on her, her alibi comes from an unlikely source—a young woman who has been stalking her. Shay wants to keep her distance from Talia, but once she gets to know the younger woman she can't keep feelings from developing. This is a story about community, and how it comes together in dangerous and devastating times. When you don't know who to trust, you better have friends who will rally around you. Will Talia and Shay find the answers they need to the mystery of the murders on the parkway, or will justice be elusive? Will they survive their quest for the truth?

Confined Spaces—Renee MacKenzie Andie Waters spends her days pulling waste samples for environmental testing and at night, she tends bar at The Cave, a popular hangout for straights in a small Georgia town. Serial monogamy has grown stale for her, so she's content working to pay off her debts and hanging out with her old hound dog. Or so she thinks, until a beautiful lesbian drops by The Cave. Andie suspects her involvement with the woman will be only temporary. Little does she know no part of her life will be left untouched. Kara Travis likewise anticipates nothing more than a brief fling upon meeting Andie, especially given her reputation as both a personal ice princess and a corporate hatchet wielder for Royal Environmental. What luck to find a hot lesbian bartender in nowhere rural Georgia. Andie and Kara spend a passionate weekend together and find that their notions of no strings attached are far from accurate. Their supposed short-term ideal diversion of a commitment-free romp hits a major complication when they come face-to-face with one another at Royal Environmental's offices Monday morning. While carrying out her duties, Kara discovers crimes being committed by and against Royal Environmental employees. Will Kara be forced to shut down the Georgia Division of the company? If she does, Andie will lose her job. Worse yet, Kara may lose Andie before she's really even sure she's got her. Corporate politics, complicated romance, and long distances conspire to keep Andie and Kara all boxed in. Can love triumph despite the Confined Spaces?

Reece's Star—TJ Vertigo Reece Corbett watches over the dancers in her gentlemen's club with the blue, razor sharp eyes of The Animal. Few know that resting comfortably in her office is her newest love, a tiny MinPin named Smudge. What happened to The Animal, known for her rapacious appetite for women and danger? Faith Ashford is what happened to The Animal. Faith and Reece have been together a while now and they have settled into something resembling domestic bliss. This bliss alarms Reece. It's one thing for Faith to see her softer side, that's vulnerability enough, but to let her friends see it…no. Not the best plan. Under Faith's guiding, loving hand, will Reece successfully traverse the rocky road of emotion and embrace the positive changes in her life? Or will she panic and be unable to control that Animal part of herself? Will she take that next step to declare herself fully capable of love and devotion? This third installment in the popular series that began with *Private Dancer* continues the passionate and often hilarious romance of Reece and Faith as they both grow in love and in trust.

Flight—Renee Mackenzie It's 1983 and Kate Hunter is a student at a small, private college in Virginia. When Lana coaxes her onto the back of her beat-up scooter one night, Kate's education starts to encompass more than just her pre-vet studies. Kate has always done as expected of her, so when she starts staying away from home on weekends to spend time with her new lover it's way out of character for her. Lana is secretive, but Kate accepts things as they are and gives Lana her space. When she feels the sting of betrayal, will she be able to continue giving Lana her privacy? Kate's sister April is a high school student playing with fire as she parties with her older boyfriend, Boyd. After finding someone overdosed the morning after a big party, April grows weary of all the drugs and alcohol. Will she be able to convince Boyd that they should slow down? Will she be able to pull it together before it's too late? Kate and April are forced to face up to events from their younger years, their mother's desertion, and their long-deteriorating relationship with one another. Some lives will be lost and others changed forever when the sisters' lives intersect. Will they be consumed by the wreckage, or will they be able to pick themselves up and take flight?

Reflected Passion—Erica Lawson Where passion, reality, and destiny combine. Dale Wincott is a 27-year-old woman born into Bostonian wealth and groomed to marry into the social hierarchy. Her mother is a hard-hearted society matriarch, but her father feels for his daughter and helps Dale find a life on her own as a furniture restorer. Françoise Marie Aurélie de Villerey is a 28-year-old Countess, born into the French aristocracy and forced to marry a count much older than herself. For ten years, she was his trophy wife, forced to endure his perverted desires, until the day he finally died. He had broken her emotionally and she no longer cared for what life had to offer, slipping from one sexual partner to another as often as she changed her clothes. Until...that one night when Françoise looked up during a sexual encounter and saw Dale watching her from the mirror. A veritable angel, full of innocence and curiosity, who touched her very soul. Through the mirror, Françoise embraces life anew, while for Dale it is

261

a powerful awakening, forcing her to discover not only her sensual nature, but the inner strength she possesses.

The One—JM Dragon 2015 GCLS Winner for romance, intrigue, and adventure. Phil (Philomena) Casters loves her work as a pilot, above everything else in her life except Ming, her married lover. Phil needs to enhance her status in the community before asking Ming to leave behind her wealthy husband. Rosa Moran a teacher, raised by missionaries in China after the death of her parents. She loves the country of her birth and the people. Her English grandfather desperately wants her to live with him to atone for the guilt he feels about the death of her parents. He sends her a letter requesting her to come home. When Phil flies to the mission to deliver the letter to Rosa, neither can envisage the chain of events about to take place. It starts as a collaboration to save four children, leading them to the surreal private paradise of Langshow. Could this be the perfect place for the children and Rosa to settle? Phil is not so sure. Chang, an old friend from Rosa's childhood, lives in Langshow and makes no bones about the fact that he wants Rosa. All thoughts of Ming disappear as Phil tries to fight her attraction to Rosa. However there is the little matter of an innocent misunderstanding—Rosa thinks Phil is a man. *The One* is a romance with everything, love, intrigue, misunderstandings with a happy conclusion—the only question—who gets the girl?

E-Books, Print, Free e-books

Visit our website for more publications available online.

www.affinityebooks.com

Published by Affinity E-Book Press NZ LTD
Canterbury, New Zealand

Registered Company 2517228